BECAUSE YOU LOVED ME

BECAUSE YOU
LOVED ME

Christa Allan

Originally published in 2012 by Summerside Press as *Love Finds You in New Orleans*

ISBN: 978-0-6925639-4-6

Dear Reader,

If you enjoyed my novel, I'd be ever so grateful if you would leave a review on Amazon. It doesn't need to be lengthy; a short review is fine. They really do make a difference for both the author and other readers.

Thank you for spending time with my characters.

Sign up for my newsletter, and you'll receive *lagniappe* (that's Southern speak/French for "a little something extra."

The link will be on my Author page at the back of the novel.

I promise to respect your inbox and send updates about new releases, specials and other reader-related info to rock your world! No pictures of my grandgirls or dogs unless they're absolutely adorable.

DEDICATION

In loving memory of my precious parents,
without whom I would not have been born
in New Orleans.

ACKNOWLEDGMENTS

Writing a novel about finding love in New Orleans meant finding helpful friends and family from sea to shining sea. My gratitude is extended...

Thanks to Jenny B. Jones and Ginny Yttrup for reading, re-reading, re-re-reading, and continuing to answer e-mails and phone calls even after they knew they were from me.

To my brother, John Bassil, for accompanying me to museums and antique stores without complaint.

To Stacey Alexius for her fact-finding missions. To Michelle Mecom, for providing reference novels and sanity breaks between classes, and to Adam Rowe, for clearing out his Louisiana history collection.

To the monthly GNO group who, even when I couldn't tear myself away from the nineteenth century to join them, checked on me to give me glimpses of the twenty-first century.

To Elizabeth Pearce, culinary historian at the Hermann-Grima Historic House in New Orleans, for answering my food questions. Along the way I discovered the Southern Folk Artist & Antiques blog written by Andrew Hopkins. His lovely photographs and detailed descriptions were invaluable.

To the Starbucks crew on Barataria Blvd., I appreciate your allowing me the corner chair to write away the day.

To Shea Embry and Cam and Will Mangham, thank you for welcoming us home to Camellia Manor and being a part of rewriting our history.

And last, but never least:

To my husband, Ken, for entertaining himself during my time travels and welcoming me back from the 1840s in the most unexpected and delightful way.

To my children for continuing to support and encourage me.

And to a most loving God who reminds me that I'm not the boss of Him and who has been generous beyond measure.

Saint Louis Cathedral   French Quarter

New Orleans is a city much like the gumbo for which it is famous. Populated by the Indians, founded by the French in 1718, and later inhabited by the Spanish, the Germans, and the British, various cultures have simmered for centuries, creating a stew of rich, hearty, and vibrant people.

Called "the Crescent City" because its communities expanded along the half-moon curve in the river, New Orleans is as genteel as it is raucous, as flamboyant as it is understated, and as historic as it is contemporary. In one day, visitors can admire the towering triple steeples of Saint Louis Cathedral, the oldest cathedral in North America; meander into the French Quarter for Sunday brunch and listen to jazz in the lush courtyard of the Court of Two Sisters; shop for antiques along Magazine Street; stop at Plum Street's Snoball Stand, where the treats are served in Chinese takeout containers; dine on the two-hour Natchez steamboat cruise along the Mississippi; and end the night with coffee and beignets at Café du Monde, the original French Market coffee stand.

Soulful jazz spiraling from clubs on Frenchmen Street, lavender wild irises and pink azaleas splashed along Creole cottages, beads and doubloons tossed at Mardi Gras parades, streetcars clanging along St. Charles Avenue, and fleur-de-lis–flocked Saints fans chanting "who dats" all the way to the Superdome—New Orleans wraps her arms around you and hugs you so close, you can feel her heartbeat.

Christa Allan

CHAPTER ONE

January 1841

G RAND-MÈRE AND ABRAM WERE due home from the French Market at any moment, and Charlotte could not convince Henri to leave her bedroom.

"You know Abram will throw you out the door, and after Grand-mère is finished with me, I may never leave this bedroom. Forever a prisoner of this house." Well, forever until the day of her coming-out party. Lottie knew there would be no missing that event even if she wanted to. And most days, she wanted to forget the event entirely.

Henri yawned and stared back at her.

"If your belly wasn't so full, you wouldn't be so content."

He stretched and blinked a few times as if to say, "Whose fault is that?"

Of course he was right. Lottie reached for her mattress and pulled herself up from crouching on the floor to have her one-way conversation with the calico cat that eluded capture under her four-poster bed. She'd started feeding Henri the day she spotted him wobbling after the milk lady's cart. Madame Margaret delivered the milk to Grand-mère and went on her way, but the cat with the pleading gray eyes stayed behind. Her grandmother begrudgingly relented when Lottie begged to feed him, as long as she promised he would never, ever cross the threshold into their house.

Still wearing her nightgown, all Lottie could do was peek through the muslin curtains. "Only two houses away," she whispered, as if the words might alarm Henri. She turned around just as the spotted cat started to make his escape, and in a movement so swift that she almost toppled into her armoire, she snatched him.

Even before Grand-mère made her entrance through the wrought-iron gate at the rear of the house, with her basket sprouting colorful vegetables, Lottie had deposited the cat on the front steps. She hurried through the library and the parlor and up to her bedroom—just in time to see Agnes pick up the china saucer left under the bed.

Agnes looked over Lottie's shoulder and then behind, toward the gallery, where Lottie's grandmother, Marie LeClerc, could be heard already discussing dinner with the cook. "Now, Miss Genevieve Charlotte…" Agnes lowered her voice from its usual trumpet blast and set her chestnut eyes right on Lottie's guilty face. "You forget your cup this morning when you fount the coffee?"

Without waiting for an answer, which they both knew would be one step away from the truth, Agnes slipped the saucer into the wide front pocket of her white apron. "I'm taking care of this"—she patted her pocket—"while you taking care of getting dressed for the day."

Lottie wanted to hug her, but Agnes backed away and waved her arms in front of her to ensure her distance. "You best wash that cat off your hands before wrapping your arms round me. No telling where that mister been since you last saw him." Agnes secured the mosquito netting to the four posters of Lottie's bed, surveyed the room, and looked into the ceramic basin on the dresser. "Well, your water is fresh. Your grandmother gonna start calling your name if she don't see you soon." She walked out of the room.

After Lottie splashed water on her hands and face, she pulled the blue chintz day dress from her armoire and laid it across her bed. The skirt and bodice showed some wear, but for Lottie, that meant she could soon cut it down to sew dresses for the orphan home. Weeks ago, she had gone to the home for the first time with Gabriel when he delivered food there. She had taken a homespun summer dress covered with pink, blue, and yellow flowers that no longer covered her pantaloons. Grand-mère had been appalled the last time she'd worn it, so Lottie had decided her grandmother wouldn't mind if she gave it away.

Not that Lottie had told her about giving it away yet. Even though her dress could clothe at least two of the girls, she feared her grandparents would not want her traipsing to an orphan home—with Gabriel, no less. How many times had Grand-mère droned, "Picking up

3

strays again, dear?" Gabriel, the orphans, Henri—all defined as strays by her grandmother.

I'll tell her after my twentieth birthday. It's nearly two months away. Lottie laughed at the thought that she would be old enough to take a husband into the house and a dress out of the house on the same day. She might even write that in her letter to her parents, one she would compose later when she sat at her desk to share her day with them, as she had almost every day for the past ten years. Lottie told no one about her letters. They would have called her foolish to write to people who were never going to write her back.

GRAND-MÈRE INFORMED LOTTIE OVER BREAKFAST that she would be taking music instructions from Madame Fontenot because "playing the piano-forte reflects a lady's culture and sophistication."

"Why do I need to be cultured and sophisticated?" Lottie reached for a second croissant, but Grand-mère whisked away the basket and handed her a bowl of strawberries.

"Why, Charlotte, suitors appreciate ladies who can play music, especially something as entertaining as the pianoforte." Grand-mère placed the basket of croissants next to her own plate, sighed, and mumbled as if speaking to the tablecloth.

As usual, when her grandmother spoke to the air, Charlotte pretended not to listen. She had spent years not hearing what she was certain Grand-mère expected her to hear.

"Entertaining? Will that require years of lessons?" Actually, Lottie hoped so. Anything to put distance between herself and the prospect of suitors.

Her grandmother settled her coffee cup in its saucer. "Certainly not. Unless, that is, you show promise. In that case, your lessons could continue even after you are married."

Had she not just bitten into the sweet strawberry, Lottie might have tasted the sourness in her stomach as it rose to her throat. But, as always, she would defer to her grandmother's plans. She brushed off the croissant crumbs sprinkled on the bodice of her gown and patted her mouth with her napkin. "May I be excused?"

"Of course," Grand-mére said. "But before you leave, it might brighten your face to know that I've arranged for Justine to join you in your lessons."

Lottie smiled. "Thank you. It does make me happy to know that she and I will be sharing the time." *And the suffering*, she thought.

"What are your plans for the day?" Grand-mère folded her napkin over her breakfast plate and stood.

"Justine and I planned to work on our samplers this morning since we both need more practice with stitches. She should be here within the hour." Lottie followed her grandmother into the butler's pantry to rinse their dishes.

"If I finish planning the week's meals with Cook, I

may join you. If not, you can show me your progress later."

Lottie nodded as she dried her plate and hoped for a difficult menu planning.

———∽∽∽———

"I SUPPOSE SUITORS APPRECIATE LADIES who eat only one croissant at breakfast," Lottie told her friend Justine Dumas as they worked on their samplers in the library. Looking behind her to make certain her grandmother hadn't slipped in, Lottie lifted her sewing and snapped the end of her thread with her teeth before staring at the half-finished piece. "I wish the alphabet didn't have so many letters." She tugged a green thread from the bundle of string. "Look, Justine, it's the color of your eyes. I'm going to sew the *J* with it."

Justine leaned over the arm of her chair to get a closer look. "No, that is the color of celery." She smoothed the almost-completed needlework on her lap and raised her head with an air of mock sophistication. "My eyes are like two glittering emeralds."

Lottie smiled and pulled the threads into a knot. "Somewhere between there is the truth. Like the truth I learned this morning."

"Maybe your grandmother doesn't want you to outgrow your corset." Justine giggled and coaxed her needle through the muslin. "But isn't it exciting to think about being courted, then engaged and married?"

"No. All that excites me is that you will join me in

those piano-forte punishments. I will have a partner in suffering." Lottie placed the back of her hand to her forehead and swooned in imitation of Emmeline, Justine's cousin, who joined them for Spanish lessons with Señor Marino. At least once a month, Emmy felt faint and always managed to fall into his arms. Perhaps there would be an engagement announced soon.

"My mother was delighted to have one fewer lesson to schedule," said Justine. As the youngest of seven, Justine often orchestrated her own social life since her older siblings, and now their children, kept her mother in a perpetual state of obligation and confusion.

They slipped into comfortable silence. The afternoon sun bowed out of the sky as if its dance with the day had ended. Shadows lazily drifted through the tall windows while the girls collected their threads and samplers to continue another time.

Agnes's orders to Abram vibrated through the rooms. "Why you not out there lookin' for Mr. LeClerc? Go wait by that *porte cochère* where his carriage come in. Remember, the doctor said he got a weak heart." Lottie imagined Abram's usual response of shaking his head in what Agnes called his "what you gonna do with her" way. Agnes and Abram had been with Lottie's grandparents longer than she had. Before Lottie had reached the age of ten, old enough to join her grandparents at dinner, she had felt like Agnes's daughter. Often, she wished she was.

Justine adjusted the bow of her bonnet, even though

Lottie had remarked earlier that the evening shade didn't require a bonnet at all. She had just reached for the door latch when she suddenly grabbed Lottie's arm as if she'd fallen into the swamp. "Charlotte, I have the most wonderful idea." Her face certainly reflected the excitement in her voice.

"Is the idea that you will not squeeze my arm again?"

"You are so silly." Justine let go, smoothed the sleeve she had mangled, and leaned toward Lottie. "We could have our coming-out parties together, even though you are older. Everyone understands the fright over contagion because of the fever in the city. Your coming-out party was not the only one delayed."

Justine's words ran out of her mouth so fast, they bumped into one another. The speed of her words wasn't a problem, but her ever-increasing volume was. Lottie pressed a finger against Justine's lips. "Shush. No talking about this now. I am hoping my grandparents forget—"

"Forget?" Justine pulled back and looked at Lottie as though she'd just told her she'd met Andrew Jackson. "Do you really think your grandmother would forget such an important event?"

Important for her. A chance to market me to a rich man she can boast about. Lottie didn't have to think of an answer, because they both knew what it would be—and because someone knocked on the door.

Benjamin, one of Justine's older brothers, waited outside. He nodded in Lottie's direction, looked at Justine as Lottie imagined only an annoyed older brother could, and said, "Mother sent me for you."

Lottie laughed. "You live four houses away."

Justine stepped out of the house. "Charlotte, that kind of thinking is your problem. It's not the distance. A lady should not walk the streets in the evening without a chaperone."

"That was one of the best 'elegant lady' statements I've ever heard from you. Our deportment teacher would be so proud."

Justine giggled. "I will be back tomorrow for our first pianoforte lesson."

Again, Benjamin nodded toward Lottie, and the two walked away. Lottie watched as they moved down the *banquette* and maneuvered around sludge that was too thick to slip into the ditches. The gaslights swaying from the ropes fastened to tall poles along the street seemed to blink as they passed.

Lottie pushed the door closed and wished she could close the door on her dreams as easily.

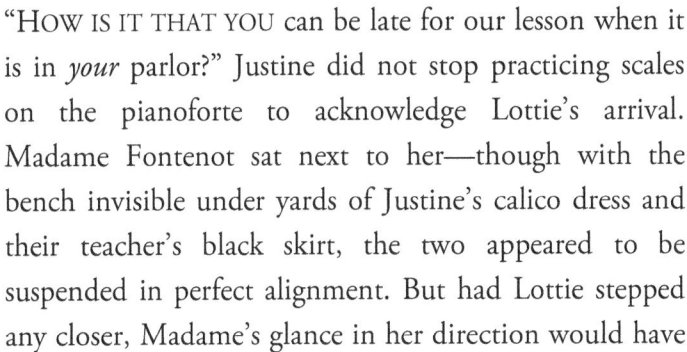

"HOW IS IT THAT YOU can be late for our lesson when it is in *your* parlor?" Justine did not stop practicing scales on the pianoforte to acknowledge Lottie's arrival. Madame Fontenot sat next to her—though with the bench invisible under yards of Justine's calico dress and their teacher's black skirt, the two appeared to be suspended in perfect alignment. But had Lottie stepped any closer, Madame's glance in her direction would have left cuts. Justine and Lottie often joked that Madame Fontenot paid Marie Laveau, the voodoo queen, for those chilling expressions.

Lottie closed the parlor doors behind her and mentally pinched herself to avoid saying something to Madame or Justine she might later be made to regret. She was not going to tell either one of them that she overslept after staying awake longer than intended so she could write a letter to her parents.

Lottie sat in the padded chair facing the tall windows at the front of the house and waited for Justine's lesson to end. As far as she was concerned, Justine could have Lottie's lesson time too.

Lottie watched a carriage pass, its curtains drawn, and wished she were in it, headed down Rue Royale. Instead she listened to Madame Fontenot as she reminded Justine, "Wrists up, fingers curved," and dreaded her own practice. She tapped her feet on the thick Turkish carpet; waves of pale blue chintz swished back and forth, keeping time with each key that Justine's fingers touched. Lottie felt as gray and as restless as the clouds outside. *Maybe Grand-mère will allow a trip to the opera this evening—*

Charlotte, Justine has finished her lesson." Madame Fontenot waved her over to the bench.

"I will be in the library. Your grandfather invited me to select a book," Justine said to Lottie. She opened the door and pressed her gown to her side as she passed through the opening.

As Lottie lifted herself off the chair, she spotted a familiar *tignon* making its way across the street, made even more familiar by the young man behind, who carried a large woven basket. Whatever hope Governor Miró had that requiring free women of color to wear the knotted headdresses in public would make them less attractive surely had not counted on women like Rosette Girod. The handkerchief swirls of orchid-shaded silk framed her exotic face. Without the tignon, Lottie knew, she and Rosette could have walked together in the French Market and no one who passed would have identified Rosette as a free woman of color. Her features were echoed in her son Gabriel, who, as a child, explained his light complexion to Agnes by telling her that before he was born, God had dipped him into a pot of café au lait. As she watched, Lottie saw Rosette point in the direction of her home.

Lottie's time with Gabriel had been severely curtailed since he started helping Rosette at her Chartres Street café a few years ago. What started as a stand selling coffee and hot *calas*—the deep-fried rice cakes eaten for breakfast—had, over the years, become an outdoor café with chairs and tables. Churchgoers who poured out of Saint Louis Cathedral on Sunday mornings spilled right into the café that bore Rosette's mother's name, Café Elizabeth.

Fueled by the possibility of talking to Gabriel, who actually cared what she thought, Lottie hurried past the piano bench. "I will return *tout de suite*," she told a tight-lipped Madame before heading to the library. Justine truly was reading. *Romeo and Juliet,* of course. Lottie plucked the play out of her friend's hands. "Rosette and Gabriel are on their way to visit. Tell Agnes the lessons are almost over. See if they can stay until we finish." Lottie felt as surprised as Justine appeared by the urgency in her voice.

"We?" Justine returned the volume to the *étagère,* sliding it between *Macbeth* and *The Tempest.* "I'm finished. So what I'm actually asking is if they can wait on *you.*" She held a small silver tray she'd found on Grand-père's desk up to her face and smoothed her hair along each side of her part.

"Charlotte." Lottie didn't need to see Madame's face to assess the level of her irritation. The second syllable of her name sounded as heavy as an anchor. An anchor that landed on the *t.*

At that moment, Lottie mentally thanked her grandmother for deportment lessons. She turned around, cast her eyes downward, and clasped her hands loosely at her waist. "Forgive me, Madame Fontenot. I did not want to forget to deliver an important message to Justine."

"I have other students today, so your lesson will have to end right on time. Come with me. You have already wasted enough time."

Lottie nodded and, when she sat next to Madame on the piano bench, produced a genuine smile and said, "Let's begin."

CHAPTER TWO

I F A SHAKESPEARE CHARACTER COULD write about music to her ears, then an orchestra waited in the courtyard for Charlotte.

The melody of Agnes's round voice, Rosette's words riding on the wave of emotions, Gabriel's steady hum as he talked to the cook, and, like an unexpected clash of cymbals, Justine's laughter as she spoke to Grand-mère. They were all gathered around the cypress table near the outdoor kitchen, the women's dresses an explosion of soft hues amidst the fruit and magnolia trees. Agnes, Rosette, and Gabriel wrapped pairs of pecan pralines in madras squares. Standing away from the smoke that curled like soft gray ribbons through the lemon trees, Justine and Grand-mère chatted, their heads tilted toward one another like flowers whose blooms are too heavy for their stems.

How is it that my grandmother converses with my friend, even pats Justine's hand, and yet her talks with me seem like an obligation—sometimes a nuisance? Grand-père says I'm too sensitive. Maybe Grand-mère isn't sensitive enough.

Lottie picked up her skirt to avoid tripping on the steps that led from the screened gallery onto the slate pavers that surrounded the garden. Had it been summer, no one would have ventured far from the back room that opened to the courtyard, allowing even the whispers of breezes. The New Orleans summer wrapped such a steamy blanket around the city that most residents fled for summer homes in the country or across the lake. Grand-père owned a cottage in Mandeville, so they sometimes spent cooler days enjoying the lake breezes. Families not so fortunate dressed in lightweight linens, slept on their porches, and prayed for an early fall. But today, the January sun treated them to warm breezes. Winters rested in New Orleans.

Lottie headed in Grand-mère's direction, because to do otherwise would be to risk her sharp-edged tongue later.

"Madame Fontenot had another class scheduled. She apologized for not speaking to you before she left. She said she will be back next week," Lottie said.

"So, Charlotte," Grandmother said, glancing at Justine for a wisp of time, "did you enjoy the lesson?"

Lottie glared at Justine, who appeared to be entranced with the slate paver on which Lottie stood. "Well, I think the lessons will be interesting." She wouldn't be dishonest, especially since she suspected that Justine had already suggested Lottie's lack of enthusiasm.

Grand-mère frowned at Lottie. "You must listen more closely to your deportment instructor and eliminate 'well' from your conversations." She turned toward Justine and placed her hand on the young woman's cheek. "My dear, you must have your bonnet, or else this dreadful sun will scorch your lovely ivory skin."

"Oh, you are so right," said Justine. Lottie watched, almost blinded by the glow of gratitude on her friend's face. Rosette could have sweetened her pralines with Justine's smile instead of brown sugar. "I think I left it on the sofa in the parlor."

But before Justine could place a slippered toe toward the house, Grand-mère held up her hand. "Wait. I can send Agnes to retrieve it."

"Agnes is helping Rosette. I can fetch it for her," Lottie said, aware too late that *retch* could have replaced *fetch* and sounded equally offensive.

Justine immediately averted her eyes. Grand-mère looked composed, but disapproval tightened her jaw and Lottie knew this would not be the end. As she'd gotten older, she'd become more aware of social distinctions, but she still couldn't understand her grandparents' attitude toward their slaves. Abram and Agnes filled the well of Lottie's earliest memories. Their firm, warm grasps as she skipped between them on their way to buy croissants at the French Market…her giggles when Abram scooped her up and twirled her around an antidote to Grand-mère's harsh words…and always, the familiar smell of chicory and gumbo *filé* when she rested her sleepy head against Agnes's neck as she was carried upstairs to bed.

It wasn't until Lottie grew older that the differences were explained to her: *gens de couleur libres* were the free people of color who carried papers to prove they weren't slaves bought and sold at market. Slaves like Agnes and Abram. But then, even some free people of color owned house slaves. Ownership of someone else just did not make sense to Lottie. It was exactly the reason, too, that Lottie dreaded the day she would have to marry. She didn't want to be a wife owned by a man.

Lottie knew her grandmother's pinched face had more to do with Lottie's tone than her offer. Disrespect was not tolerated, of course, which likely accounted for children being "seen and not heard" in many households. Once Lottie had overheard her grandmother telling her dressmaker that she wondered some days if children shouldn't even be seen. Today, Lottie wished she could be both invisible and mute. *When will she notice that her own granddaughter's head is bare?*

In that suspended moment, she hoped she could issue an apology before the waves of her response crashed against the wall that was her grandmother. Lottie attempted to look and sound more penitent than she felt. Softening her voice, with her eyes cast down, she said, "Please, forgive—"

The sudden presence of Gabriel silenced her. He turned briefly to Lottie and murmured, "Excuse me," then faced Grand-mère and Justine. Dressed simply in the dark blue trousers and white shirt he wore when he helped Rosette in the café, Gabriel lowered his head to avoid a tree branch posing no threat to the women. "Here is your bonnet, Mademoiselle Dumas," he said, holding out the handcrafted lace bonnet as if he had placed it on a silver tray. His voice reminded Lottie of the velvet dresses she wore in the winters—elegant, yet comforting in its warmth. It could have belonged to a man twice his age. When they were younger, Gabriel had told Lottie he was glad God gave him that voice. It made him seem older and better able to provide for and protect his mother and sister after his father left them.

Justine placed the bonnet over her wilting curls and chirped, "Why, Gabriel, what a kind gesture."

He nodded then turned his attention to Lottie's grandmother. "Madame LeClerc, my mother and I would like to leave some pralines for you. A little *lagniappe,* as it were, as thanks for allowing Agnes to spend time with us."

"Of course, of course," she said and waved her hand as if to dismiss him, yet all the while glaring at Lottie.

"Perhaps…" Gabriel blinked in that honey-eyed innocence Charlotte recognized from years ago. The one he'd use to avoid Rosette's wrath when he'd been mischievous. He looked at Lottie and ever so slightly nodded his head. "Mademoiselle Charlotte could make the selection and then retreat to the house, having no bonnet herself."

To hide the smile about to make its presence known, Lottie held her hand over her mouth and feigned a slight cough. Were it not for the weight of the situation, her skirt, and his status, she might have hugged Gabriel. But the wiry boy who taught her how to pull crawfish out of ditches had disappeared inside the muscular young man who stood in front of her today. Hugging this version of Gabriel could, if she allowed herself, take on more meaning than friendship. But her future would be shaped by society and her grandparents. And it didn't include Gabriel.

Lottie recovered from the onset of her throat disturbance, smiled at Gabriel, and, before her grandmother could speak, said, "I would be happy to help Grand-mère by doing that."

She walked to the table with Gabriel, leaving Justine, whose mouth had formed a perfect circle, and her grandmother, whose lips had formed a perfect line between her nose and her chin.

"It was kind of you to protect me from my grandmother," she whispered as they walked away.

"I knew she would not be rude to me as she would to you. And how else could I thank you for standing up for Agnes?" He grinned.

Lottie blushed, thinking of an answer to the question.

AFTER THEIR DINNER, LOTTIE ROSE to carry the china to the butler's pantry, where she and Grand-mère would hand wash and dry the table settings. When she had grown old enough to join her grandparents for meals,

Lottie was deemed old enough to participate in cleaning the dishes too. The two women carried the Sevres china plates and serving pieces themselves because Grand-mère didn't entrust the pieces to the house servants. What confused Lottie about the ritual was that the slaves were allowed to carry the dishes to the table. Agnes had told her, "No worrying about that. I'm glad Miz LeClerc don't want me touching them plates, if they that temperamental. Beside, they probably cost more than me."

As Lottie reached for her grandfather's plate, Grand-mère said, "Charlotte, I will take care of the china. Your grandfather and I have decided that the two of you have matters to discuss." She looked at her husband. "Isn't this so, Louis?"

It wasn't truly a question.

Louis LeClerc stood, straightened the front of his frock coat, and motioned toward the library. "Come, Lottie, we will talk before I return to work."

Lottie's confusion left her motionless for a moment. Usually her grandfather rested for a while after their large midday meal, avoiding the sweltering sun, and then he would go back to his office. Since his heart problems, sometimes he even napped on one of the daybeds that was pulled out to the gallery at the end of dinner. So for him to spend that time engaged in a conversation with Lottie meant that her grandmother had found time before they ate to inform him of the morning's events. And since Grand-mère had already carried the serving dishes into the pantry, her part in the conversation was already over.

Lottie brushed her fingertips down the front of her dress in case piecrust crumbs had landed there. "Yes, PaPa," she responded, as if there would be another answer.

Not that she didn't expect repercussions.

Grandmother was quite predictable when it came to doling out consequences. Quite often, the more severe the offense, the longer Grand-mère waited before she dispensed the penalty. The time Lottie hid in the carriage house just to see if she was missed, she'd begged her grandmother to administer swift punishment, but Grand-mère had waited until the next morning to inform Lottie that she would spend the night sleeping in the one empty stall in the stable. Her grandfather must not have agreed with the decision, because when a disapproving, mumbling Agnes escorted Lottie across the courtyard, they were accompanied by the crescendo of her grandparents' voices from their upstairs bedroom. Lottie remembered hearing Grand-mère mention her mother's name, but the rest sounded like a cartful of bells that had been thrown down the stairs. Agnes and Abram took turns checking on her that night. Agnes had given her a warm praline that not only melted on her tongue like snow crystals of brown sugar but sweetened the air a bit too. That next morning, Lottie awoke to a pair of arms scooping her off the hay and the soft tickle of her grandfather's beard as he kissed her on the forehead and whispered, "*Je t'aime ma petite fille jolie*" when he tucked her into the cool soap-scented sheets on her bed. Nothing Grand-mère could ever do would erase the memory of his voice telling her he loved his pretty little girl.

By now, Lottie understood that the delay between action and reaction was an element of the punishment. It typically did not involve her grandfather, which made this meeting all the more unusual. *But at least I can spend some time with him.* Lately, he left for work earlier and arrived home later. He recently told Lottie, when she asked why he was gone so often, "I thought at one time I owned the business. Now, I'm afraid the business owns me." She didn't know if his shoulders sagged from sadness or exhaustion or both, as she watched him walk to his carriage that morning.

Instead of sitting in his desk chair, Louis LeClerc moved the mahogany chairs flanking the tall bookcases against the wall to face one another. He looked at the chairs, then at Lottie, back at the chairs again, and said, "This would not be comfortable for either one of us, would it?" He laughed when Lottie shook her head. "Of course it wouldn't," he agreed and moved the chairs back to their original spaces. He reached for his granddaughter's arm, linked his around it, and patted her hand. "To the parlor we go."

Lottie smiled, glad that he looked relaxed and relieved. She sank into the silk settee and her skirt billowed around her, the relief of its weight as welcome as Grand-père's calm demeanor. She chided herself for allowing her stomach to practically loop around itself. She'd rather talk to Grand-père on a bad day than Grand-mère on a good day. Hands clasped in her lap, Lottie waited for her grandfather to mete out whatever consequence her grandmother had decided he should, confident that he would soften it. *Should I remind him that I am almost twenty years old?* But using her age could well be a disadvantage, if he used it to remind *her* that she should act more like an adult.

The sun streamed through the shutters, leaving slices of light along the carpet. No sounds drifted through, not this time of day, when the entire city lay drowsy and waiting for even the slightest suggestion of dusk. On the wall behind Charlotte was a painting of her father, the likeness between them obvious to even a stranger. The dark brown eyes beneath the thick, arched eyebrows, the firm set of the chin… Quite often, the portrait of her father was mistaken for that of her grandfather as a young man. Louis glanced at the painting of his son as he loosened his ascot, tugging the knot away from his neck. He straightened against the wingbacked chair and rested his arms on the softly worn *manchettes*.

Louis leaned toward Lottie. "Are you, my *p'tit*, such *un tonnerre a la voile* that I should have you confined to jail for a night?"

Wild and uncontrollable? Does Grand-mère think that of me? Spurs of anxiety rippled through Lottie. She readied herself to protest, but then she saw her grandfather's lips curl into a smile. "Maybe two nights," she answered.

"I am making light of this," he said. He looked over his shoulder for a moment then back at Lottie. She wondered if he feared his wife may have overheard him. "But you know you are to be respectful to your elders, especially in the presence of others."

"Yes, Grand-père, of course. I will apologize to Grand-mère and ask her to forgive me." Lottie hated to disappoint her grandfather, and it would be for that reason that she would be especially contrite when she spoke to her grandmother. "But you know how I feel about how Agnes is treated—"

"Stop. We are not going to discuss this further. We have more important business to talk about."

"But that was all that happened today." Lottie heard herself whine and winced. That would not go far in supporting her maturity.

"Part of what happened today is because you are a young woman and, in your case, a strong-headed young woman. By now, you should have already had your coming-out party, engaged, married. But the yellow fever, then my unexpected sickness, delayed all that."

Lottie grasped the arm of the settee. "But, Grand-père, I understood. You know I've never complained. We will have time when you are feeling stronger." Ever since the doctors suggested his need to rest because of his heart, Lottie was careful to not upset him.

"You will soon be twenty. Some might say we have

waited too long."

Too long to make a suitable match? Too long to be told what man would be chosen for her to spend her life with? She could not even make her grandmother happy. How would she ever please a stranger? "Please, PaPa, please." Lottie reached for his hands. "I am not ready to be a wife. Why do we have to follow someone else's rules?"

"Oh, my dear Charlotte, you are so much like your father." He gazed at his son's portrait then at his granddaughter. "But we are doing this for you. For your future. In a few months when we have your party, you will see."

"But I do not want to see."

"I know. I know. And neither did your father."

CHAPTER THREE

G ABRIEL GIROD FORCED A SMILE when André Toutant strolled into his mother's café. It wasn't that he disliked André, but his cousin flaunted his wealth, or at least that of his mother's protector. If Gabriel had the wealth of his own mother's protector, he could have joined André in Paris, attending the school the man had promised him.

Both of their mothers lived well as the *placées* of rich Creole men, white men who provided for them in a system of "left-handed marriages." As free women of color, they were not allowed by law to marry these men, but they could become their life partners. Care of the women included jewels, gowns, and homes—like the Creole cottages on Rampart Street where both André and Gabriel lived. And for the first ten years of their lives, they both enjoyed the benefits that came with being the sons of rich men. One of those benefits was being sent to Paris for an education. But Rosette Girod changed that when she decided she valued self-respect more than money.

All Gabriel remembered about the night his father

walked out of their home was harpoons of lightning slashing the night canvas followed by thunder that roared and rumbled. The kind of thunder Tante Virgine said could "break a boy's bones." Huddled in the corner of his bedroom, Gabriel didn't know if he feared the fury of the storm outside or the one he overheard inside. The one that ended with his mother's tears.

In the years since, Gabriel had helped his mother by working in the café. During that time, his cousin left New Orleans as a gangly, credulous kid and had returned a gentlemanly, cosmopolitan young man.

"When did you arrive in New Orleans?" Gabriel handed André a steaming cup of café au lait and sat at a small table, one protected from the sun by a canvas awning.

"A few days ago." André answered Gabriel, but his eyes surveyed the small stand.

He thinks he is above this simple place. That I have sunk to a different class. Gabriel shifted in his chair. "Tante Virgine must be quite proud and happy that you are here. We don't see as much of her because of"— Gabriel motioned toward the stand and shrugged— "well, we have the business now." He sounded guiltier than he meant to, thinking André might interpret it as apologizing for having to work. And work seemed as foreign to André as André's double-breasted frock coat and broad, pleated, starched linen shirt did to Gabriel.

André sipped the coffee and leaned back, comforta-bly slouched. "Yes, yes, she is. Cooking as if I have not eaten for the past five years, which"—he patted his stomach—"does not seem to be the case. But I doubt she will be excited for long. I plan to return to Paris. I am studying to be a medical doctor."

"Excuse me," Gabriel said to his cousin, relieved that a couple approached the stand and gave him a reason to walk away. The realization of all he could have been throbbed in his chest, a knot of dreams pushing its way out. *This is now my life.* He reached for the pots, holding one of almost-scalded milk in one hand and coffee with chicory in the other, and poured them together into each cup.

Gabriel returned to the table and hoped that disappointment had not settled like a cloud on his face. But it didn't need to. His cousin already knew that the distance between them was more than miles.

"So, a doctor of medicine," Gabriel said. He hoped his words car-ried pride instead of envy. "What school will you attend?"

"The University of Paris has accepted me," André said, sounding almost apologetic and only glancing at Gabriel. He stared at a trio of nuns on their way to the cathedral. "To dress in so much black, with hardly a hair showing, in this depressing heat… Now *that* is showing a commitment to God. Something my mother wished I had taken to Europe with me all those years ago. But maybe I will find it again while I'm here."

Gabriel opened his eyes so wide, he felt his eyebrows wrinkle his forehead. He stifled his laugh when he saw the look of confusion on his cousin's face. André's years in Paris, European clothes, living as free as any white man, attending medical school…what more evidence did André need of God's commitment to him?

"What amuses you?" André seemed confused.

"Only that the person least committed to faith has the most to be thankful for."

"Yes, but none of it can I find here. Home. With my family and friends. And yet, what is humorous to me," André said, "is that the friend I leave surrounded by voodoo, slavery, and crime continues to believe."

"Some days more than others," said Gabriel. "I need to close early today. With Rosette gone, I will be walking home."

"I have a carriage. You don't need to do that," said André.

A part of Gabriel wanted to refuse, to prove that he didn't need the comforts to which André was accustomed. But he remembered that soon his cousin would be thousands of miles away, and he didn't know if or when he might see him again. He nodded his thanks, and André waited as he closed up the shop.

"I saw your mother and Alcee at the French Market buying shrimp," said André as they climbed into his carriage. "Alcee still laughs like the little girl I knew, not like the young woman she is becoming. How old is she now? Thirteen?"

"Not yet. She just turned twelve," Gabriel said. Without Alcee, he might have joined André in Paris.

Maybe his father would have stayed, with one less person to depend on him. But, no, he had seen his father's face soften with delight, his generous smile when he held his sister. Money flowed too freely from the river of the landed gentry into the stream of the Girod home for that to be the reason he left.

"Your mother, is she…?"

Gabriel flinched. He knew the question before his cousin finished it. "Is she still alone? That is what you meant, yes?"

André bent forward to grab the reins. "It was not an accusation. I wanted to ask if she was happy." He urged the horses forward.

Gabriel saw a glimmer of the boy who'd played tag with him and Lottie, the one he would trip so Lottie could win a race. He realized in that moment that he didn't need to mistrust everyone who asked about Rosette. Since he had become the only man in the house, he felt responsible for protecting his mother. They had moved beyond the clustered whispers when she passed or the wide space someone would take on the banquette that forced his mother to step in the vile muck of the street. When she opened her café and started selling coffee and pastries before and after church or during holidays and weekends, Gabriel prayed for customers. Prayed that she would not be made to look foolish, standing alone when people passed her by. Those prayers had been answered in abundance as Rosette's stand grew into a café with places for her customers to sit. His mother had proven that a head for business could coexist with a beautiful face, a cultured upbringing, and a pampered life.

"I'm sorry. I'm not accustomed to questions from people who truly care about my mother beyond what gossip they can bring with them to the dressmaker," Gabriel said. "Yes, she is content. She's worked hard to provide for us, and she's proud of her success."

"And you? What about your plans to attend *L'Ecole Centrale* to become an engineer? If you're still interested, maybe we could arrange a way for you to return with me. You know my mother would have a mind to help. I'm her only child. She has the means—"

Tales of Virgine Toutant's extravagances were legend in the city. She spent money, Agnes said to Rosette one day, "like people spend time. She just lets it go by, always thinking there be more tomorrow." Usually Agnes followed her observation with a "hmph" and a tally of the merchants grateful for Virgine's existence. Or at least the existence of her protector, cotton-exchange broker Bernard LaFonte. Gabriel, however, did not want to add his name to the list of those indebted to Virgine.

"It is a generous offer, but no. My mother needs my help."

"Do you truly believe she would want you to throw away your dream, your future, if she knew you had the opportunity?"

"No, she wouldn't. So, please, do not discuss this with Tante Virgine or Rosette. I know my mother would want me to go. She never asked me to sacrifice anything to help her. First, her dream. Then mine."

The carriage stopped in front of the Girod cottage. "Have you given up your other dream as well? The one you should have forsaken years ago?" André asked.

"I'm not sure what you mean. Being educated in Paris *was* my dream."

André tilted his head. "You really don't know what I mean, do you? It can't be because you think of it as something real, something not a dream." André placed his hands on his cousin's shoulders, gently shaking him. "Tell me the truth."

"I would if I knew what you meant."

"Charlotte LeClerc. That dream." André released Gabriel's shoulders and reached for the reins.

André's words stung him, and Gabriel's hesitation was his answer.

"Even though we were young, her presence pulled you like a mag-net. Obviously that hasn't changed. But you know, you're following the wrong dream. One you have no control over. It does not matter that with your skin, your hair, you could pass for white. You will always be Rosette's son. *Comme il faut.* You will always be a free man *of color.* And Charlotte will always be white."

André spoke the truth. A truth like hundreds of bee stings. A truth he would one day have to face.

GABRIEL WATCHED THE CARRIAGE WHEELS churn as

André made his way home through the thick mud, dredging up garbage and untold muck that littered the narrow street. The sun intensified the mingled odors, and the humidity made them almost palpable. Were it not for the fragrances of the gardenias and violets planted in the neighboring gardens, leaving and entering the house would be even more of an assault.

The scent of Rosette's gumbo filé welcomed him and would certainly pacify the beast that growled in his stomach and reminded him he had not taken the time to eat lunch today. Rosette had left the café early to consider enrolling Alcee in Michel Seligny's *l'Academie Sainte-Barbe*. The school was within walking distance of the business, which was important because it enabled Alcee to join her friends in private lessons. Unlike most of their mothers, Rosette worked to support her family, and taking time away to transport Alcee to and from lessons was almost impossible. Gabriel hoped they had been pleased with the school. If not, the conversation between the two females in the house might be spicier than the gumbo, in which case he and his food might escape to the *garçonnière*. Like most of the separate quarters built by families of wealth allowing their young men to go and come as they pleased, his had been built above the outdoor kitchen.

But instead of finding two women in the parlor, there were three. The one who didn't live there wiped her red-rimmed, watery eyes with the lace sleeve of a dress scattered with nosegays so vibrant they could have been plucked from the gardens along the rows of cottages. Her tignon, bands of watercolored silks, complemented the flowers spilling over the yards of taffeta that surrounded her. The cane chair Gabriel knew she had to be sitting on had disappeared under the wide bell-shaped skirt. Living with his mother and Alcee, Gabriel had learned more than he wanted about fashion and fabrics. He knew enough, though, to know that the young woman's gown could pay his sister's tuition for a year.

To get the food he wanted required walking through the parlor to the dining room. Or walking outside and through the narrow alley to the rear of the house. But he had already made eye contact with his mother, who looked too relieved to see him. He was trapped.

"Look, Alcee, Gabriel is home." Rosette sounded very much as she did on Carnival when he and Alcee were younger and she attempted to distract them from the long wait for the procession by pointing out pirates and devils and strangely-put-together animals. Even now, his sister brightened, much happier to see him than on most days. Perhaps because her penance had ended and she could be released from her mother and the visitor.

Rosette moved from the ornate wood-and-cane settee in one fluid motion, walked to the door, and escorted Gabriel to the young woman, who, despite the soft hiccups and tears, managed to appear striking. The damp fringes of eyelashes, the full lips, even the wisps of dark brown hair that strayed from her stylish tignon might have, on a dance floor, seemed calculated to entice.

"This is my son, Gabriel." Rosette paused. "This is Mademoiselle Serafina Lividaus. She recently moved to a house on Rue Esplanade."

Serafina looked up at Gabriel and nodded without extending her hand, which would have been awkward, since only moments before she had wiped away tears from her eyes and nose.

"I am pleased to meet you," he said. She didn't look much older than Alcee, but something about the dullness in her eyes suggested she had already experienced far more than his sister. He felt the soft press of his mother's hand on his back and mentally groaned, anticipating being steered to the settee. Instead, she turned him in the direction of the dining room.

"Alcee, p'tit, please show your brother the meal I saved for him while Serafina and I stay in the parlor to finish our discussion."

"Yes, Mother," she said and moved with uncharacteristic speed to Gabriel's side.

Rosette patted his cheek. The scent of the eucalyptus she'd used earlier in the filé lingered on her hand. "Thank you for your help today."

The white embroidered lace tablecloth from their earlier meal still covered the table. Gabriel served himself rice then lifted the top of the tureen to ladle the still-steaming shrimp and gumbo into his bowl. Alcee carried three chunks of bread from the sideboard, served two to Gabriel, and kept the other for herself. She pulled out a chair across from him and then, as if she'd changed her mind, walked to the edge of the dining room and pulled the secreted doors closed.

"Now we can talk," she said.

"My stomach talked to me and told me to feed it. I'll listen while you tell me about the visit to the Academy this afternoon."

"Well." She breathed in and out like she was preparing to start a footrace, glanced to her right, then looked back at Gabriel. The ringlets in her hair, which had been pulled to one side, continued to sway from the motion, too playful an action for the serious expression on her face.

Gabriel tore a piece of bread and chewed it with deliberate slowness to prevent a smile. From the first time Alcee had toddled over to him, demanding to be taken to the market and pummeling his leg with her plump little fists until he relented, Gabriel knew she would not be afraid to ask for what she wanted. Over the years, she'd learned when to push and when to pull and was growing into a strong young woman because of her confidence. Unfortunately, that was not a quality considered attractive to men or sometimes even other women. And it often placed her in an orbit outside the universe of her peers.

"The director writes short stories, so I am certain he can teach writing. The school is in a nice building." She handed him a piece of her bread, which meant she wanted it dipped into the gumbo and returned, continuing to talk as she waited. "But the students did not spend much time talking to me after Mother left to talk to Monsieur Seligny. I don't think they liked me."

Gabriel handed Alcee her bread then served himself another bowl. His sister was not one to be pacified with platitudes. He dismissed responding as he might to his own friends, telling them that things would get better, to give it another chance, or, depending on the friend, to pray. "Did you talk to them? Politely?"

She shifted in the chair and started making crumbs with the thin crust of the bread. "Yes. I think so."

"So." Gabriel kept his voice light, stirred his gumbo, and watched the shrimp as they chased the okra around the edge of the bowl. "What did you talk to them about?"

Alcee made what had become known in the Girod household as her "oyster" face—that medley of pain and disgust that transformed her face from winsome to wicked when offered a raw oyster on the half shell. She swirled bread crumbs in circles on the tablecloth. "I just asked them why manners classes were important only for the girls and why we couldn't be enrolled in whatever classes were offered for the boys."

"I see," he commented, and as he dipped his spoon into his bowl, he raised his eyes and saw two fat tears stream down her cheeks.

CHAPTER FOUR

G ABRIEL AND ALCEE WASHED THE DISHES, removed the tablecloth, and discussed the idea of cake. But his sister decided she wanted to relieve her body of the weight and heat of satin, petticoats, camisoles, and a list of other garments he would have preferred she'd not mention. "I may sit outside on the back gallery and finish *Romeo and Juliet*. Or I may sleep," she'd told Gabriel before she glided out of the dining room. He had attempted more conversation about the school, but she said tomorrow would be better because she would have more time to think about the day.

About to retire to bed himself, Gabriel heard his mother's *"Mon dieu!"* before she slid open the door that separated her from the dining room. She stepped in and rubbed her temples with her fingertips. "I must learn when to stop listening," she said. She collapsed into the closest chair, her skirt billowing around her in waves of silver silk. "Alcee has gone to bed?"

"Yes. She said she might read, but she hasn't left her bedroom." Gabriel opened the shutters, hoping for a cool night breeze, then sat in the chair next to his mother. "It seems she had an eventful day."

Rosette smiled. "How kind of you to call it such." She leaned closer to him. "You and I can talk at the café, so there will be no danger of her only pretending to be asleep while we talk. She's already learned far too much using that ruse."

Once a friend of Rosette's complained that the hairdresser they both used made no effort to learn the latest styles. The next month when Eliza came to the house, a then-eight-year-old Alcee informed her that Madame Chatengier thought, "Eliza is too old or too slow to bother to learn what fashionable ladies want." Fortunately, Rosette had time to tell Louise Chatengier what happened before her appointment with Eliza, else, as Rosette said, "Louise may have never needed a hairdresser again after Eliza finished with her hot irons." His mother and sister had had a long discussion about eavesdropping and the danger of angering a woman who could make wearing a tignon necessary inside the house as well as outside.

"André stopped in at the café today. He brought me home in his carriage."

"And nothing happened in between?"

Of course she already knew the answer to her own question. In fact, Gabriel supposed she knew his cousin would be visiting him at the café. The Tremé neighborhood didn't need a newspaper as long as André's mother lived there. Tante Virgine reported whatever she heard to whoever would listen. She knew how many of Old Man

Mouton's Creole tomatoes the Beranays' mutt trampled when he ran through Mouton's garden chasing the one-eyed calico that belonged to the German family whose daughter secretly met an American, whose family might be on the verge of bankruptcy because of the father's frequent racetrack visits.

"Would I be able to tell you more than Tante Virgine told you?"

"Maybe this time, because you are home before André and she keeps too busy entertaining him to stroll here with gossip." She patted her cheeks with her palms and looked around the room. "The evening is not as cool as expected. Have you seen my fan?"

"Yes, I did." Gabriel had spotted it earlier, surprised to see it on the corner of the breakfront. She didn't use it often. He handed it to her, sat again, and watched as she separated the carved ivory sticks to reveal an explosion of flowers hand-painted on sapphire-blue silk edged with lace.

"It is exquisite, isn't it?" She held it in front of her and gazed at it as if it spoke a language only she understood.

Perhaps it did. The first Christmas Jean Noel Reynaud did not join them for dinner, a carriage delivered three packages. Rosette gave one to Gabriel and one to his sister and sent the other back with the driver. The next Christmas was the same, except that four packages came. Rosette handed two back, gave one to him and the other to Alcee. By the third year, when three packages were delivered for Rosette, she stopped returning them. Jean Noel sent her a fan every year after she ended their relationship. Gabriel wondered if Madame Reynaud knew the destination of the carriage at Christmas. Or did she, like almost all wives of men who had placées, choose to ignore anything connected with the woman her husband protected? Except in Rosette's case and by her choice, his mother no longer defined herself by her relationship with Jean Noel.

"So, you do not want to discuss your visit with your cousin?" She paused. "Were there harsh words between you?"

No, just a harsh reality. "We aren't boys fighting over who really won at marbles."

Rosette's raised eyebrows warned Gabriel that his remark bordered on insolent. Over the years, he learned that that expression tended to precede what Agnes referred to as a "come to Jesus meeting" that almost always ended in tears or unhappiness for Gabriel or his sister.

"Forgive me," said Gabriel. "The conversation was pleasant. And he looks well."

His mother's face softened. She closed her fan and set it on the table. "Sometimes I forget that talking to your cousin is difficult."

"I am content where I am." Not happy, but she did not need to know that. "I want to hear about your young lady visitor, but let's move to the parlor where we can be cooler." Gabriel followed his mother to the front room and lifted the windows to open the shutters.

"Our café needs a cooler January," Rosette remarked, opening her fan again. "My visitor Serafina resides in a cottage built for her by Paul Bastion. You understand?"

He nodded. Gabriel did not need Rosette to explain the relationship any further. The white Bastions were cotton brokers and landowners, more than happy to fill anyone's ear with tales of their wealth. Madame Bastion did not flaunt their money as much as her husband and sons. She seemed to have misplaced her *joie de vivre* not long after her daughter's marriage to a plantation owner who moved her away from New Orleans. But whatever joy of life she'd lost, her husband Emile made up for in his new interest in ships and riverfront property. Paul, their son, spent money with a vengeance. "So, he is her protector."

"*Pauvre ti bebe,*" Rosette said, shaking her head in dismay. "Monsieur Bastion must have been exceedingly and uncharacteristically charming to the poor little thing the night of the ball, else she would have rightly refused him."

Gabriel recoiled at the thought of his mother or his sister as one of those young women, girls groomed to attract rich white Creole men. He shifted his eyes to the ornate French enameled ormolu clock on the side table and then turned his attention back to his mother. "And now?"

"And now she is worried the Bastions may one day become grand-parents of a child they will never acknowledge."

THE NEXT MORNING, WHILE ROSETTE walked an uncertain Alcee to the Academy, Gabriel readied the last batch of pralines to take to the café that day. Cooling on a marble slab, the creamy brown-sugar-and-pecan candies smelled as sweet as they tasted. His mother's recipe used more pecans than the other vendors who roamed the market balancing their baskets of pralines on their tignons. It meant spending days shelling the pecans that rained from the surrounding trees and avoiding the temptation of eating more than were tossed into the basket for cooking. But that effort meant Rosette sold out of pralines almost daily.

Business in the café had increased every year since Rosette first opened her small stand. Gabriel remembered Agnes and Rosette's conversations about money those first few months after Jean Noel stopped coming to their house. Gabriel would crouch in the dining room behind the closed parlor doors, his bare feet ready in case he had to dash into his bedroom. The first visits involved mostly Rosette's sobbing as Agnes hummed any number of hymns about Jesus. Eventually the crying and hymns gave way to practical issues. When Gabriel heard that Agnes would teach Rosette how to cook, he covered his mouth with his hands so as not to expel a yelp of gratitude. Letting go of Jean Noel had also meant letting go of their servant Olivia, which meant letting go of mouthwatering meals. In the years since, Rosette had evolved into a competent cook and an equally competent businesswoman.

Before he saw his mother return from the Academy, Gabriel heard her talking in French. He hoped her conversation was with herself, because some of the words he didn't recognize, and if words could stomp their feet, hers certainly would be doing so. She emerged from the alley between their house and the neighbor's, snapped her parasol closed, and clenched it in her hands as if it were a branch she wanted to snap in half. Although tempted to speak first, Gabriel decided it was best to wait for her boiling emotions to simmer.

"Your sister was almost expelled from the Academy before her first class." She sounded angry, but her neck and cheeks did not have the crimson flush that generally accompanied her ire. She stared blankly, as if in hearing herself, she'd realized her own confusion.

Gabriel broke a praline in two and offered her half. "Would you care to taste this batch?" He saw the "no" in her narrowed eyes and put it back on the table. Since she remained quiet, he knew he needed to ask. "What happened?"

"Alcee asked Monsieur Seligny if she could enroll in the Greek or Latin classes. He informed her that girls learned French." She released the parasol, held it by her side, and gently tapped it against her lemon-and-white-striped linen skirt. "She asked him what would happen if the girls learned the same languages as the boys. He said he didn't know and it didn't matter. That's how the school had always taught and would continue to teach." Rosette stopped tapping, turned her face upward for a moment, and sighed. "Then she wanted to know, if she wore trousers, could she be in the class."

They looked at one another, and though Gabriel wasn't sure which of them laughed first, the exasperation on his mother's face surrendered itself to the humor of Alcée's persistence.

"And could you imagine my daughter being told she would be someone's placée?" She shook her head. "Never doubt, Gabriel, even when you do not understand situations or decisions, that God has a plan and a purpose."

When Gabriel continued removing the hardened pralines from the slab and didn't respond, Rosette placed her hand under his chin and turned his face to hers. "Even when He does not reveal it right away," she said so softly it could have been a prayer.

After the experience at Alcée's school, Gabriel didn't want to disagree with his mother. It wasn't that he doubted God's plans. But what should be obvious to her was some things God could not change. Even if his skin was lighter than that of the riverfront workers, they would always be white and he would always be a free man of color. And even though he enjoyed Lottie's company, admired her honesty, and shared her compassion, his feelings for her would stay locked in his heart with his other dreams. Dreams of a life of his choosing. Dreams of a love of his choosing.

CHAPTER FIVE

"AND JUS' WHERE YOU THINK YOU headed out to, Miss Lottie, with that cat tucked under your arm?" Agnes looked up from where she sat in the courtyard, stitching a piece from the rippled mound of cream-colored gauzy fabric covering her lap and feet.

"Are you mending a tablecloth or Grand-mère's summer dress?"

Agnes stopped sewing, leaned over, and, with an abundance of care, rearranged the delicate folds of the froth. Lottie figured she didn't want her to see her laugh. But even though she concealed her face, Agnes couldn't hide or control the pulsating top of her body. She straightened herself in the chair and adjusted the gray tignon she wore. She squint-eyed Henri. "You better get a holt of that cat. If he get loose on this, he'll be finding himself lost in that swampland behind Tremé."

"Agnes, his name is not 'that cat.' It is *Ahn-ree.*" Not at all impressed with the discussion of his name, the cat squirmed and meowed his dissatisfaction. Lottie transferred him to the other side of her body and hoped she could escape Agnes before Henri escaped her.

"En don't you go changing what we talkin' about. Whenever you do that, I knows trouble is arount the corner." She pulled the thread through the fabric as if the needle were a thin sliver of a silver whip. "We been together too many years. When my heart don't hear the truth, it most beat out of my chest. Like it doing now."

Why did I think I could deceive Agnes? She isn't Grand-mère, whose heart beats rules and manners. "Is my grandmother at the dressmaker's?"

Agnes looked at Lottie as if she'd asked for permission to play in the Mississippi River. "Why? You want to meet her there?"

"Of course not. I told Gabriel—" Henri let out a mangled meow and then bolted from Lottie's arms, leaving behind pulled threads on her new violet day dress and a trail of scratches on her arm underneath the sleeves. A rogue cat on tiptoed paws and with an arched back, covered with a patchwork quilt of black, brown, and white fur, had ambled into the courtyard. As soon as the intruder hissed, Henri bounded in the opposite direction.

"Maybe your cat tryin' to teach you something. When trouble around the corner, best be close to home." Agnes tied a knot and bit the thread free of what Lottie could now see was her grandmother's cream-colored cotton skirt. Agnes smoothed the section where she'd been stitching, moving her dark hands back and forth across the fabric like Lottie had seen her do so many times. Her hands, always moving, always doing something for the LeClercs. Sewing, cooking, cleaning, washing. The cycle only changed by more of some, less of the others. And she and Abram lived in a room half the size of Lottie's bedroom.

"Now you know you not suppost to be sneaking around. And Agnes is not going to lie to your grandparents." She gazed up and spoke to the sky. "Jesus, you know I am a faithful woman."

"I'm not sneaking. I'm telling you where I will be, and I promise to be home before Grand-mère." Lottie didn't want to speak to the sky to ask Jesus about the difference between sneaking and waiting until her grandmother left the house. "The orphanage is just a few blocks away."

"You not parading up and down the Vieux Carré without a chaperone. Miz LeClerc hear about dat and…" She looked skyward again. "She don't want to know, Jesus, how Agnes would suffer for that."

"Gabriel is meeting me here to walk with me. Rosette gave him food to deliver there." The longer this went on, the less time Lottie had to spend at the orphanage and with Gabriel. They hadn't seen one another in the weeks since Justine's bonnet led to the remarks Lottie had made to her grandmother, followed by the discussion with her grandfather. Gabriel helped her make sense of her life. A life that, as she grew, became more confusing. And their latest decision about her coming-out party only added to it.

"Your chaperone here. You better hurry on." Agnes

waved her hands much like she did when she ordered Henri to "shoo" from the house.

Lottie didn't know if Agnes's face softened from growing tired of their conversation or from the sight of Gabriel as he swung open the black wrought-iron gate. Seeing him, Lottie's anxiety gave way to joy and she smiled at her friend. His tan frock coat tapered from his shoulders over his brown trousers, and he walked with self-assurance, comfortable in himself. Gabriel and André were no longer annoying boys dragging disgusting creatures out of gutters, the streets, or the river and pestering her with them. Gabriel had become this confident, handsome young man who appeared before her, and Lottie felt a door opening in her heart. And he was stepping through it.

Holding both her hands in his, Gabriel stood back at arm's length and looked at Lottie, his eyes appraising her from head to toe. "This is new, yes? I don't recall ever seeing you in this color. Very pretty. It brightens your face."

Her smile in response felt clumsy on her face. She didn't want to tell him that what brought the flush of crimson to her cheeks was not the dress. Gabriel's touch warmed her in a way it never had before. And even though she enjoyed her hands being enveloped by his, she wondered if perhaps she should. *We fished together. Pushed one another into puddles. Am I supposed to feel this way? Do I want to feel this way?*

"Just what she need for that orphanage."

Gabriel must have been as startled by Agnes as Lottie was, because he released her hands so unexpectedly that she almost lost her balance. He walked over to Agnes, who stood with Grand-mère's dress draped over one arm and the other bent at the elbow, fist on her hip, as if she dared him to move closer. Not at all intimidated by her scowl, one that could wilt bricks, he performed an over-exaggerated bow then tugged her fist from her side.

Agnes swatted his head as if a fly had just landed. "Go on. Don't you think you can mind your manners after you already forgot them. Walk right past me." She sniffed loudly—and if Gabriel had not glanced at her right at that moment, she might have continued the pretense. Instead, she let him hug her. Grand-mère's skirt billowed between them until Agnes patted his back with her free hand and, in a voice that could rock an infant to sleep, said, "Honey, I understand. Some habits hard to break."

Lottie realized what Agnes meant and shamefully wished she didn't have to. In their social structure, it made no difference that Agnes had loved Gabriel as a grandson for years. Slaves were invisible until they were needed.

As soon as Gabriel let her go, Agnes wagged her finger at Charlotte. "You best be sitting on that divan when your grandmother open the door." She shook her head and looked up at Gabriel. "*Une tête dure,* that one," she said and tilted her head toward Lottie. "Too hardhead for her own good. She had best not be that for me."

He nodded. "I understand," he answered with his charming voice. The one that made Agnes grin.

Lottie walked toward the gate but stopped when Gabriel said, "Don't forget your bonnet." He laughed as she scampered past him into the house.

———

FINALLY ON THE OTHER SIDE of the gate, Lottie handed Gabriel a box. "Hold this, please, while I tie this ridiculous ribbon." She looked up and down the street as she fashioned what seemed like miles of fabric into a bow that flopped underneath her chin and ear on one side of her face. "Where is the carriage?"

"No carriage today. We're walking." Gabriel handed the box back to her and picked up the two large baskets he'd set outside the gate before he walked into the courtyard earlier.

"Walking? To Poydras Street? Walking?" With each question, her volume had increased so that by the last one, Lottie had attracted the attention of a passing *marchande* selling tiny nosegays of Spanish jessamine and carnations tied together with lace. She held out a bouquet to Lottie. "*Un picayune?*"

Gabriel could not even see Lottie's face. Just a field of lilacs on cream-shaded linen swaying side-to-side. "No, no. I do not have any coins," said the bonnet. The merchant shrugged, returned the flowers to her tray, and continued down the street. She probably had regular customers who lived on the street, especially in this section of the city. The flowers did not simply serve as an adornment for a lady's dress. Their fragrance provided a bit of perfume to the air for both the wearer and those around her to compensate, in a small way, for the offensive city smells. Sooner or later Lottie would be purchasing nosegays herself. When she lived in her own home. With a husband. Which is exactly what Gabriel did not want to be thinking about.

"We are going to the boys' home on Chartres Street, a few blocks away. Last time we visited the girls. I thought today, the boys." He had to lean over just to be able to see her face under the wide brim. "May we start walking, or else the men will be lighting the lanterns on the street when we return."

Lottie shifted the distance of a whisper when she saw his face. "Of—of course," she said. He didn't know if she appeared to be uncomfortable because he had startled her or because she didn't appreciate his being so close to her. This awkwardness between them was unfamiliar, and even though Gabriel didn't like it, he sensed that it moved into their relationship like an uninvited relative with no money. And he would have to boot it out or learn to live with it.

"I brought a few bananas and oranges I'd asked Agnes to save for me." Lottie opened the lid of the box she held and showed Gabriel the fruit inside. "She didn't ask why I wanted them. I suspect she knew they were not for Henri, after our last visit to the girls' home." She closed the box, and when she spoke, her voice sounded as delicate as her features looked tucked inside her bonnet. "Grand-mère didn't even know these had not been eaten."

Gabriel wanted to tell her that her grandparents probably did not concern themselves with what happened to food left over, either. Agnes, he was certain, managed it wisely. "How fortunate for the boys we'll see today that the fruit wasn't eaten and that you thought of them."

He suspected that Lottie's compassion for the orphans grew from her own parents having died before her second birthday. She spoke little of them and had shared with Gabriel that her grandparents did not encourage questions, saying that to talk about their son and his wife caused too much pain. Not one portrait of her mother or her parents had even been shown to her. Too afraid to ask her grandparents why none existed, Lottie had asked Agnes, who told her there had not been time for portraits.

But if not for her grandparents, Lottie might have been one of those downcast, heart-starved young girls they visited weeks ago. And because of his parents, Gabriel did not have to fear being one of the boys they would soon see.

Between what they carried and Lottie's skirt requiring most of the space on the narrow banquette, the two of them didn't converse much on the way to the orphanage. A few times, Gabriel had to set down his baskets to pull a board over the foul ditches along the street so Lottie could cross. Even maneuvering the banquettes necessitated her lifting layers of the skirt and petticoats she wore to avoid dragging her hem along the refuse, much of it questionable. And when they passed the rotting carcass of a dog or a slave emptying chamber pots, Lottie's gloved hand would fly to her face to pinch her nose and cover her mouth. Gabriel, had his hands not been holding baskets, would have done the same. He held his breath until he saw evidence of a reprieve or was about to collapse.

"I am sorry we won't be able to stay long today," Lottie told Gabriel as he lifted the iron door knocker at the Asylum for Boys.

"You don't need to apologize. It is generous of you to come here at all," he answered.

The door opened and one of the Sisters Marianites of the Holy Cross who ran the home greeted them.

"May I help you?" She appraised them with the experience of one accustomed to having people on the doorstep, her eyes quickly moving from their faces to their feet. A collar of stiff white fabric encircled her head and a band of it covered her forehead, so that it appeared as if she peeked through a flowing curtain of black. "Oh," she said and smiled broadly, "you are here to help us. Come." She opened the door wider. "Come in, please."

"My name is Sister Mary Catherine. I am responsible for this home." She folded her arms, her hands disappearing into the opposite sleeves of her habit. "And you are?"

Gabriel placed the two baskets on the worn wooden floor that faded into a dull white in places. He introduced Charlotte, who handed the Sister the box she held, and then introduced himself.

"We have food to donate and"—he reached into the pocket of his trousers—"and this." His handful of coins moved Sister Mary Catherine's arms rapidly from their hiding place. Gabriel placed the money into her outstretched hands. "It is a small amount, but—"

"Monsieur Gabriel, we appreciate whatever God provides us." Sister reached for the baskets. "I will take these to Sister Josephine to empty into the pantry." She smiled. "Then I will return your baskets for you to fill again. Do you have time for me to show you around?"

Gabriel turned to Lottie. "Yes. A quick tour would be fine," she said.

"Wait here while I find Sister, and then I will come back so we can begin." Sister Mary Catherine walked down the long hall underneath a gallery of religious pictures. The home smelled of bread and cinnamon with a touch of little boy.

"You did not tell me about the lagniappe." Free of her box, Lottie slipped her bonnet under her arm and pulled off her gloves. Their color was a deeper version of the violet flowers in her dress. "If I had known you were bringing something extra, especially money, I would have contributed."

Her tone confused him. Was she annoyed? "I didn't know I needed to tell you."

Lottie brought the gloves to her forehead, about to blot the perspiration that glittered there. Then, as if she'd heard an inner voice of reprimand, she frowned and, with one bare hand, wiped her forehead and then patted her dark hair. She sighed, bit her bottom lip, and looked down. "You did not have to tell me. How would you have, anyway?"

Sister Mary Catherine called out from beyond the foyer, "I am almost there."

Lottie barely lifted her head and said, "I forget that everyone does not hold me to Grand-mère's standard."

"BLESS YOU FOR COMING HERE today," said Sister Mary Catherine as she walked them out. "I am certain the boys were surely pleased to have someone who did not tire so easily. Not to mention making any attempts to do much more than walk in this." She held out her black habit.

"I do understand that," said Lottie as she looked down at her own gown. "Were women not meant to run?"

"Clothes came with the fall, but their design with man. So it seems like we could but cannot. That did not answer your question, but you entertained them by reading fables. Your audience was enthralled."

Lottie laughed. "It is kind of you to say so. The boys might have been enthralled and sleepy after Gabriel ran their legs off."

"Some of these children have not had the experience of an adult reading to them. Sadly, for a few of them, their parents were forbidden to learn, because an educated slave is a dangerous slave. If uneducated people are necessary to carry out slave owners' plans, the problem is with the plans, not with the people." Sister's voice was low, but her passion was high. She held Lottie's arm. "We were so close to changing that. Maybe only a few people at a time. But Sister Anna has been ill, and we could no longer continue."

"Are you talking about teaching slaves to read and write?" Lottie said in a lowered voice. "Sister, what a courageous act."

Sister turned the thumb-worn beads of her rosary. "It's been a terrible disappointment to us all to stop."

Gabriel saw the answer rise like the sun in Lottie's eyes, and he knew she had just adopted a mission. "Lottie, I'm not sure that is a risk you need to be taking."

"You're not sure of my risk? You do not need to be." She shifted her attention to Sister. "I could do this for you."

"The question is not that you could. The question is whether you should. Jail, Lottie. You might be prepared to spend a year in jail, but are your grandparents ready for you to?" Gabriel hoped he could convince her, but he prepared himself for the inevitable—teaching at the orphanage.

"Please, I did not mean for you to take up the cause.

It is not something you should decide so suddenly. You could be placing your grandparents at risk. Pray about this," Sister urged.

"Sister, I understand that you want to be cautious. But this is something I want to do. I can teach on Sundays after our regular visits."

"Then you will have two teachers. I will be here with her," Gabriel said as he opened the door for them to leave.

CHAPTER SIX

"**Y**OU DON'T HAVE TO PROTECT ME," Lottie told Gabriel.

"Who else would be aware of where you spend your time? If something happened to you, I would not forgive myself. As long as you refuse to be honest with your grandparents about where you are, someone needs to watch you."

"There isn't much I do that Grand-mère approves of. I stopped trying to make her happy on my own. It is easier for me not to think and to just do what she tells me when she tells me to do it, no matter how I feel about it."

"Well, you are visiting the poor. Would that not make a difference?"

"To my grandmother, who cares what everyone thinks of her? Maybe if these visits had been her idea first."

"What about your grandfather? He has always impressed me as a man who is reasonable. Surely he would not disapprove of your helping out."

"I don't know. Sometimes he is so strong, but other

times, he seems afraid to disagree with my grandmother. I've overheard them a few times, talking about decisions he had made and the consequences of them. And I do feel so much closer to him. But, because of that, I do not want to do anything that would hurt him. Or have it be the reason for a fight between him and Grand-mère." Then Lottie countered, "But what about you? Why haven't you been honest with your mother?"

"Of course Rosette knows about these visits. I am not pilfering food and clothes from the house to supply the orphanages." He scratched his head. "Why would you ask such a thing?"

"Because these visits are not what I am referring to. You have helped Rosette in the café for years, and yet you don't discuss with her that you still want to study abroad."

"Rosette needed my help, and she still does. And my not talking to her about school is not the same as your hiding what you are doing."

"Is it not? You are hiding. You are not sharing what you really want."

"I don't discuss it with her because she would ship me off on the next boat. She would never want to stand between me and my dream. And that is precisely why I do not tell her. When the café is more profitable, then I can leave her on her own. Until then, I choose to stay."

Ahead of them, a maid washed the banquette in front of a house, splashing water on the brick dust she used to clean the steps. When Gabriel gently held Lottie's elbow and steered her away from the murky brown puddles, Lottie wished for a succession of puddles just to feel the warmth of him. The woman stepped aside as they passed. When Gabriel dropped his hand from her arm, Lottie saw the eye contact between Gabriel and the dark-skinned woman wiping her hands on the stained skirt of her faded calico dress.

"Does she know?" Lottie asked him. They stopped at the corner as a carriage made the turn from one street to another, the uneven cobblestone paths causing it to teeter in a way that reminded Lottie of inebriated men making their way home from Carnival.

"What do you mean?"

"Which one of us isn't white." Lottie covered her nose with a gloved hand as they crossed the street to ward off the foul smell emanating from the gutter.

"I don't…why are…?"

Lottie explained, "Because if we were a white couple or gens de couleur libres, we would not be seen so suspiciously or with such judgment. But how could someone looking at us know the difference? And could they know which one of us was which?"

"Is that what you thought? That the servant knew the difference?" Gabriel sounded surprised.

"Yes, and I just don't understand why it matters." She meant to sound observant, not frustrated.

"This is unlike you to be so, well, angry."

"I know. I know. So much is changing in my life, and I have so little control over it. And…" Lottie turned her face away and pressed her gloved hands to her eyes to blot them before Gabriel could see her tears.

"What are you talking about?"

"My grandparents. They are planning my coming-out party as my birthday party."

GABRIEL WATCHED AS CHARLOTTE WALKED through the courtyard and into her house. Each step took her farther from him, until she disappeared through the doorway into a world he would never be able to join. Loss was not unfamiliar to him. But this…this was more than loss.

A coming-out party meant a prelude to finding a husband. Well, at least to her grandparents, who were finding a husband for her. Marriages in Lottie's world were business transactions completed for the mutual benefit of both parties. For some, the match kept land in the family. For others, it might bring money. The result was the same. Women often found themselves in arrangements where husbands provided a home, children, financial security. In exchange, wives pretended not to notice that their men spent nights away with their placées, dining in their homes in the Tremé, sleeping in their beds. Creole women, raised to exhibit all means of propriety at all times, could hardly compete with those often exotic, alluring women raised to entice men. Women like his mother used to be.

Gabriel recalled the conversation he had with his cousin. How André warned him about the futility of this attraction to Lottie. But to know in his head, logically, that whatever he felt for Lottie would be considered impossible in their society, was one thing. To feel that knowing in his heart was something else entirely. Just that morning he had walked the same streets to the LeClerc house. But now those streets spanned a distance that would forever be more than physical.

"MY GRANDPARENTS HAVE DECIDED IT is time for me to marry." Lottie stabbed the back of the sampler with her needle, pushed the needle through the fabric, and missed the edge of the border. She tried and missed again and felt a hot sting, which was followed by a crimson blot on the fabric.

Justine froze, her sampler in one hand and her needle in the other, as if she sat for a portrait. "What wonderful news. How exciting!"

"Please, stop being so excited," said Lottie, her voice as sharp as the needle that had drawn blood from her finger. She released the unfinished sampler from its hoop and rolled it closed. "I can't do this now." She shivered in the glinting morning sunlight that poured over their shoulders as they sat in the gallery.

Her friend set her sewing on the nearby table, moved her chair closer to Lottie's, and, pushing the jumble of pin-striped muslin skirts aside, reached out and held Lottie's hands in her own. "Why are you so distraught?"

Lottie lifted her head to meet Justine's gaze.

"It's...it's so sudden. I hoped..." She hesitated. "I prayed, even, that they would wait until I was ready."

Justine cocked her head. "Sudden? We have been raised to be wives and mothers. Our families have never kept that a secret."

Lottie looked away for a moment and wondered if Justine were capable of understanding the confusion, the frustration, and the fear that shadowed her, kept her awake at night, met her in the morning when she awoke. And could she confess that the one man she felt she could entrust her life to was the one man who would be forbidden to her? "Yes. But why does no one ask if we want to be or if we are ready to be wives?" Lottie slipped her hand out of Justine's and slid her damp palms down the garnet-and-cream-striped skirt of her gown.

Justine leaned against the back of the wicker chair. "They don't ask us because—"

"Because our answer doesn't matter," Lottie retorted, standing and pushing the chair aside as she started to pace the length of the room. "What makes women different from slaves? Agnes, you, me—we may look different, but we really are not that different at all."

"My word, Lottie," Justine gasped, "how can you say such a thing?"

"I can say it because it is true. Are we allowed to pursue the same jobs as men? Do men take classes in music or how to keep one's eyes downcast or what to discuss while they are dancing? Are they trained to be husbands and fathers? We are all kept from being something or someone we want by people, by a world we have no control over. For Agnes, it is because she is a slave. I am white, but I am a woman. In my world, it seems women have a color all their own."

Justine picked up her hoop and resumed sewing. "I suppose you think me foolish for looking forward to being married, to having babies."

Lottie sat across from Justine again. "No. I do not. Not if that is truly what you want."

With the right man, it might be what she wanted too.

CHAPTER SEVEN

G RAND-MÈRE MANUFACTURED A POLITE GREETING
for Reverend François as she, Lottie, and Grand-
père passed him on the way out of Saint Louis Cathedral
on Sunday. The poor reverend probably had no idea that
Grand-mère thought him *un blanc bec* because he chose
not to adhere to the smallest details of protocol. She told
her husband almost every time they attended services
that only a novice would be so negligent. "He would
bury a thief with full sacraments. Does he not understand that *laisser les bons temps rouler* does not apply to
the holy church? The good times rolling by should be
confined to Carnival," she'd say.

Grand-mère paused before the steps and opened her
parasol, twisting it so that the heavy gold fringe untangled itself before she lifted it over her head. Grand-père
held his hand out for her to hold as she made her way
down the worn stone steps. Lottie noticed that after her
grandmother descended and reached her grandfather, he
pressed her hand between both of his and gave her
grandmother a smile Lottie wasn't used to seeing. A
smile like she and Justine shared when the deportment

teacher pretended to be a woman when teaching the curtsy. Each knowing what the other thought. Grand-mère rewarded him with a flimsy upturn of lips as if a more enthusiastic smile might be costly.

"You and Charlotte go ahead of me. I see Emile Bastion, and I need to talk to him," said Grand-père. He walked toward one of the booths along the iron railing surrounding Place d'Armes. Most Sunday afternoons, vendors lined the park selling peanuts, ice cream, and fruit. As she watched him move through the collection of churchgoers, Lottie's memory followed, remembering Sundays years before, when she was young enough for her dresses to be just below her knees, no one caring if her petticoats showed as she skipped alongside him. He introduced her to ginger cake, *estomac mulatre,* which she nibbled while he drank *bière douce,* ginger beer cooled in large tubs. Grand-mère would wait for them in the café at the corner of St. Ann and Chartres Streets where she and her friends gathered for coffee and gossip.

"Charlotte? Charlotte, come along." The voice pulled the skipping little girl back into the one that stood before Grand-mère. "Open your parasol, dear. You must protect your skin from the sun."

A familiar admonishment from her grandmother, who thought having skin the shade of a snake's underbelly desirable. Lottie resisted the temptation to snap the royal-blue-and-beige parasol in two and, instead, complied with her request.

"Are we stopping at Rosette's on the way home?"

Lottie didn't care about the café au lait. Having a chance to talk to Gabriel made Sunday afternoons more bearable since she didn't even have Agnes to talk to when they arrived home. One concession most slave owners made was giving their slaves a day off on Sundays. Agnes and Abram always spent the day away from the LeClerc house. Lottie didn't blame them. She wouldn't be within shouting range of Grand-mère either, if she did not have to be.

"Not today. We need to begin making plans for your party. I have made an appointment with the dressmaker for you. We will meet her this week to discuss the evening gown for your debut party." Grand-mère measured Lottie with her eyes and sighed. "Surely Madame Olympe will know what to do."

Lottie looked down, almost expecting something about her body to have changed since she'd dressed that morning. No, she still wore the patterned dress, each flounce edged in what Agnes told her was robin's-egg blue. Not that Lottie had ever seen a robin's egg, but she was not going to argue. Clearly, she did not have her grandmother's ample proportions, above or below. But even without the dreaded corset, her waist measured twenty inches.

Lottie did not see the necessity in spending more time or more money on something of no interest to her. Two things, actually: the party and the dress. "But, Grand-mère, I already have a beautiful evening gown that I have worn only once. The gold silk dress with the long sleeves, remember?"

"No sensible young lady would think to wear a dress already worn to one of the most important social events in her life. Especially when the young lady is making her debut later than most," said Grand-mère.

Charlotte heard the unspoken "tsk, tsk" in her tone and decided not to pursue the discussion. Evidently she was not a sensible young lady.

TWO DAYS LATER LOTTIE AND JUSTINE decided to take advantage of a ready chaperone in Agnes and accompany her as she shopped for the day's meal. They strolled around the French Market within shouting distance of her. She had threatened them with eternal punishment if they wandered out of range. The two young women would not have been all that difficult to distinguish in the crowd. At that time in the morning, vendors and servants of the wealthy mingled, creating a swell of conversations. The soft ripples of Spanish and Italian, punctuated by the gravelly German voices and the melodic French, became a gumbo of languages. On the fringes of the market, Indians wrapped in coarse-fibered blankets sold blowguns.

"Be careful," Agnes said as she pointed to the wagons threading their way through the people—one carting bushels of plump tomatoes, another filled with mountains of cabbages and lettuce, and none of them paying much attention to the shoppers. "Stay out they way cuz they not going to stay out of yours."

"We promise. I asked Grand-mère for money for calas and coffee. Did she remember?" Lottie asked.

Agnes reached into her apron pocket. "She sure did. I made sure to remind her that you two girls need to eat something for breakfast."

"Thank you," Lottie said as Agnes handed her the coins. She looked at the money in her hand. "You know, Justine, I think we can squeeze out enough to buy Agnes breakfast too."

"Well, then, hurry on you two, so you come back soon. Don't want no cold calas. Like trying to bite a rock." Agnes smiled as she walked away.

Lottie surveyed the vendors. "Justine, I don't see the calas lady. Let's go to the other side of the market."

"Do you think your grandmother will approve of that? Spending her money for Agnes too?" Justine asked while she fiddled with her lace glove. "Perhaps you should have mentioned to her before we left that you intended to buy food for Agnes."

"Oh dear, Justine," Lottie said and stopped. "Did you lose a button on your new glove?" She stared at her friend.

"Why...why, no. I thought it might be loose." When she answered, Lottie saw the pink flush on her friend's neck. Lottie remained silent and waited.

Justine twisted her hands together. "I know you are upset because I'm questioning how you are spending your grandmother's money. It surprises me."

"Surprises you? Justine, the only person I'm not related to that I've known longer than you is Agnes. Why would I not want to do something for her?"

"I don't know, Lottie. It seems at times you forget she's just a…"

"Slave? Is that it?"

"Well, yes. I mean, it's like you don't understand your place. You treat her as if she is a part of your family. What about days ago when you didn't want her to leave Rosette to find my bonnet? I know it is a small example—"

"Small. Exactly. Perhaps because you have a mother, you can't understand what Agnes has meant to me. Perhaps Grand-mère loves me, Justine, but Agnes shows me she loves me."

Ahead, a tall ebony woman strolled fluidly and sang, "Calas, calas, *belle* calas. Tout *chaud*!" as she held onto a large basket balanced on top of her tightly wound tignon.

Lottie tugged Justine's sleeve. "Come. Let us buy our calas while they are fresh-baked."

"YOUR COUSIN IS LEAVING TOMORROW. Will you be talking to him before then?" Rosette handed her son café au laits to take to the two ladies in the café.

"We discussed attending the opera at Theatre d'Orleans, to see *Robert le Diable*," said Gabriel. He didn't mind seeing André. Talking to him was what he minded. He returned with empty mugs left by other customers and handed them to his mother. "Have you checked the pastries today?"

"The pastries are fine," said Rosette. "They are not roaming around the café with a face as long as a broomstick." She moved the milk kettle sitting on the hearth closer to the fire. Pouring equal parts coffee and milk into the cup at the same time meant one had to be as hot as the other.

Gabriel wanted to tell Rosette what Charlotte had shared about her grandparents arranging her marriage. But not now, especially in public, because he did not know if he could trust himself to remain composed. He had already revealed his feelings about Lottie to André by what he did not say when his cousin confronted him. If André told his own mother about the conversation, then surely she would tell Rosette, either before or after the entire Faubourgs—the neighborhoods of Tremé and half the Marigny—knew.

"We can talk about this another time," he said.

"Yes, we could. But I am concerned about you during this time." Rosette readjusted the simple white linen tignon she wore when working.

"But we have customers, and—"

"Not anymore," she said and turned to the two women as they were leaving. "*Merci beaucoup.*" Rosette wiped her hands on her apron, moved two stools together, and patted one. "Sit," she directed her son.

A part of Gabriel wanted to run, but the other part

was grateful that the exiting customers forced him onto the stool.

His mother straightened her apron over her dress, and he suspected she was straightening her thoughts as well. He knew she rarely began serious conversations without saying a brief prayer. She had told him that years ago after explaining why Gabriel would probably no longer see his father. He had shouted words he heard men in the streets use, words never allowed in the house. Instead of a harsh punishment, she brought him the Bible and pointed to Proverbs 12:18. "*There is that speaketh like the piercings of a sword: but the tongue of the wise is health.*" It was then Gabriel realized that some punishments stung more than a hand.

"I am proud of the young man you are becoming," she said now. "I wish you had an older man to guide you. There are times, perhaps, when only a father can provide the words a son may need to hear." She placed her hand on his shoulder for a moment. "So I understand that this may be one of those times."

For his entire life, Gabriel had thought of Rosette as his mother. As only a mother. But now, listening to her, he sensed a clarity he had not felt since learning to read. How remarkable to learn that those lines and curls and circles formed meaning. And for the first time, he looked at his mother and saw a woman. A woman who loved a man and bore him two children. A woman who still loved a man but learned to live without him.

Gabriel understood her pain in a way that only someone who must endure loss can.

CHAPTER EIGHT

"I SUPPOSE IT IS APPROPRIATE that I should look like a very large ball of cotton for my debut." Lottie eyed the yards and yards of watered white silk Madame Olympe presented her grandmother.

The dressmaker launched a barrage of French Creole that ended in "*une 'tite poule grasse*" in the direction of Grand-mère. Lottie figured Madame did not just call her grandmother a little fat hen and certainly would not, if that had been her intention, until after they left the shop.

Lottie held a panel of the silk that threatened to make her resemble a fat white hen. Standing in front of the mahogany cheval mirror, she draped herself in the milky fabric to assess Madame's opinion.

"You are beginning to speak like those rude Americans in the Garden District," Grand-mère declared. "Since your first remark seemed to be an insult, Madame simply stated that she had the ability to transform you into something quite unattractive." She smiled at the dressmaker, who stared at Lottie. "Not to mention, she could stitch your lips closed, my dear."

Did Grand-mère truly intend to be funny? Lottie

might have remained statue-like longer were it not for Madame's response. Only the dressmaker's hands covering her mouth prevented waves of laughter from reaching the ears of nearby shoppers. Not even being the target of Grand-mère's humor could detract from Lottie's wide-eyed surprise at the playful tone in her voice. She would have expected the words from her grandmother to be disdainful, for she rarely, if ever, bantered with Lottie.

Perhaps this party, this rite of passage, marked a shift in their relationship. Lottie imagined she might come to know her grandmother as more than someone who dispensed rules in her life. The idea of gaining a grandmother appealed more than the idea of gaining a husband.

Madame Olympe flittered around the store, her fingers pecking at ribbons and laces and tulle. A mound of her choices grew on the table. "A few more selections and we will begin," she said…though she appeared to be addressing the gold buttons in her hand instead of her customers.

"Is there a pattern selected already?" Lottie moved to the chair near her grandmother and hoped the question might keep open the door to this new space in her heart.

"Pattern?" Grand-mère said the word as if it hardly had the right to burst forth from her lips. "Why would I go through the trouble of a dressmaker for a…well, something anyone could sew?"

The door slammed on Lottie's heart. *Because you have*

a pattern for everything else in my life. The dress, the party, the wedding, the marriage. Her role was to be present. Lottie feared that if she exhaled all at once, her corset would need replacing. She knew what her grandmother wanted to hear.

"You wouldn't."

AT MIDNIGHT, THE STILLNESS OF RUE ORLEANS broke with the streams of people leaving the theatre, their passages home made possible by the gaslamps hanging from ropes stretched across the streets. Reflectors and the slight breezes made the faint gold light shiver against the brick and stucco of the homes along the way.

Gabriel buttoned his frock coat as he and André walked out. The air was unusually chilly for a Louisiana night becoming early morning. When they reached the corner of Rue Bourbon, Gabriel heard someone behind them call his name. He turned and saw Nathalie Chaigneau waving a blue glove at him. The well-dressed group she walked away from stopped and folded in, talking to one another.

"Where have you been, Gabriel Girod?" She tapped him on the shoulder with her lace fan. A panel of white wrapped around her bare shoulders and edged the sleeves of her dark-green gown. She stared at André. "Are you—"

"Excuse my rude cousin, Mademoiselle." André bowed slightly. "I will introduce myself—"

She examined him in the way that one might view a

laboratory specimen then interrupted him with a delighted gasp of recognition. "André? André Toutant? I have not seen you for years. Not since…"

"Since he was as tall as you are now?" Gabriel could have patted the top of her head if not for the elaborately tied tignon of moss-green fabric accented with rows of clear glass beads along one side. "André, the three of us tried to learn how to play the piano. We all had lessons with Monsieur Plessis. This is Nathalie Chaigneau."

"Ah yes, Nathalie Chaigneau. You always wanted Gabriel and me to start the lessons. Remember?"

Gabriel nodded. "Of course. She wanted Plessis to be too tired after our lessons to care how she played."

Nathalie batted her eyelashes in feigned innocence. "Do you think I would do such a thing?"

"Yes!" Both Gabriel and André laughed. Gabriel was about to ask why he had not seen her for several months when he heard her name coming from her friends.

"Nathalie, aren't you coming with us?" A young woman parted from the circle and walked halfway to where her friend stood. She held out a nosegay of violets as if intended to entice her to rejoin them.

"Yes, yes, of course," Nathalie answered, waving her away. "Tell them one minute more."

The woman with the pink dress shrugged and turned around.

"We are all going to Vincent's for dessert. Please join us." Nathalie reached out as if she planned to pull Gabriel and André along with her. "We will be able to talk more." She glanced over her shoulder, and Gabriel's gaze followed hers. One of the waiting men pointed toward them, his face solemn. Nathalie looked back at him and André. "I need to join them. After all, tonight was a celebration for my returning home."

"Home from where?" So that explained why Gabriel had not seen her.

"Oh, had you not heard?" She placed one gloved hand on either side of her face and shook her head. "My parents sent me to school in New York. But…" She leaned forward and cupped her hands around her mouth as if telling a secret. "I broke every rule until the school finally sent me home."

Neither Gabriel nor André expressed shock upon hearing the news of her expulsion. "Well, since I have not horrified you with my behavior, will you come with us?"

André explained that he needed to prepare to return to Paris. Gabriel declined, saying that he would need to open the café soon.

"Then I will visit you there soon, Gabriel. But I doubt I will be allowed to travel for quite some time. So, you"—she swatted André with her fan this time—"will see me when you return. Yes?"

Nathalie didn't wait for responses. She picked up the front of her skirt and scampered back to the group.

"I do not remember her being so engaging," André mused as the two continued their walk home.

Gabriel loosened his cravat, ready to exchange the

stiff formal clothes for his usual shirt and trousers. "That could be because, at age ten, not many girls are engaging in the way Nathalie looked tonight."

"I didn't mean in that way," said André.

Gabriel raised his eyebrows.

"Maybe I did, but are you telling me you missed her expressive brown eyes, the curve of her lips, the hollows of her shoulders..."

"No, I am certainly not blind to the fact that she is a beautiful young woman. It's that she is not—"

"She is not Lottie, is that what you were going to say?"

"I was going to say that she is not someone I would be interested in," Gabriel responded, though he felt the doubt he knew his cousin would hear in his voice.

André did not respond.

"The LeClercs have planned a birthday party for Charlotte. The yellow fever delayed her coming-out party, so they decided that it is time now, since she will be twenty."

"So, that is it then," André said.

"Yes, of course." Gabriel wished he did not see pity in André's eyes. For years, he had endured this pity from his cousin after Rosette sent his father away. Tonight it agitated him. Would he forever be frustrated in achieving his dreams?

"I understand the desire to have something— something achievable. But Lottie will never be. You knew that from the day we first learned what *de couleur* meant. And, more importantly, what it did not mean."

Gabriel saw Alcee, not yet five, sitting on the parlor floor, Rosette's favorite porcelain bowl filled with water by her side. The little girl held her hairbrush, dipped it into the water, and scrubbed her legs to "make the dirty go away." Alcee had stopped trying to be white years ago. Maybe he should take a lesson from his sister.

CHAPTER NINE

"WHY ARE CHARLOTTE AND JUSTINE outside our cottage?" Rosette set the basket she had packed for the orphanage on the side table in the parlor.

"Why are you asking this question?" Gabriel pulled on his light gray gloves. "You know they are not waiting for Alcee." Had they not discussed Lottie that afternoon in the café, his mother would not be questioning her presence this afternoon. He realized, too late, that any time spent with her now would arouse Rosette's suspicion.

"*On lave son linge sale en famille,*" Rosette retorted in her angry-mother posture: one hand on her hip, the other free to wag a finger at him as she spoke. "Now that you have washed your dirty clothes in your own family, why are you dragging them down the banquette for all of Tremé?"

"Charlotte does not know about my feelings for her, nor do I want her to. So I am not going to change what we do as friends because of the plans her grandparents are making."

"Do the LeClercs know where she is now? Do they

know whom she is with?" Rosette had stopped the finger-wagging.

"'Ask me no questions, I will tell you no fibs,'" Gabriel said. He reached for the basket. "Oliver Goldsmith, *She Stoops to Conquer.*"

"'A froward man soweth strife: and a whisperer separateth chief friends.'" Rosette handed him his gray top hat. "Proverbs 16:28, the Bible."

LOTTIE HEARD THE TIGHT, CLIPPED VOICES of Gabriel and Rosette as she and Justine waited outside their home. If Justine overheard the tension, she prattled on as if she didn't. When Gabriel walked out, the coil of anxiety in Lottie's chest unwound. She feared the conversation between him and his mother might mean the visit would not happen. And the shame that now warmed her cheeks was because she could not deny that she cared more about seeing Gabriel than the children they were going to see.

"So, ladies, are we ready?" He glanced from one to the other. "I will be a thorn between two roses today."

No thorn would be so well suited. His black frock coat wrapped itself around his shoulders and down the length of his body to his waist, where it tucked in right below his partially buttoned waistcoat. A long navy-blue silk cravat, fastened with a pin, wrapped around his neck and fell down the length of his chest.

Justine touched the brooch at the neck of her peach

dress then smoothed the layers of curls that grazed her shoulders and spilled from her pale-green bonnet. She looked up at Gabriel then quickly cast her eyes downward. "How very kind of you," she said.

How very coquettish of Justine. Perhaps she was practicing her flirtations on Gabriel...not that she would ever admit such a thing. Lottie almost asked her if she had missed that lesson in their deportment class, but what gave her pause was Gabriel's reaction. Instead of joining Lottie in a mutual rolling of eyes over Justine's obvious, cloying behavior, he didn't even look in her direction.

"Three roses," Lottie said. "Agnes is joining us."

He lowered the basket, setting it on a concrete step. "I see."

Gabriel's lack of confusion coupled with his lack of enthusiasm stunned Lottie. Agnes had never before joined them on a visit to the orphanages. Why wasn't he at least curious as to why she was today?

Justine, who could fill gaps until they choked with information, provided the unasked answer. "Lottie's grandparents are visiting Judge Rost and his wife, Louise. They finished remodeling their plantation in Destrehan and invited the LeClercs." She locked her arm with Lottie's. "My parents said Lottie could stay in the city with us. And we've stayed so busy preparing for her birthday party—haven't we, Lottie?—that I can hardly believe it is already Sunday afternoon. And Agnes is coming because she wants to be sure nothing happens to

Lottie today, because her grandparents will be back tonight." If Justine's story had a cover, she could have closed it with "The End."

While Gabriel's attention was focused on Justine, Lottie focused on him and waited for a reaction. But how could she look at him and not see the man who made her wish it was his arm linked with hers? If only she knew at what point in their friendship she'd begun to think of him differently. When had she begun to worry that standing next to him would make her insides melt like candle wax until she puddled on the ground? When had she begun to understand that her heart would ache? If she only knew and could return to that time, she could retreat.

This morning, the relief of knowing she would be able to join Gabriel at the girls' home without the nagging worry of her grandparents finding out soured with disappointment.

Gabriel surveyed the street. "So where is Agnes?"

Lottie peered in the direction she expected to see Agnes appearing. "She should be here soon. The three of us left my house at the same time."

She untied her bonnet—a selection by Justine, whose daughters might one day resemble walking peacocks if left up to her. White, with lavender ribbons and white feathers, the bonnet crushed the looped hair she had allowed Justine to gather. Another ridiculous decision by Lottie in their preparations for church. She welcomed the breeze that cooled her scalp and regretted not having her parasol so she could free herself from the annoying headpiece.

"Agnes stopped so many times on the way, she finally told us to run along and she would meet us." Lottie avoided including that what continued to interfere with their walk was people who wanted to talk about the upcoming party.

But Justine piped up, just as Agnes's white parasol turned the corner, "I didn't think we'd arrive here before sunset with all the questions Agnes had to keep answering about Charlotte's party. The LeClercs must be inviting the entire city."

Gabriel spotted Agnes and put on his hat. "No, Justine, not the entire city."

And that's when Lottie understood what had changed in Gabriel.

"OH, I AM SO GLAD YOU are finally home." Alcee closed her book and jumped up to meet Gabriel as he stepped into the back gallery.

"Finally?" From experience, he knew that if his sister used that word, there was a plan waiting to happen. But the only plan of any interest to him required a meal and a bed. "Is your book not interesting to you?" He removed his coat and draped it over the arm of the couch. "Where is *Maman*?"

She cocked her head and drilled Gabriel's face with her eyes. "What happened?" She followed as he walked to the dining room.

"Nothing." He lifted the lids of the serving bowls on the sideboard. Jambalaya in one, green beans in the other. "You didn't answer my question. Either question." He served himself a mound of jambalaya then sat at the table.

"I'm reading *Mansfield Park*, and Fanny Price has just been pitifully cast off by her parents to live with relatives in Northampton—"

Gabriel held up his hand before Alcee recounted every chapter of a novel he thought questionable for her to be reading. "Do you have permission to read that novel?"

She folded her arms over the book, her head held high. "No one said I couldn't read it."

It impressed him that, despite the fault in her logic, Alcee demonstrated she could assert herself. That quality in her personality reminded him of the one person he most wanted to think about the least. "That is between you and Mother anyway. Assuming you are honest with her and tell her that you are reading it." He set down his fork and wiped his mouth with his napkin. "Speaking of which, you have not told me where she is."

Alcee set the book on the table and removed the two ivory combs holding her hair away from her face. She had not yet reached the age where her hair would never be seen, except for Mardi Gras masquerades, on the streets of New Orleans.

"She went to Serafina's. Now, I have answered all

your questions. You have not answered the only one I asked."

Gabriel leaned back in his chair. "Ah, that's where you are wrong. I did respond to your question."

"No, that's where *you* are wrong." Alcee's slow smile and narrowed eyes should have been warning that she intended to trump her brother. "You rarely use 'Maman' when referring to our mother. I have only heard you use it at times you were pained or worried. Answering the question like a *homme de paille*? It is not like you to be a man who intends to mislead."

Alcee had inherited Rosette's ability to sift through pretense, which was both a blessing and a curse, for them and everyone else. But Gabriel did not believe it proper to be confessing his feelings about Lottie to his sister, especially since she was not yet thirteen. Alcee was not too young to comprehend the social order of the world in which she lived. Society's laws could be broken, but too often those who broke them were fractured most. Even though love had no color, it resided in the hearts of people who did.

"I DUNNO WHAT WEAR ME out most. Rocking those babies or listening to Miss Justine from there to here. Her folks might oughta find some beau for her can't hear too good. That the onliest way that man survive." Agnes shook her head and reopened her parasol after they left Justine's. She tilted it to shade both herself and Lottie, whose bonnet had once again found its way off her head as they walked the short distance home.

"Justine ought not know he can't hear, because she will start screaming like a steamboat whistle to get his attention," Lottie added. "I'll be sure to suggest your idea to Madame Dumas the next time I see her."

"And you be sure to get to the slave market to buy me after I get sold for saying such a thing."

Lottie smiled. "They would have to sell me too. I don't know what I would do without you."

Agnes threaded her arm through Lottie's. "We not going to hafta find out. I know you'd never be no disrespectful person and tell that poor girl's parents that."

"Of course not. Because," she paused to take a breath to push down the storm she felt rising in her chest, "I do what I'm told. Whether I want to or not."

Agnes stopped, reached for Lottie's chin, and turned her face toward her. "Now, we almost home. Maybe your grandparents be there already. Maybe not. Either way, you try not to be so sad all the time. I know this is not what you want."

Lottie's chin quivered, and Agnes pulled her handkerchief out of her pocket and blotted Lottie's eyes and cheeks. "It's so unfair. They're going to arrange this marriage, and I have no choice. None. I might as well be…"

"A slave?" Agnes gave Lottie the damp handkerchief and closed the parasol.

"I'm so sorry, Agnes. I didn't mean…."

"Well, you real close to the truth, child. Real close to understanding life without too many choices. But you gotta start trusting God to find a way, you hear?"

Lottie nodded, though she wanted to ask Agnes how God was going to make Gabriel white so he could be the man her grandparents would choose.

They neared the house and saw Abram, his hands shielding his eyes, looking up and down the street. As soon as he spotted them, he headed in their direction.

Lottie grabbed Agnes's hand. "Why is he waiting for us? Something must be wrong."

"That not the face of trouble," Agnes said and pointed at Abram, his mouth stretched into such a wide smile that even his eyes disappeared behind his cheeks.

"We got one more day," said Abram. "I wanted to tell you right off."

Lottie was as confused as Agnes looked.

"That other family the LeClercs followed to the plantation, they come by the house and say they staying one more day."

Lottie felt as if she'd just been handed a gift. "Can we not go to the house yet? At least for now? We have time to stroll along the levee, and the weather could hardly be more perfect. And we'd still have time to be home before curfew when that dratted cannon pounds the city with its noise, telling everyone to go inside."

"What you think?" Abram asked Agnes, who held her parasol like a cane and tapped the end on the cobblestones. He reached out and stilled her hand with his. "You waking up the devil?"

"I hopes not," she said. "Some days I think somebody already did."

"So, Agnes, can we go? Please?"

When she still didn't answer, Abram told her, "Now, Agnes, you know we can't let Miz Lottie promenade all over creation without chaperones."

"You right. If our Charlotte tell us she was going to go sashaying down the levee, we hafta be there with her."

"Abram, if I were still five years old, I would hug you right here on the street," Lottie said.

"Miz Lottie, you just hug me with your heart. That be good enough."

CHAPTER TEN

6 February 1841

Dear Mama and Papa,

Last night I didn't write because I stayed with Justine's family while Grand-mère and Grand-père traveled to Destrehan. Grand-mère said her friend Louise was one of fourteen children in the family. How much time they must spend cleaning dishes after meals! Since they did not arrive home tonight, Agnes sleeps in the sickroom downstairs because she does not want me alone in the house.

Abram and Agnes and I strolled on the levee and watched the sun as it began to retire. This winter is unseasonably warm, and the cool evening air was a welcome relief to staying within the confines of this room. I was reminded of the fascination I had as a little girl, being brought to watch the rumbling steamboats with their deep whistling horns and all the cargo ships like metal monsters burping out steel containers and wooden crates or eating bales of cotton.

I confess, I was relieved by my grandparents staying at Destrehan, and Papa, please forgive me, for I know they are your parents and you loved them as I love you. You know Grand-mère would not approve of my having visited the girls' orphanage today even though Justine and Agnes joined Gabriel and me. I don't think Gabriel will invite me again when he makes these trips. I told him about the party, and he was not the same Gabriel afterward. I wanted to tell him I understood, because I do not feel as if I am the same person either. For an instant today, his actions brought me a glimpse of joy. Surely, I thought, he must care about me to be so different. Then it saddened me. How odd to discover that the only way you learn about someone's feelings is when the person will never be free to express them.

How I wish you could be here. My unanswered questions are constant companions. Seeing how distressed Grand-mère becomes when I want for more information about the two of you, I decided it would be wise to simply discontinue the asking. Grand-mère brings me for dress fittings, Mama, and I asked her about your coming-out party and engagement to Papa. She tells me he met you at the theatre, where most of the parties occurred. And that you dressed beautifully. I asked her to show me where they lived, and she said, Papa, that you traveled to Paris for business, and I was born there.

She does not discuss how or when we came to New Orleans. On All Saints' Day, when many in the city are placing flowers at the graves of loved ones, Grand-mère remains at home. She refuses to allow me to visit, even with Agnes. I have thought, lately, that I should find a way to the cemetery on my own.

If only I could know, Mama, whether you feared becoming a wife, or if you, like Justine, counted the days until your coming-out. How did you come to care about Papa? Maybe my feelings for Gabriel are not love. Perhaps I confuse the love between friends with that of a husband and a wife. We spent so much of our childhood together. I have come to trust that he would protect me, and he believes women can do so much more than we are allowed to do. He encourages me to be true to myself. I know that when I am with him, I feel as if I am home. Is it foolish to believe a husband would be a friend?

My party is February 27, now only a few weeks away. Agnes says having it on my birthday makes it more special and blessed, though I am sure she was trying to console me. Grand-mère is taking me to my final dress fitting in a few days. I must admit, when Madame Olympe stands me in front of the mirror, I feel as if I am a princess. Madame said it is a dress to attract a prince. We shall see.

My love and affection,
Genevieve Charlotte

LIFTING HER WHITE SILK DRESS higher than any woman of low breeding would consider, much less one trained in the social graces, Lottie raced through the Place d'Armes, the train of her gown wet from weeds untrampled by her soft leather shoes. Grand-père shouted words in French as she approached and then caught Grand-mère as she swooned in his arms. Abram and Agnes held the lines to the steamship, preventing it from leaving for Paris. Exhausted, Lottie pushed herself to run faster, but she could not bridge the distance. It was as if her feet spun the earth underneath them, leaving her in the same place. She was afraid that if she stopped, she might fall over the earth's edge.

Agnes's calling her name pierced the dream. Lottie was trying to capture the images before they drifted away when a warm light exploded near her face. She covered her eyes with her hands and summoned her voice from the girl left running that Agnes made disappear. "Make it go away. Make it go away," she begged, before rolling over and mashing her face into her pillow.

"That sun going nowhere till evening."

Lottie lifted her head only long enough to mumble, "I can wait."

"A girl might not be so ornery in the mornings if she don't go to bed late."

The new torture of the pillow almost suffocating her and Agnes's comment moved Lottie to turn her head and squint as one panel of the heavy damask drapes closed.

"That better? You ready to join the living now?"

"Yes," she answered, knowing that even if she had disagreed, nothing would change. *Like most things in my life right now.* Lottie propped herself up on her elbows as Agnes stood at the foot of her bed picking up the bed linens that had spilled onto the carpet. *Maybe I ran harder than I thought.* "What makes you think I stayed up late?"

Agnes folded the down comforter in sections at the end of her bed. "See that candle on your desk?" Her hands now busy with the blanket, she nodded her head in that direction. "When I come in here, I see hain't nothing hardly left to burn on the candle. So, you maybe forgot to put it out 'fore you went to bed, but since the house still standing and we still here, then it's something else. Some mornings I come here, like this one, and that foolscap still on your desk. That quill a-yours all dis away and dat." She moved her hand up and down as if holding the quill. Agnes walked over to the desk, picked up the blank sheet of writing paper, tucked it into a drawer, and closed the inkwell.

Lottie sat up in bed as her stomach plummeted, hitting bottom like a carriage wheel in a sinkhole. Could there have been times she forgot to put her letters away? Suppose Grand-mère had read one? If so, that might explain why her grandmother soured in her presence. She wanted to simultaneously leap out of bed to inspect the bundle hidden in her armoire and also slink under the bedcovers. Agnes could know about the letters. Lottie could accept that. Even her grandfather... Lottie trusted that he would not only understand, but he would respect her privacy. But her grandmother? Given a choice, she would rather wear only her petticoat to church. "Agnes, could you close the window, please? There's a chill in the room." Lottie rubbed her arms while she thought of a response.

"No window open, Miss Lottie, but I close this curtain." Agnes picked up the candle stub. "Just so you remember. Agnes is the first person that comes in this room every morning. And you don't have nothin' to worry 'bout with me. Even if I could read those words you write, I'd never tell."

"I know, Agnes. I know." Lottie hugged her knees to her chest. "I only wish you had the choice."

As a child first learning to read, Lottie had sat next to Agnes, opened her books, and read out loud. When she stumbled on a word, she'd look up at Agnes who, every time, would pat her hand and whisper, "You just go on. We pick it up next time." No one seemed to mind, the two of them side by side in the gallery or outside in the courtyard, shaded by one of the lemon trees. No one, that is, until Madame Narcisse visited and reminded Grand-mère about the year-long imprisonment for anyone caught teaching a slave to read or write. Lottie wasn't allowed to read with Agnes after that. She told her grandparents she would go to jail, but she wanted to share her books with Agnes. Grand-père laughed and said, "Ah, my p'tit, you are so small, you would slip right through the bars." It was only when he gently explained the risk for Agnes that Lottie promised to never do it again. She had cried, thinking of Agnes being flogged at the public whipping post or losing part of a finger or a toe.

"Miss Lottie." Agnes now lowered her voice. "We learning to read. Maybe writing come later. But we so bad wanted to read the Bible for ourselves. That's why Gabriel spend so much time here and us there. Every chance we gets, we learn more." She stepped to the side of Lottie's bed and pulled a folded square of paper out of her apron pocket. Agnes opened it with such attention that Lottie imagined the words might slip off the paper were she not so careful. "We got this from Proverbs." She pointed to the word on the top line and smiled. "I carry 'em with me so's I can practice. And don't you worry. We always been careful.

"First, when Gabriel start tearing them pages out of the Bible, I waited for something powerful to rain down." Agnes refolded her treasure and returned it to her pocket. "But he told me Jesus would rather us tear up the Bible so we can read than just let that book sit there with all those blessings locked inside."

So, Lottie thought, *Gabriel has been doing all along what I volunteered to do at the orphanage.*

CHAPTER ELEVEN

AGNES AND ABRAM LEFT FOR the French Market to prepare for the LeClercs' return, and Lottie finished the breakfast of coffee and fruit that Agnes had brought her before they left. Moving the tray off her lap and onto the bed, Lottie mashed and fluffed the mound of pillows behind her. Somewhere between deciding what to do for the rest of the morning and the thumping from downstairs, she drifted off to sleep.

Thinking they had returned with the hot calas she had given them the money to buy, Lottie slid out of bed and decided to risk Agnes's wrath and venture downstairs in her bare feet and nightgown. In the time she'd need to grab a calas or two, she figured she could be back in her bedroom before Agnes ever finished her tirade. But as she stepped out, it was her grandparents' voices she heard over the shuffle of bags. Lottie almost called to them but realized they would have expected her to be dressed for the day, not for bedtime. Her stomach rumbled in disappointment, and she had started to back into her room when she heard her grandfather mention her name.

"I do not think this is the proper time to have this

conversation, as Lottie could hear us."

The soft clinks as cups met saucers and chair legs bumping along the carpet as they moved from the table meant they had settled in the dining room. Lottie perched on the floor in the small alcove outside her room and hoped Agnes and Abram were taking their time at the market.

"If she were here, we would have seen her by now. Agnes and Abram are gone, so she is either with them at the French Market or she stayed with Justine another night," her grandmother said.

"As I tried to explain to you earlier, there are more considerations than making sure of the marriage arrangements. We cannot ignore them, and I am concerned. More so than you, I fear."

"I am not unaware." Grand-mère's words sounded like whips whistling through the air. "But we are in a situation ourselves. We were fortunate the Bastions happened to be at the event this weekend and that they decided to stay another day so we could talk."

Bastion. That is the man Grand-père spoke to after church.

"No, my sweet. That was not fortune. That was planning. I invited Emile after receiving word from Judge Rost that he and his wife would be welcomed as our guests. I thought it would work in our favor to spend time with the Bastions in a more comfortable social setting before we went any further."

"Oh, then..." She paused. "You were correct."

If the intention of the party was for several eligible men to attend, why was their son singled out? The one person who might be able to tell her about the Bastions was the one person Lottie couldn't ask. Gabriel, because of the café, was acquainted with people from political to poor. If a name was not familiar, it traveled the lines of communication until it reached again, who could then attach it to a face, a cottage, a business, or, in some cases, one to avoid. But just the thought of asking after a man she did not care about from the man she did made her stomach turn. As Lottie unfolded herself from the floor, Agnes and Abram returned to the house and interrupted the lull in her grandparents' conversation. Grand-père asked where his granddaughter was and when Agnes expected her home.

When she heard Agnes answer, "She home right now. Miz Charlotte stay while Abram and me went to the market," Lottie tiptoed into her bedroom, tucked herself under the comforter and sheets, and burrowed into the pillows. If her grandparents planned to be angry with her, it was better to be because they thought she'd overslept than overheard.

GABRIEL ENTERED THE WELL-APPOINTED STORE of Cordeviolle and LaCroix tailors on Chartres Street, where distinguishing between their employees and customers was made complicated by the popular dress of both. Himself a free man of color, François LaCroix elevated his business with imported silks and linens and fabrics from Belgium for the particular tastes of his clients desiring the latest styles. Even the store's elaborately scrolled billhead, designed in Paris, reflected LaCroix and Cordeviolle's attention to detail for "fashionable articles pertaining to the Gentleman's Wardrobe, imported, and kept constantly on hand."

Gabriel was there to pick up his new wardrobe—after losing the discussion with his mother several weeks beforehand regarding his need for it. He might have come away victorious but for his one fatal declaration: "Maman, perhaps you should be more mindful of how you spend your money."

They had been working on a fresh batch of pralines. Gabriel shelled the pecans, and Rosette chopped them to add later to the mixture she had just moved over the fire. He'd stopped to roll up the sleeves of his shirt when she remarked that the cuffs appeared to be frayed.

"Hardly," he'd said and shrugged. "Where do I go that it matters? The café, to visit the homes? It's fine." He rewarded himself with a few of the fresh halves then pushed the hill of shelled pecans across the table to his mother. She scooped the chopped pieces into a bowl then rocked the half-moon blade back and forth over the ones just peeled.

"You attended the opera with André. I doubt his cuffs were worn thin."

"He lives in Paris. Styles there change too quickly for anything to show signs of wear. Except maybe the dressmakers and the tailors." He rolled more pecans out of the firkin onto the table and set the wooden bucket on the stool next to his.

"Still. I know you devote much of your time to the business. And to me and to Alcee. But it is important for you to have some *joie de la vie*, especially while you are still young."

Not bundled in the yards of fabric required in public, her hair gathered loosely at her neck by a scant piece of lace, Rosette looked far younger than her thirty-eight years. A stranger would not suspect that she no longer lived a pampered life, except for a few places on her hands and along her forearms that had healed darker after being burned. At times, the praline mixture boiled over, sending the thick mixture onto her arms and hands and taking a layer of skin as it did.

"You could use some joie de la vie as well." Gabriel knew she cut down and reworked some of her own dresses for Alcee. Later, Gabriel realized he should have shared his heart instead of his head because his next statement was, "Maman, perhaps you should be more mindful of how you spend your money."

If the look on her face could have baked bread, the torrent of French assaulting his ears could have sliced it. Caught off guard by his mother's considerable reaction, Gabriel decided that riding out the storm of her vexation would be the wiser course. But the damage had been done, and he paid the cost of repairing his mother's dignity by submitting himself to the tailors.

But what he'd just heard from Monsieur LaCroix was prelude to another tempest.

"I do not understand. Who might have settled my account?" Gabriel lowered his voice, hoping the tailor would do the same. Overheard, the news of the son of a former placée discussing a mysteriously paid bill would appear in the next day's *New Orleans Bee,* published in both French and English so as to cause more embarrassment.

LaCroix examined the bill again. His finger scanned each line as he read. "Tan trousers"—he looked up at Gabriel—"with the dark blue pinstripe, of course." Gabriel nodded, so the tailor continued. "One tan waistcoat and a black frock coat with pocket flaps at the hip." He placed his hands on his hips and eyed Gabriel again, who nodded once more. "Oh, the frock coat shows flared open-cuff sleeves, and there are two white shirts. One with pleats, one without. And two silk cravats, one yellow and one dark blue, of course." LaCroix stared at Gabriel as if waiting for applause.

"The payment?" This time it was Gabriel who pointed to a line, where the balance of almost two hundred dollars had been subtracted.

"Yes, yes. I will ask Etienne." He walked off with bill in hand, toward the back of the store where Monsieur Cordeviolle held out a black tailcoat for a young man wearing a white waistcoat and black silk pants. The man's long sideburns, mustache, and goatee had not disguised his protruding jaw and lower lip, which was heavier than the upper one. Tante Virgine would describe him as having *une gueule de benitier,* a mouth like a holy water font. And, no doubt, she would not be as discreet as Gabriel hoped LaCroix remained.

The tailor moved away from his customer to talk to LaCroix, their conversation peppered with a symphony of gestures. Gabriel examined a selection of silk top hats displayed on a nearby table while he waited. Next to him, a gentleman who should have been refitted for his frock coat forty pounds before spoke to one whose chin identified him as the father of Etienne's customer. As Gabriel walked over to look at the wool felt bowlers, he overheard the LeClercs' name mentioned in their conversation. He kept his head down, passing the brim of an ordinary derby hat through his hands with meticulous care. Not that he had to make an effort to appear invisible. As a homme de couleur libre among two white men, especially ones of wealth, Gabriel was already disregarded, unless, like LaCroix, he resurrected himself in a successful business.

The rounder of the two pointed his cane in the direction of the younger version of the man to whom he spoke. "So, Benjamin is being fitted with a new wardrobe. What does he think about this LeClerc soirée?"

Gabriel moved on to a bowler, treating it with the same painstaking interest. He looked in the men's general direction, but only briefly and always with his head down.

The young man's father yawned, adjusted his spectacles, and said, "Benjamin and I share a strong physical resemblance. Benjamin and his mother share a strong propensity for spending. He will be equally satisfied with a new wardrobe or a new wife."

Equal fulfillment. Lottie and a set of clothes. *If this is what fathers teach sons, then I'm grateful mine left before this lesson.*

Indignation and restraint met Gabriel as a child after Rosette had explained to him that the word *illegitimate* and the one used to taunt him meant the same. "But people give the other word more power. Never forget, we decide the degree of power we allow words to have over us," she said. Later that evening, he had sat next to his father, who went through the Bible and showed him passages about everyone being children of God. He never directly answered Gabriel's question that night about whether he really was "the nicer word" those boys screamed at him after pitching handfuls of mud and telling him "that's ya real color." His father started talking about God's laws and man's laws, but Gabriel didn't remember much. The next day, Rosette told him he'd fallen asleep. "And that's why you never ask lawyers about the law."

Ever since then, Gabriel understood that indignity might burrow into his gut at any time, and if he didn't allow restraint to take over, that sick creature could win. *Though, at this moment, I would welcome it.* He clenched his hands and, when he felt the damp wool, realized he'd molded part of the brim into a felt tube.

Gabriel returned the hat to the table, turning the part he'd bent to resemble one of Alcee's curls to the back. On his way to meet LaCroix, he walked past the two men, who did not pause their conversation as he went by. They might be blind to him, but he was not deaf to them. From Benjamin's father he heard something about a front-runner by the name of Paul, the son of Emile, a prosperous ship-industry family.

Paul Bastion. That name seemed familiar to him.

CHAPTER TWELVE

"**M**ONSIEUR GIROD, I HAVE THE ANSWER to your question." LaCroix folded the bill in half and handed it to Gabriel. "However, according to my partner, the person does not want to be known."

"How is it the person knew I had ordered this wardrobe?"

LaCroix pressed his palms together and rested his chin on his fingertips. "Hmm. This, I do not know." He stared, eyebrows drawn together, and appeared as if he might be praying for an answer. Pointing to Cordeviolle, he said, "If you will excuse me, it may be better for you to speak directly with him." He showed Gabriel to a seating area off the main showroom. "You would be more comfortable here, yes?"

Gabriel sat in one of the two mahogany chairs that flanked a round table. This had become more than he expected, and he had promised Rosette he would return with the fiacre so she could take the coach to the market. Once again, the partners engaged in a conversation punctuated with finger-wagging and forehead-holding.

He forced his thoughts to solving the mystery of the

donor. Though he knew a broad spectrum of people because of the café business, most were acquaintances with little knowledge, as far as he knew, of his personal affairs. Considering those who had the means to accomplish paying his debt narrowed the possibilities to less than a handful. For Tante Virgine and even André, the money owed was not beyond their reach. But his aunt would never undertake such a stunt for fear of her sister's wrath, which displayed itself in ignoring Virgine. And for someone who required human contact to survive along with air, food, and water, that separation would be a death. André, while able to use his money freely, probably had no knowledge of Gabriel's visits to the tailors. More importantly, he would not undermine Gabriel's pride.

Having exhausted the list, Gabriel stood to look for Monsieur Cordeviolle. The tailor headed in his direction, but alongside him were the father and son Gabriel wanted to ignore. Watching the three men, Gabriel then realized the one person he had forgotten. His father. Certainly his pockets were deep, but his responsibility to his family with Rosette hardly necessitated a pocket at all.

Gabriel heard Cordeviolle's farewells to the two men. Then, walking over, Cordeviolle motioned for Gabriel to sit as he took the other chair.

"Monsieur Girod, please accept our apologies. This is, you understand, a most unusual situation."

"Of course. As I am sure you understand that, depending on the person responsible, I must initiate appreciation or an offer of compensation."

Cordeviolle sighed. "The gentleman responsible requested that we not reveal his identity. And he has been our customer for quite some time now."

Gabriel's frustration was tempered by the tailor's apologetic tone. He respected the man's unwillingness to be dishonorable. "It is not that I don't appreciate the gesture, it is that it creates a certain sense of obligation." He stood and said to Cordeviolle, "Please thank Monsieur LaCroix for his help, and thank you for yours as well."

"You are most welcome." He nodded. "Please, wait here, and I will bring your wardrobe to you."

Moments later, he handed the clothes to Gabriel and then, in a voice so low Gabriel hardly heard him, said, *"C'est son père tout craché."*

YEARS OF PRACTICING RESTRAINT ENABLED GABRIEL to delay his reaction to Cordeviolle's observation until he reached his carriage. In commenting that Gabriel was the spitting image of his father, Jean Noel, the man accomplished both honoring his promise to the father and acknowledging the confusion of the son. And if not to convey the identity Gabriel sought, why would he have mentioned the resemblance? And why would his father choose to do this now?

This was the first time Gabriel had placed such a costly order. He still didn't know how his father knew the information, unless the tailor who'd helped him had made the same remark. As hommes de couleur libre themselves, they understood the system of *marriages de la main gauche.* The tailor knew Jean Noel and Rosette had what some called a "left-handed marriage," in which neither were bound to the other but in most cases resembled marriage in every way. With the exception that placées willingly, consistently, and generally happily participated in the physical aspect of the marriage. Ironically, the system disfavored the free men of color like himself. The choice between a protector who provided well for her or someone like Gabriel who often struggled to attain or maintain success was not difficult for most women of color. Sometimes, if cast off by their protectors, the former placées would consent to a marriage with a free man of color. Except for his mother, who defied the system by telling Jean Noel that she would no longer need "protection."

Gabriel could count on one hand the number of people who knew that his father did not leave willingly. To spare him humiliation, one of Rosette's concessions was allowing others to believe he no longer desired her. It might have been inevitable, but unlikely. Before Rosette ended their relationship, Jean Noel appeared content, comfortable, when he visited. After it ended, he tried to arrange time with his children and, at the same time, avoid Rosette. He looked like a starving man allowed to attend a banquet but forbidden the food. And now Gabriel understood his father's pain because it was his pain as well.

Though he didn't have much time to spare, he could pass by his father's law office and still arrive home without delaying Rosette. Gabriel mentally played out the scenario at his father's office. He would explain that the tailors hadn't revealed Jean Noel's identity, but that he had come to the conclusion himself. If they could not spend time together today, they could arrange another. For if there were ever a time he needed his father, it was now.

He stopped and waited for his insides to stop trying to break through to his outsides. Just as he started to exit the fiacre, his father stepped out of the office then turned and closed the French shutters over the door and long windows. Gabriel paused for a moment, not wanting to call out his father's name and yet giving him time to finish. Gabriel had started to cross the street and was a few feet behind when he saw his father wave to a woman and a boy about Alcee's age, who both waved in return as they walked to meet Jean Noel.

Whatever Gabriel's father had intended to accomplish by paying for his wardrobe, seeing him with his other son could not have been his intention. At least he hoped not.

CHAPTER THIRTEEN

L OTTIE FOUND A DEAD MOUSE on the steps outside, which meant Henri couldn't be far away. After the first time this happened, she had grown less repulsed, eventually realizing that in his cat brain, he thought he'd delivered a treasure.

Today, the prize showed up at the steps leading to the gallery. She swatted it with her foot into the flower garden. Henri sauntered from alongside the house, stretched as easily as bread dough, and arranged himself close enough for Lottie to be able to scoop him up. She did and carried him inside, where she could hold him while she rocked in the same chair her grandmother had rocked her father. The faint needlepoint flowers on the seat and back showed the years of use, and the mahogany rails were almost as worn as the arms. Sitting in it, Lottie imagined a gentler version of Grand-mère. A mother cradling her child—her father—and it served to comfort her. Especially during times like these when her sole comfort came from ignoring the future that awaited her.

Henri turned around twice on her lap then settled into a round, furry patchwork pillow of brown, black, and white. "Where will you deposit your mice when I no longer live here?" He lifted one eyelid and turned his head to the opposite direction, either bored or bothered or both. Lottie looked down at him. "I'll continue to pet you, even though you are being quite rude. It is possible that I could take you with. Maybe you should reconsider."

"Are you having a conversation with that cat?" Justine closed her parasol as she walked up the steps into the gallery. Startled by Justine's entrance, Henri leaped from Lottie's lap, snagging threads in one of the lace cuffs on her sleeve and leaving a collection of hair scattered over her pale yellow dress. He darted around Justine's plaid skirt, which elicited a yelp from her, and then fled down the stairs. "Why do you want that thing near you?"

"Well, you did surprise us both," said Lottie as she brushed the cat hair from her dress and examined the loose threads hanging from the lace. She rummaged through the sewing basket next to the chair, found a pair of scissors, and snipped off the loops that Henri had created in his flight. "There. Good as new," she said, tossing the scissors back into the basket.

Before sitting, Justine scrutinized the seat of the chair across from the rocker. "That will only cause the lace to unravel more," she warned. "And is that one of the new dresses made for you?"

"Yes, it is one of the 'Lottie gets a husband' dresses." She held out the cotton lawn skirt to show the rosettes spilling down the center of the dress. "I actually like this one. It's rather simple, like me. With the exception of this." She pointed to the white lace collar that ruffled around her neck and was joined in the front by another lace rosette. "But since Agnes will be walking with us to class, I imagined Grand-mère thinking this the perfect dress for a promenade."

Justine rolled her eyes. "Sometimes I don't know if you are being serious or silly. I doubt she would consider walking to Monsieur's house an opportunity to stroll just to be seen. Perhaps on the levee in the evenings…" Her voice trailed off as she tapped her mouth with her forefinger and, as she often did, looked off into some space she supposed the answers hid. The quirk served her well during lessons when she stalled for an answer, making it appear as if she'd forgotten it when she didn't know it in the first place.

"If I have it, I might as well wear it," Lottie said. *Then the more it will wear, and the faster I can donate it.* Lottie couldn't think of the orphanages without thinking of Gabriel. He'd opened her heart to those children, and she would be forever grateful. But she missed him. She missed watching him play kickball with the older boys or jumping rope with the girls, who giggled at his clumsiness. And she missed looking into his eyes and feeling like she would never be cold again.

"I guess," Justine answered, without sounding at all convincing. She stood and peered through the open doorway into the main house. "Where is Agnes? We should be leaving."

"Wait here. I will find my gloves and Agnes."

"Your bonnet. Don't forget," Justine cautioned, before smiling.

Lottie heard Agnes's voice coming from the foyer, so she headed in that direction. Halfway there, she saw him...standing with his back to the front door, his hat in hand, speaking to Agnes. It being too late to retreat, she continued toward them and willed her voice to sound normal.

"Gabriel, so good to see you." She smiled as evidence and clasped her hands so as not to wring them dry in front of him. But the smile he returned barely turned up his lips. Lottie felt the awkwardness of having intruded, like the way she had when, much younger, she'd slid open the parlor door and witnessed her grandparents kissing. No one could truly pretend it didn't happen, and yet that was exactly what they did.

"He just now leaving. I told him you and Miz Justine had a lesson," said Agnes as she patted Gabriel's arm.

Whatever caused him to be so solemn and to find Agnes here, it had to be important. Lottie didn't want him to leave without what she suspected was the solace he sought. "Yes, but we have time. Please, finish. We can wait in the gallery." She nodded in Gabriel's direction. "Please give your mother and sister my regards." Lottie glanced at him and wondered how "handsome" and "anguished" could coexist in his face.

"Lottie, I appreciate your kindness, but Agnes and I are finished," said Gabriel.

What Lottie wanted to say was, "We chased one another with slimy frogs, hid from Agnes in the stable, and dared one another to eat a raw oyster. What happened?" Instead, she replied, "Thank you."

———

"If my mother insists on these lessons being in the afternoon, then either Monsieur Gautier will have to come to one of our houses or someone will have to drive us in a carriage," Justine said, holding her gloved hand over her nose. "A parasol and a bonnet have no value when it is chilled outside."

Agnes and Lottie, walking behind Justine, shared a small shrug. "I have a heavier, longer cloak—would you like to wear it? I would be comfortable in yours." Lottie started to untie the ribbons of her dark blue quilt-patterned cloak, but Justine looked over her shoulder with an expression that caused Lottie to check her hem for mud splatters.

"You're supposed to be promenading, remember? My faded brown mantelet over your dress would be most unappealing. People would think your grandmother raised a ragamuffin." She covered her nose with her hand again and continued walking.

Lottie started to speak, but Agnes shook her head, leaned toward her, and said quietly, "We almost there. Ain't no point discussing now."

She didn't know what the point was until Agnes, as Justine walked through Monsieur's door, said, "Sometimes it's hard for people to see somebody get what they want. Especially when the person who got it don't want it."

CHAPTER FOURTEEN

"L̲ADIES, WITH M̲ADEMOISELLE L̲ECLERC'S PARTY so soon, we should review behaviors appropriate to genteel society. We would not want you to disgrace your families." Monsieur Gautier stared thoughtfully at the ceiling then returned his gaze to Lottie and Justine perched on the settee. "Or your deportment teacher."

The list of bad habits certain to forever doom them as models of rectitude included never admiring themselves in a glass, laughing immoderately, placing their hand upon anyone ever, taking snuff from or giving it to a stranger, winking, or crossing their legs. Lottie, fearing she would demonstrate another unladylike habit by nodding off to sleep while he spoke, waited for him to take a breath before she said, "Monsieur, perhaps it might be more to our benefit to simply relate what we can do, since the list of undesirables is so lengthy."

Monsieur rose from his murky-yellow upholstered armchair, clasped his hands in front of him, and pierced Lottie with his stare. "Mademoiselle, you have just illustrated an unpleasant aspect of gentility in conversation, which is that sarcasm is most unbecoming to a lady."

Justine affected a cough behind her hands and whispered to Lottie, "You are doomed to silence." Justine's response, and their mutual amusement of both the rules of deportment and their teacher, dissolved the previous tension between them. Lottie reached over and squeezed her friend's hand, a gesture that signaled all was well.

"In closing, regarding your conversations, of utmost importance are modesty, simplicity, and avoiding the appearance of possessing wisdom if one has none."

Lottie brushed an invisible thread from her skirt to avoid eye contact with her teacher.

"Now, I need for you to stand for our next lesson." Monsieur readied to instruct them in the proper lifting of a skirt when on the street, to avoid, he said, "the foul mud that would soil your gowns."

He moved his chair to the side then stood before Lottie and Justine, holding the legs of his trousers out as if he were wearing a skirt. Lottie forced herself to not look at Justine for fear that they would both be banished from class for eternity.

"You must hold the folds of your gown with your right hand." Monsieur looked up to make certain they followed directions. "Now, with the same hand, you draw the skirt to the right." That demonstration presented a problem since his trousers could not be drawn at all without risking his knees giving way.

"Oh, Mademoiselle Charlotte, we must not seem as if we will be pulling our skirt off. Gently, draw." He said the word "draw" for as long as it took him to carefully sweep his imaginary skirt to the right. "Again." He motioned for Lottie to practice her technique. "Very good. Now, ladies, we must never, ever show more than just a little peep of an ankle, yes?" His peep sounded remarkably realistic, which caused another concentrated effort on Lottie's part to suppress laughter.

"And we must never, ever do this." Using both hands, he pretended to raise his skirt on both sides. "Lifting skirts on the streets in such a way is vulgar." He placed his hands on his cheeks. "You would be labeled demimondes, or at least on your way to such a life."

As they readied to leave, Monsieur informed them that only Justine would return for a lesson the next week. Relieved but also surprised, Lottie asked why her grandmother had not scheduled another class. "I am not in the habit of questioning my clients, mademoiselle."

While Grand-mère had a reputation for annoying instructors with her demands, she did not make frivolous decisions. With all the details of the party occupying her, she must have neglected to mention the missed class to Lottie.

Buttoning her gloves, Justine said, "Maybe gentility is only important before the marriage, not after it."

"I will see you this week for our pianoforte lesson," Justine said as they stood in front of her house. "And, Lottie..." She looked down for a moment before she spoke. "I am sorry for my petty remark earlier. As your party draws near, I think I'm realizing I am also nearer to losing my friend."

Lottie drew back. Justine's words stung no less than a hand slapped across her face. So occupied with dreading what the future held with a man who wasn't Gabriel, she had not considered the changes in her friendship with Justine. Living close to her, spending time with her family, their lessons together…it would all be different after the wedding. "I—I hadn't thought about what would change between us. Not because it didn't matter. I expected…I don't know…"

"That your husband would move into your grandparents' house and we would all play together," Justine said softly.

Lottie nodded like a contrite child.

"Me too," Justine said. "Me too."

ON HER WAY UPSTAIRS, LOTTIE asked Agnes why Gabriel had stopped by to talk. "Is he feeling well?" Lottie hoped her voice sounded the same as when she asked what was being served for dinner.

In the storeroom, checking the inventory of spices and flour, Agnes replied, "He's fine," and continued to open and shut the lids of boxes and barrels.

"He didn't look fine," Lottie countered.

Agnes shooed her away from the door, locked it, and placed the key in her pocket. "On lave son linge sale en famille," she said, adding, "I'm going to set the dishes on the table."

"Wait," Lottie said. "What does that mean?"

"It mean," Agnes said, "wash your dirty clothes in your own family." She walked into the china pantry and Lottie walked up the stairs.

Lottie sat with a volume of poetry near the tall windows in her bedroom. They had been opened just enough for her to smell and hear the rain that started moments before she and Agnes arrived home. It was a friendly rain, the kind that fell as soft as an apology. But the slight wind carried the mist through the window, so she closed the book of William Blake's poetry, a gift from Grand-père on her sixteenth birthday. When young enough to still sit near him, her head on his shoulder and his arm wrapped around her, he would read to her. She loved his rendition of "Tyger! Tyger! burning bright, in the forests of the night…" and never forgot how he explained the tiger that, at first, frightened her. "Some people see the ferocious tiger as evil, but it was a creature made by the same God who created the gentle lamb. Remember, God is always smarter than any man. So God created everything for a reason."

She expected that, as she grew older, she would understand more of life. Instead, she understood less. She asked more questions but received fewer answers. The party, the marriage, Gabriel, Justine, her parents, her grandparents. Agnes and Abram, who had no control over the color of their skin, now had no control over their lives. *But isn't that true for all of us?* The God Grand-père explained all those years ago seemed then far less confusing than He did today.

And now her grandparents' voices drifted through her window, but no one had yet called for dinner. Lottie watched the rain exhaust itself, leaving behind drops on the lemon trees, a shine on the bricks in the courtyard. She decided she was tired too. She closed her eyes and waited. She just wasn't sure for what.

CHAPTER FIFTEEN

O F COURSE SHE WOULD BE there. It was her house.
Gabriel left the LeClercs' house hoping his day
of disappointments ended soon and that Rosette would
be understanding about his being away so long. Neither
one seemed likely.

First, he had watched as his father, the man he intended to visit in moments, turned to meet his wife and
son. The reunion Gabriel plotted in his head became as
useless as he felt. Knowing he didn't want to tell Rosette
what happened, Gabriel went directly to Agnes. The
thought that he might have to endure the awkwardness
of seeing Lottie didn't occur to him. That is, not until he
finished explaining to Agnes what happened and then
saw Lottie walking through the hall. And there was no
way out for either one of them.

He saw how the delicate yellow of her dress high-
lighted the honey gold in her eyes. And when he had
averted his eyes from Agnes, having heard the rustling of
Lottie's dress, he saw that she smiled. That she held one
hand with the other, he knew signaled her nervousness.
Their first few times visiting the children's homes, days

they'd walked and she'd talked about her grandmother's distance from her, she'd clasped her hands just like that.

The discomfort he sensed between them was sadly reassuring, because it reflected what they could not openly acknowledge. It pained him to be so close that he could take her hands, draw her to him, and no longer need to wonder what it would be like to bend to kiss her, knowing it would be welcomed. And worse, her grandparents might have already decided on her husband, and yet she didn't know. He wanted the party to be over, perhaps more than Lottie.

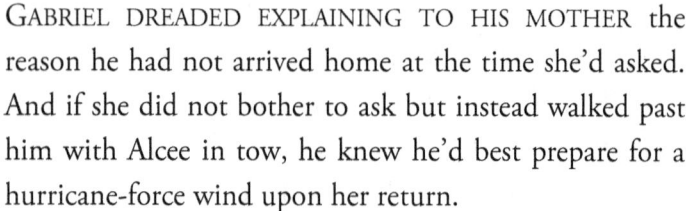

GABRIEL DREADED EXPLAINING TO HIS MOTHER the reason he had not arrived home at the time she'd asked. And if she did not bother to ask but instead walked past him with Alcee in tow, he knew he'd best prepare for a hurricane-force wind upon her return.

He heard a medley of voices as he approached the house. Probably Tante Virgine. But entering through the open French doors of the dining room, he was surprised to find unfamiliar faces gathered around the table.

"Gabriel, so glad you are home." Rosette sounded as if she meant it. "Finally."

Ah, there it was.

His arms occupied holding his wardrobe, he simply nodded and wished he had first gone to his garçonnière and perhaps stayed there.

Excusing himself from the guests, Gabriel brought

his clothes to his room and laid them on his bed. Rosette expected him to join her and her guests, so he quickly splashed water on his face, dried off, and returned to the dining room.

Most everyone had already finished eating, and, judging by the smell of fresh coffee, dessert would be served soon. He hated feeling uncomfortable in his own home. He served himself a bowl of red beans and rice then sat at the table across from his mother. Tearing the heel off the crusty French bread on the serving tray, he set it on his plate. When he lifted his spoon to his mouth, Rosette decided to start the introductions.

"This is my dressmaker, Madame Barrier. She graciously came here after Virgine told her we were without transportation." Rosette gestured to the lady on her right, whose high white lace collar had been fastened by a rectangular brooch. The pink-and-gray horizontal stripes of her dress made for a surprising contrast, as Gabriel would have expected on a younger woman. Perhaps the lines around her eyes made her appear older.

"And this is Monsieur Joseph Joubert. He is a builder."

Curious. "Pleased to meet you. And what is it you build?"

"Cottages, town houses, and stores. Most of my designs are traditional, but I do my best to know current trends. I provide floor plans, sketches of the completed project for my clients. I also renovate, which is what brought me to Madame Girod's home today."

He spoke with the practiced assurance that comes from knowing his clients wanted someone trustworthy, competent, and confident. Had he not introduced himself as a builder, Gabriel might have mistaken him as someone who worked on the river. Joubert had the well-developed arms of a man who spent the major portion of his day carrying objects the size of which might make another man, like Gabriel, collapse. Considerably darker than the Girods, Joubert's close-to-his-scalp, tightly curled hair may have defined him as entirely black had his eyes not been as green, his lips not as thin.

Gabriel mixed the mound of red beans atop the rice, the creamy gravy barely visible. The night before, Rosette and Alcee had sifted through them to remove small pieces of rock or hard mud that sometimes hid in them. After scraping the beans into the pot, Rosette covered them with water. Alcee used to say they got "fat" overnight. This morning, Rosette drained the old water, started with fresh water, onions, and spices, and then cooked them for most of the day.

While his mother, the dressmaker, and the builder shared stories about strange occurrences during Carnival, a conversation that could go on for years, Gabriel leaned over to Alcee and said, "I am sorry if I spoiled the day you were to spend with Maman. I can explain later."

"How much later?"

"Hmm. When you are twenty?"

"Maman looks like she thinks she might be twenty again."

At first, Gabriel thought his sister's over-dramatizing was a result of her reading *Mansfield Park*. The wretched treatment of poor orphans made for highly impassioned and sob-wracked voice scenes in the parlor. She told Gabriel and her mother that "happily ever after" challenged her acting skills.

Rosette had remarked, "Exactly." But Alcee continued playing the suffering heroine and pleading with Rosette for permission to quit school to perform. Their palaver one particular night sent Gabriel back to the quiet of his garçonnière. They continued to quibble, but not with regularity. Rosette told Alcee she could act by pretending she liked school.

But he watched his mother across the table and noticed the shift in the brightness of her eyes when she spoke to Joubert and the dress-maker, the natural smile for one, the polite smile for the other. Gabriel waited for an opportunity to join the conversation, which kindly presented itself when Rosette went to the pantry for dessert plates.

"Excuse me. I will see if I can be of help to Maman." Alcee kicked Gabriel ever so slightly under the table before she left.

"Monsieur Joubert, did you escort Madame Barrier here?"

The builder looked across the table at the dressmaker. "No. No. Of course…" He smiled then continued. "Of course, I offered to escort her home."

Madame Barrier nodded. "He is very kind, especially

since…since Monsieur Barrier is no longer with me." She withdrew a lacy handkerchief from one of her long sleeves, patted her eyes dry, then pushed it back into her sleeve.

"Monsieur Joubert, I wasn't aware Rosette knew any builders," said Gabriel.

"I am here because your mother and I talked at the café about the possibility of bringing the kitchen to the house. Many homes have been safely remodeled to do this, and it seemed an idea that would be of great help to her."

Rosette walked in, holding a tray of Dresden cups and the coffee service. Alcee followed with dessert plates.

"Gabriel, remember how we talked about the Gallier home and the indoor kitchen?" Rosette walked to the sideboard for the sugar bowl.

He wanted to say that they had discussed a number of houses for a number of different reasons. But tonight was not the night. "Yes, I do recall that conversation."

"When Monsieur Joubert showed me how we could increase our business at the café with simply a few changes"—she stopped to smile at the builder as she passed him a cup of coffee—"that's when I asked about our kitchen."

Gabriel prepared himself. Witnessing his mother's demeanor around Monsieur Joubert, he suspected the café might not be the only change at the Girod household. He hoped Rosette understood that most all renovations required tearing down the old to accommodate the new. And it couldn't be one brick at a time. He passed Alcee his empty bowl and waited for the next cup of coffee.

Joubert had the muscles for the job. But did he have the heart?

CHAPTER SIXTEEN

THOUGH CONSIDERED MILD BY ANYONE north of New Orleans, the winter brought enough of a chill to warrant velvets, cloaks, and fireplaces. Business increased in the café as the aroma of the calas mingled with the café au lait and lured customers in to warm themselves and wrap their hands around the steaming mugs. Sundays before and after the masses at the Cathedral were especially busy.

The morning after dinner with their guests, Gabriel looked around the café at the scattered groups standing near tables and admitted that having more seats would be of benefit.

As he bent to pick up empty cups and plates from a table, Gabriel felt a tap on his shoulder. A bundle of silver velvet brushed against his hand as the dress whisked past, and then Nathalie stood in front of him. "Is anyone sitting here?" She placed her silk fan on her face, revealing only her large, inviting eyes. She blinked like Alcee when she exaggerated her adoration of him to plead for some favor. Nathalie, though, seemed much more practiced, especially in the way she slowly lowered her fan from her round eyes to below her full lips, revealing a smile as curvaceous as her body.

Without waiting for an answer, she glided onto the stool and unbuttoned her mantelet, a delicate pink that matched the bow just below the hollow of her neck and the small buttons down the center front of her dress. She looked at him with the expectancy of a woman awaiting a compliment.

Not sure if his temporary inability to speak was due to Nathalie seeing him as a server or his seeing Nathalie, Gabriel thought the best course of action was to dispense with the jumble of cups and plates he held. "So good to see you. Would you excuse me? I need to take these to Rosette." He mentally kicked himself for sounding as uncomfortable as he felt.

"I won't go away. I promise." She started removing her gloves as if to prove that she would not be leaving.

He deposited the china inside the deep wooden tub they used for washing and dried his hands. Rosette handed him a fresh cup of café au lait and nodded in Nathalie's direction. "Is that—?"

"Yes. Little Nathalie Chaigneau." He saw Rosette's eyebrows arch even higher and her mouth open to speak. "I know. I know. She's not so little anymore."

His mother smiled. "Well, at least you noticed. That's a beginning."

Her remark unnerved him. He set the cup down on the counter. "Why do you say that?"

"Because you need to hear it." She reached for more

cups. "We can talk later."

"I don't have anything to say. Not now." Gabriel walked away before she could answer and made his way to Nathalie. He set the cup in front of her. "I suppose I should have asked if you wanted coffee."

"Why else would I be here?" She moved her gloves to her lap. "Thank you. I will probably need another soon." She glanced around the café.

"Oh, you are meeting someone." Of course. Why would someone as attractive as Nathalie find herself alone in a café drinking coffee?

"Yes. A friend I haven't had an opportunity to spend much time with since I returned." She sipped her coffee. "How have you been? I don't see you out much."

"No. I spend most of my time here or helping Rosette at home with her pralines." Hearing himself, he realized how feeble that must sound. At least he escaped having to admit that in front of the man she was there to meet.

She tilted her head. The simple yet tightly wrapped dove-gray tignon, two soft pink feathers banding one side, drew more attention to her face. "Then we must change that. A group of us will be at the opera Saturday. Why don't you join us?"

He didn't have a reason to refuse. "Yes. Yes, I will do that."

She clapped her hands. "*C'est magnifique!* Great news. I look forward to it. We usually meet at six o'clock outside the theatre. My family has seats. I will be sure to save one for you."

At some other time, Gabriel would have argued against a ticket being provided for him. But the café was not the place nor Nathalie the person for that discussion. "Thank you."

She smiled but looked past him and waved. "My friend. She is here."

The tall young woman, elegant in her expensive French silk-and-lace dress and triple pearl strands, moved in their direction. Not only was she *au courant* with fashion, but she wore money with the self-assurance displayed only by those who had it in abundance. That the wealth did not originate with her was revealed by her equally understated but bejeweled tignon.

She looked familiar, and when Nathalie introduced her, "This is my friend, Serafina Lividaus," Gabriel remembered exactly where he had last seen her.

"I am pleased to see you again," she said.

Serafina.

The woman Rosette comforted in their parlor.

The woman who thought she might be pregnant with Paul Bastion's child.

THE FIRST FEW MONTHS AFTER ROSETTE ended her relationship with Jean Noel, Gabriel heard the maids and children of other placées weave the most elaborate tales about his mother and father. All of them involved a version of how, why, or when Jean Noel left, because a placée asking her protector to end their left-handed marriage would be so unusual as to be unbelievable. When he heard stories of his mother wanting more children, not wanting more children, spending too much money, not pleasing Jean Noel, or whatever the tale *du jour*, Gabriel said nothing. His mother had promised his father not to reveal the truth so as to protect his reputation, which, ironically, made her the protector. And so Gabriel had honored his mother's request that he not disclose what he knew to be the truth. Maintaining silence and his temper were crucial, and that promise to his mother was one of the most difficult Gabriel had ever experienced.

Until today, when Rosette extracted another promise of conf identiality.

After serving Serafina and Nathalie, Gabriel severed every emotion possible. Cut their ropes, let them drift into a sea of nothingness. Otherwise, he could not have finished the day that he now stood discussing with Rosette, who confronted him as soon as the last customer left.

"Have you swallowed a ghost?" she teased when he handed her more cups. "Wait, you didn't smile." Still holding the dishes, she said, "Sit on that stool right in front of me. I'm going to put these in the tub. Don't move."

Gabriel sat and watched his mother as she walked away, her shoulders straight, her head high. Even at the end of a day, no one would guess how little she slept, how hard she worked, in her business and as a parent. He thought of Jean Noel's wife, who didn't have to concern herself with money, and his son, who could talk to his father whenever he needed. At times, Gabriel resented his mother's decision. How could half a father be worse than no father?

Rosette dried her hands on the hem of her apron then pulled up a stool for herself. "You have been bothered since earlier today. What happened that you are barely alive?"

He chose not to mention the discussion with LeCroix and Cordevialle about his clothes or about trying to spend time with Jean Noel. He related the conversation he'd overheard in the tailors' about the Bastions and then about seeing Serafina today, making the connection between her and Paul. "He already has a woman, and she is pregnant, and now he will have Lottie too? I—I cannot watch this unfold and do nothing."

"So what is it you think you can do?" Rosette unwrapped her calico tignon, letting her hair spill over her shoulders. She pushed her fingers through her hair where it pressed against her scalp. She would retie the tignon before they left the café, but Gabriel knew she welcomed even this brief respite.

"Lottie should know the kind of man Paul Bastion is. She would want to know."

"And then what?"

"Why would she want to marry such a man? If she knew beforehand, she could—"

"Refuse? That would suggest she has a choice—which she does not. And how is Paul Bastion different from any other white Creole man? How is it different from—"

"Don't," he snapped and stood, leaning to hold onto the stool. "You were going to say how is he different from my father."

"No. I intended to ask how is it different from rocking my son to sleep on the day his father married? Because this is about *your* grief. About having no control over *your* life."

He clenched the stool, wanted to hurl it across the café. He wanted to see the destruction he felt. "But I love her. When I was younger, I thought I'd grow out of it. A boyhood infatuation. But I kept growing into it."

"Have you told her?"

"Of course not. What would it change? The laws are not going to change for us."

"No, they're not. If you haven't told her your feelings, why would she even think she had any choices? But people who love each other have found ways. None of which are easy."

"Telling Lottie that I love her still may not change anything."

"Neither will not telling her. But you are not going to say anything to her about Paul Bastion or Serafina. That is not your place. She is not ignorant of the system. Lottie has known us since she was a child. How could she not know?"

GABRIEL WISHED HE HAD TAKEN ANDRÉ'S advice and found a way to go to Paris. Being within arm's reach of Lottie in New Orleans proved to be no different than being thousands of miles away from her. Except that there would be occasions to see her here, which made erasing her from his heart all the more impossible.

In her own way, Rosette understood. His mother had told him those stories when he began to ask about the balls to which he would not be welcomed—unless invited to serve food to those who were. Brought to the theatre at the age of sixteen, Rosette had followed her mother into the world of *plaçage*…not by her choice, but by her mother's. Rosette, a free woman of color like her mother Elizabeth, dressed like a princess and had been well-educated and properly mannered. All because she had a white father as a protector. Helene had decided that her daughter should maintain the lifestyle to which she had been accustomed. And being a placée, while it would not provide her with a husband, would provide her wealth. A life few women of color—ironically, even few white women—would otherwise have.

But the exquisite clothes, finely crafted furniture, and expensive jewelry failed to comfort Rosette on the nights she waited for Jean Noel after his marriage. The nights she sewed, waiting for him, nights the inlaid-wood mahogany table set with china and crystal from France, sterling silverware from England, and hand-embroidered damask linens did nothing to warm her heart when she snuffed the candle because he had not come.

***

HELPING ROSETTE DISTRACTED GABRIEL, AND IT prevented him from the likelihood of seeing Lottie. Then, perhaps because she thought he needed more to do, Rosette asked him to help Monsieur Joubert with the designs for both their house and the café. Gabriel noticed how the builder stopped in daily even before his mother approached him about assisting with the plans. When Gabriel mentioned to Rosette the frequency of Joubert's visits, she told him that Joubert needed to observe the ebb and flow of the business. It appeared to Gabriel that the design plans of interest to the builder had more to do with his mother than the customers.

The first day Gabriel met Joubert at the house to discuss the kitchen plans, he considered that he might have misunderstood the builder's intentions at the café. Instead of a discussion of the plans at the table or in the parlor, Joubert wanted Gabriel outside, demonstrating how he and Rosette worked around the kitchen area. While Gabriel modeled, Joubert asked questions and wrote notes.

"Aren't you enclosing the space? What is the purpose of this?" Gabriel never felt comfortable performing.

"Some builders do simply bring the two spaces together. But not everyone works in a space in the same manner. For instance, not everyone has to make the quantity of food that is made here. Or as often. These are important details," Joubert shared as they walked through the alley to the banquette.

Gabriel nodded. "I had not thought of building this way. To me, it is a matter of having the money, the materials, and the manpower."

Joubert smiled. "Well put." He pointed to the vocal couple across the street, whose gestures and volume attested to the conversation's contentiousness. "Think of it as a relationship. All women and men have the same construction. But that does not always mean they fit together well."

And that explains why some fall into ruins.

CHAPTER SEVENTEEN

ON THE WAY HOME FROM her last dress fitting, Lottie asked if she could be let out at Justine's house so as not to be late for their pianoforte lesson. "You know how Justine hates when people—what does she call it? Oh, 'dillydally,' that's it," she told her grandmother as the cab turned onto their street.

Grand-mère parted the inner curtain of the carriage and peered outside. "You don't have a lesson today So we are going directly to the house."

"Is Madame Fontenot ill?" Lottie couldn't imagine anything else keeping the woman away from torturing her and Justine.

"No. Justine will have her lesson today as planned." Grand-mère let the curtain fall. "With the party and the dressmaker appointments… I thought we…you did not need to be bothered with something else that needed attention."

If Justine's lesson had also been cancelled, Lottie might have celebrated the news with enthusiasm. "I will have one the week following, yes?"

Grand-mère sighed. "Perhaps. We will need to wait

until that time is nearer. But you can always practice at home."

Lottie held out her hand and placed it against the side of the carriage to steady herself as it jostled over the gutter into the flagstone porte cochère. Practicing alone only sounded inviting if the other choice were sitting alone with Grand-mère. *Why would I just begin taking lessons if I would be stopping them so soon?* A question better asked of Grand-père, Lottie decided.

Abram opened the cab door. "Be careful now, Miz LeClerc. These stones still slippery from the rain this morning."

"You'd tell me that even if the stones were dry, Abram," Grand-mère remarked, and, to Lottie's surprise, did so kindly.

While her grandmother concentrated on her footing, Abram winked at Lottie. "Yes ma'am. Don't want nothin' bad to happen to you."

Lottie hid her grin behind one hand and reached for Abram with the other.

"You too, Miz Charlotte." Abram gave her hand a squeeze and smiled.

"Abram." Grand-mère waited for Lottie to alight, and he looked in her direction. "Remember, I need you and Agnes to pick up the supplies from Monsieur Laroche's grocery. And, Lottie, I am going to take a nap. I suggest you do the same."

After standing in a dress that weighed thirty pounds, required a corset made for a twelve-year-old, and overemphasized her décolletage, Lottie needed movement. She summoned her sweetest voice to ask her grandmother if she could accompany Agnes and Abram to the grocery because, as she continued, "Some of the best families in the city shop there, and then I'd know everything available for the dinners I will be planning."

Once her grandmother agreed and disappeared inside, Lottie used the back stairs and quickly gathered the dresses in her armoire from Justine that her nieces had outgrown. She stacked them in a basket and met Agnes at the bottom of the stairs.

"You planning to shop there? I don't think your grandmother wants you spending her money." Agnes tugged the basket closer, peered inside, and eyed Lottie as if she had hidden away Henri. "Nobody at the Laroches need clothes. Specially ones already been worn."

"Shh!" Lottie held Agnes's elbow and steered her toward the cab, where Abram waited. "I'll explain."

Agnes mumbled as they walked toward the stable. "Explain trouble. That's what you about to explain. You muss want Abram and Agnes sold down the river."

"You and Alcee practicing for the next drama? If you get shipped down the Mississippi, I'll go with you."

When they reached Abram, Lottie said, "The store is around the corner from the girls' home. I'm getting out there, and by the time you and Agnes are finished, I should be too. I'll wait for you."

Abram opened the door to the fiacre. "If that's what you want, then that's what I do."

"You as bad as she is. Double trouble."

"Agnes, I'm not going to stop her helping those children. It's on the way, and she got it all worked out." Abram took the basket from Lottie. "Come on, let's get you back in."

Once they were both seated and on their way, Agnes said, "Miz Lottie, you got a big heart. But sometimes that gets you big heartache. Even when you mean it for good."

"I know, Agnes. I know."

———✦———

LOTTIE PERCHED ON A STOOL in the parlor, or "greeting room," as the Sisters called it, reading to a group of girls who sat on the carpet to listen. Sophie, a wisp of a two-year-old, whose blue eyes were set off by her honey-colored skin and dark-brown hair, wiggled her way onto Lottie's lap and rested her head on her shoulder as she read. The two little ones sitting by her feet slid their hands across the bottom of her velvet dress to touch the soft nap. A girl who appeared to be around ten years old sat cross-legged behind all the others, her round face encircled by Lottie's bonnet.

Lottie pointed at the solemn little girl, who twirled a loose bonnet tie in each hand. "Angele, this one is for you." She read the next limerick from *A Book of Nonsense,* which the girls enjoyed because the limericks were exactly what the title said they were. "There was a Young Lady whose bonnet/ Came untied when the birds sate upon it;/ But she said: 'I don't care!/ All the birds in the air/ Are welcome to sit on my bonnet!'" As she read, Lottie sensed someone's presence in the room even before she glanced at the girls and saw them looking behind her, their quiet smiles and shiny eyes signaling their delight.

The word "bonnet" at the end of the limerick had barely escaped Lottie's lips when a few of the girls skipped past her, calling Gabriel's name. She was certain the warm rush of joy at hearing his name had already risen from her neck up to her cheeks, and she was grateful for Sophie being on her lap, for she had provided a reason to delay turning around. But even the two-year-old, anxious to see Gabriel herself, flopped out of Lottie's arms and scuttled through the waves of green velvet to toddle off. And it was in her hesitation, the longing to run to him and the need to guard herself from it, that she knew for certain that their relationship was undeniably changed. In the past, she would have jumped up with the little girls, as eager as they to see him. Today, she understood the "sweet sorrow" of which Romeo spoke when leaving Juliet.

Lottie rose, smoothed her hair, which had gathered into a tumble of curls on one side, and pressed the smashed fabric of her skirt that had been under Sophie's little body. Her body reacted slowly, as if returning from numbness, pins working their way out of her skin.

Seeing Gabriel's reaction as she glided toward him, she imagined what her own face must reflect upon seeing him. That he had crouched down in the midst of a hive of giggling girls, his smiles for them genuine and his care for them sincere, made him all the more attractive.

"Sophie, Sister said it was time for everyone to eat, so follow the girls, and I will be there as soon as Mademoiselle LeClerc and I finish talking."

He patted the top of Sophie's head as she reached to hold his face between her plump little hands and said, "Oui," before sauntering off behind the other girls.

"How are you here? Not that it isn't…I mean, I'm surprised."

"I know. I am as well, actually," Lottie said. *Happily surprised.* "My grandmother sent Agnes and Abram to Laroche's grocery, so I thought it would be an opportune time to deliver a few clothes from Justine."

"Do you need to leave soon? I hoped to talk to you." He looked down for a moment. "I know the last time we saw one another was… brief, so…"

"Yes. I mean no." *Lottie, you have known this man almost your whole life. Breathe.* "Let me start over. Yes, it was brief. No, I don't need to leave soon. At least I don't think so. You know how I lose track of time."

He grinned. "That I do. Let me quickly tell Sister I'll be outside, and we can talk while you wait."

Lottie nodded, but as she watched him and his long stride covering twice the distance hers would have, she wished she had said she didn't have time. Some things are better not talked about. Once one knew the answer, one couldn't pretend that one didn't. And what if she had been the foolish one? Maybe her feelings for Gabriel were not his feelings for her. Did any of it even matter, considering the circumstances?

She decided that when he returned she would tell him she thought they'd be returning soon and they could talk later. She fingered the cameo brooch at her neck, a gift from Rosette on her eighteenth birthday. The Wedgwood-blue jasper cameo was mounted in silver and showed a woman selling love tokens. Taken aback by the extravagance, Lottie had refused the gift, telling Rosette she should save it for Alcee. Rosette told her that her daughter was not being deprived and that Lottie had been like a daughter to her, She was adamant that Lottie accept it.

Gabriel walked up, extending his arm. "Am I destined to always be recovering this for you?"

If only that could be true. Lottie smiled sheepishly and took her bonnet from him.

SET BACK FROM THE STREET, the girls' home featured an expanse of lawn and a cobblestone path that wound its way to the gate leading to the banquette beyond. Lottie appreciated the coolness, as she already felt flushed just anticipating the conversation between herself and Gabriel.

He set his hat on his head, took it off, and rotated it in his hands. "I hadn't planned to be at your house that day. Some situations happened, and I knew I could ask

Agnes to help. The point is…" He looked across the lawn and then returned his gaze to Lottie. "I probably would not have stopped if I had known you would be home."

Lottie wished she had her muff, not that the weather dictated it necessary. If she had it, she could wring out the confusion and disappointment already twisting her hands. She managed an "Oh."

He gently placed his hand on her arm. "Wait. I didn't mean to sound as if I don't want to see you. I do. But that's the problem. I—"

They had reached the gate and Lottie's attention was drawn to the approaching clip-clopping of horses' hooves. Abram stopped the fiacre and nodded in Lottie's direction. She didn't want to move, because Gabriel would have to let go of her arm, and what was left unspoken hung between them and refused to be ignored.

She lifted her face to meet Gabriel's, and she felt him grasp her arm as if to prevent her from disappearing. "Lottie, this is not what I had planned. But if I do not say this now, I do not know if it will ever be said. And even in the saying of it, I know nothing can change. I want you to know that I have avoided you not because I don't care about you, but because I do. I don't know when my heart realized that our relationship was more than just friendship. But—"

"Gabriel," she stopped him. Lottie despised herself for what she was about to do. She wanted to hear him say more, as she wished she could have said more as well.

How many times had she imagined this moment? The moment she would hear him say he loved her. These dreams all ended the same, with Gabriel drawing her close, cradling her face in his strong hands, and kissing her with a fierce tenderness.

But she had to save him from himself, from sacrificing his heart. She moved his hand from her arm. "Don't. I treasure our friendship. I hope never to lose you as an important person in my life. As for more than that, I don't want to mislead you or disappoint you."

His pain and confusion etched themselves in the furrows of his forehead, the firm set of his lips. His eyes searched her face as if she had transformed into a stranger. Then, as if she were someone he had mistaken her for, Gabriel donned his hat and took a step backward. "Then, that is what we will be. *Comme il faut.* I understand."

You do not. You do not understand, Lottie's heart screamed. But all Gabriel heard was silence.

THE DAY GABRIEL SAW LOTTIE at the girls' home, he'd thought it was an answer to prayer. But while the prayer might have been his, the answer was not the one he wanted or expected. He had rehearsed the scene so many times in his mind since his talk with Rosette that when Lottie did not follow the role he had written for her, he had no response. Before he could share with her that he loved her, she relegated their relationship to friends. And with Abram and Agnes waiting in the fiacre, was there any point in continuing the conversation?

So, instead, he'd told her he understood. *Understood?* No. Gabriel watched her leave and wished they played a grown-up version of tag so he could run after her. He could say, "You're it. Forever. You always were. You always will be." But she didn't turn back to look at him once. Lot's wife might have saved herself from becoming a pillar of salt had she the same strength.

Walking home down the side streets, Gabriel ordinarily paid no attention to anyone but Lottie. Today, he heard the lyrical chattering of women gathered on porches. Some rocked sleeping infants stretched across their laps. The others leaned against the slatted shutters, sipping coffee, their faces bronzed by the afternoon sun. Most of the dinner gatherings were ending, and families spilled from porte cochères with their lavish gardens and gurgling fountains. All of it making him aware of how alone he was.

By the time he reached home, Gabriel had convinced himself that Lottie might have saved them both. The idea of the two of them having an open relationship was as likely as the notion of flying. Would she walk away from her life? And if so, where would they go? Live a life without family, friends? Would that be a life either one of them would want?

CHAPTER EIGHTEEN

February 1841

Dear Mama and Papa,

The date draws near for my coming-out party, for it is now only seven days away as of tomorrow. In reading over letters of the last month, I was overcome by how unkind I have sounded about the event. I have decided I must no longer think of this as punishment or be ungrateful for what Grand-mère and Grand-père are doing for me. They are doing what they know you would have done for me.

I told Gabriel something today that pained me to say and him to hear. Is it wrong for me to deny my true feelings if, in doing so, I believe I am saving someone from heartache? I have come to realize that as long as I allow myself to hope there could be something more between Gabriel and me, I would always be unhappy when left alone with thoughts about my future. I care deeply for him, so much so that I believe what I feel for him is love. I think this afternoon he may have been on the verge of express-

ing those same emotions for me. I stopped him. I told him that our friendship was important to me, making it seem as if that was the extent of my relationship with him. Oh, if you could have seen his expression after my words slapped him in the face.

Would life not be easier for him to think we were merely friends? All the hope in the world would not change our circumstances. And if he believes that I do not feel the same way about him, then he would be free to make a life for himself.

I think Agnes knows how I feel about Gabriel; she tried to console me. She told me Jesus has been watching me my whole life and He wasn't going to stop now. She said I need to trust Him, that just because I am in the dark doesn't mean He's not holding a candle. Mama, when Agnes talks to me, it is like a mother talking to a daughter, and I imagine what it would be like if you were here.

And I so wish you could see my beautiful dress! Grand-mère spared no expense and, I must admit, I feel like a princess when I have it on. It is amazing that all those yards of fabric have been transformed into this spectacular gown. Madame Olympe designed the white tulle to be worn over the white silk, and it has two pink lace flounces, each headed with a quilling of black ribbon. In each of the festoons in the lower flounce is a medallion with black ribbon quillings and pink lace, black ribbon, and tulle. The right side of the bodice crosses over the left side just around my shoulders and dips low in the back. The sleeves are four puffs of silk and tulle, separated by rows of braided black and pink ribbons, ending at my wrists with frills of white lace.

Papa, I am certain that flounces and medallions and quillings are as interesting to you as my listening to Agnes talk about how to make a gumbo. Though she did tell me I needed to listen to her because I wouldn't know if the cook left something out. I said I'd just send the cook to her first!

Saturday evening Justine and I are to attend the opera with her older sister and her husband. Lucia di Lammermoor is now playing, and I have heard that it is an outstanding production. Grand-père is quite pleased that I am attending the theatre with my friend, as he says I need to enjoy my youth.

As always…my love and affection,
Genevieve Charlotte

"WAKE UP, CHILD." AGNES PATTED LOTTIE'S shoulder as she lay sprawled across her bed. "What you doing sleeping when you suppose to be readying yourself for the opera?"

"I'm awake. I'm awake," Lottie said, but her eyes remained closed and she didn't move.

Agnes attempted again, and again Lottie replied that she was awake, only this time her voice was edged with irritation.

"That's a mighty fine way of showing you awake. Maybe you don't need no opera. You putting on your own show right here." Agnes pulled the curtains open so that the afternoon sun streamed through the gray, dark room and found its way straight to Lottie's face.

"I'm tired," Lottie moaned and rolled onto her back with her hands over her eyes.

Agnes retrieved the dress Lottie had removed before resting and brought it to the armoire. "Agnes tired too, seeing as you all over the mattress I done already beat flat this morning." She placed the dress on a hook and withdrew a cranberry-striped silk with alternating stripes of plain cranberry and a lighter shade of woven flowers. "I got this new dress your grandmother want you to wear, and you better stand up now so's I can help. More hooks and eyes down the back of this dress than sense."

Lottie uncovered her eyes and squinted as Agnes drew near with the dress. "Are you sure I shouldn't wear one less fancy?" She pushed herself out of the bed, stepped into her petticoats, and held her arms up so Agnes could slip the dress over her head. The slight vee in the front of the dress was matched by one in the back, and the basque waist formed a point in the front.

"You think Agnes would forget such a thing? I tell you what she like to forget is all these hooks back here," she grumbled. "Miz LeClerc say she want you to be seen by some them young bucks gonna be at your party. At least that's what she tole your grandfather."

"I don't know if I should be flattered or insulted by

that. Maybe she wants them to see me tonight so they won't be too disappointed by what they see next week." Lottie distrusted her grandmother's calculated moves—the ones that, on the surface, appeared to be in Lottie's best interest but inevitably served hers as well. Like the time Grand-mère enrolled Lottie in art class when she was eight years old, explaining that she wanted to see Lottie develop her artistic potential. Months later, when Grand-mère no longer had to leave home for her card meetings and held them at her home instead, it seemed Lottie reached the limit of her art skills and no longer needed to attend class. Once those puzzle pieces fell into place, the rest followed the same pattern.

About ten "Jesus, help me" later, Agnes finished hooking the back opening of the dress and directed Lottie to the mirror. She heard Agnes's gasp at the same time she saw a woman she barely recognized in the mirror.

Lottie spoke as if the woman in front of her would answer. "I was born before my mother was twenty. Do you think she might have looked like...like this?" She held the sides of the skirt and twisted from side to side. Lottie would not have been surprised if the reflection in the mirror had moved too.

Straightening the linens on Lottie's bed, Agnes answered so quietly, Lottie almost couldn't hear her. "Oh, yes, I think she mighta looked just like that. Just like you."

WHEN LOTTIE ENTERED THE PARLOR to tell her grandparents that she was leaving, they greeted her with the same stunned silence as Agnes.

"Have I worn too many pearls? I asked Agnes to weave the pearl strands in with my curls, but they are easily removed."

"No. Do not change anything." Grand-père closed his book and smiled. "Turn around slowly so we can see all of it."

"With my corset and the weight of this gown, I could not move quickly if I wanted to," said Lottie. When she turned back to face them, Grand-mère was holding her embroidery hoop and sewing. Her grandfather rose, walked over to her, and kissed her on both cheeks. "You, *ma cher*, are a beautiful young woman."

When he spoke, Lottie detected the faraway look in his eyes that came when he told her stories of her father. "Marie," he said, his voice sounding as if in warning, "aren't you going to tell our granddaughter how lovely she looks tonight?"

Her grandmother looked up, smiled the same smile she bestowed on Monsieur Fonte next door, who believed the Americans to be nice people, and said, "Of course, my dear husband. Lottie, that gown suits you well." Her hoop and needle were poised to connect again, except that she seemed to be waiting for permission to resume.

"I am going to escort Charlotte to the cab," he said, extending his arm for Lottie to hold.

"Good night, Grand-mère." Lottie wanted to ask why she showed so little reaction to a dress whose fabric and design she'd selected. *Didn't Agnes say Grand-mère hoped I attracted attention?* Perhaps her reaction reflected her disappointment. She was fortunate that her grandfather provided sufficient attention for both of them.

Grand-mère had resumed her sewing. "Good night, Charlotte. Enjoy the opera." At least she looked up from her stitching long enough to convey her message.

As they walked to meet Justine, Lottie wished she could lay her head on her grandfather's shoulder. She missed the coarse linen of his frock coat that bore the faintest smell of cigar smoke and ink. It was such a comforting place to be. Older now, she missed those times with him, so she appreciated even this small chance to be with him.

"Do you think the dress did not turn out the way Grand-mère expected?" They were almost to the carriage, and Lottie hoped for some understanding of her grandmother's reaction.

He clutched her hand and shook his head. "P'tit, listen to me. I do not know what your grandmother expected. But this I do know. When you came into the parlor, you looked at us with your father's eyes. But, for that, it was as if Mignon had walked into the room, you so resemble your mother."

WHOEVER DESIGNED THE FOUR-PERSON CARRIAGES either knew nothing about women's fashions or did not care or never intended for more than two women to share one. Day dresses and visiting dresses easily measured four or five feet across, what with all the petticoats or wire cages worn as underpinnings. Evening dresses for operas and balls were often wider, with their swathes and swags of embellished silks and brocades. Travel often required patience and compromise and a sense of humor.

Fortunately, Lottie and Justine had all three qualities. They sat facing Isabelle, Justine's sister, and her husband, François Honore, who married four years ago and now had three children. François told Madame Dumas, his mother-in-law, at dinner one Sunday afternoon that if he merely looked at Isabelle across the Place d'Armes, she would be carrying another child within weeks. Justine said that after they and the children left, her exhausted mother had said that maybe the only way to solve that baby problem was for one of them to poke the other's eyes out. Tonight François's parents entertained Raimond, Marceline, and Rosalie.

"Charlotte, that dress is as stunning as you are," said Isabelle with a no-nonsense voice that echoed her mother's. Even her questions sounded as if they were definitive statements. Isabelle's face glistened, and she fanned herself with such intensity that her hair, parted in the middle and loosely gathered into a bun, billowed around her face with each sweep.

"How very kind of you," Lottie replied and held her skirt down, hoping François did not mind being trapped by her tempest of red silk. "You look pretty as well."

"Thank—"

"The two of you remind me of deportment class," Justine interrupted, "and, quite frankly, you are boring us. Right, François?"

"Justine, François has been peering out the window since Charlotte joined us. I think he was bored before we started talking."

François, whose round face made him look younger than his wife, clasped his hands around his walking stick and said, "I suggest instead of talking about ourselves, we discuss the opera."

Isabelle snapped her fan closed, and for a moment, Lottie anticipated that she would swat her husband on the head with it. And she may have, had the carriage not bounced everyone inches off the seat when the back wheels pushed through one of the many deep holes in the street. In February, the ruts stayed mostly dry. But when the rains started every April, the road became sludge that seemed to suck in the wheels of every carriage that passed.

"It's a love story. Everyone dies at the end." Isabelle shrugged. "If we sat in the theatre and stared at an empty stage for hours, I would consider it an entertaining and peaceful night."

"First, you revealed the ending, and Lottie is not familiar with *Lucia di Lammermoor*." Justine held up her lace-gloved hand to count for her sister. "Second, you are so unromantic, I do not know…well, never mind. Third, I do not remember everyone dying at the end. François, would you please tell Lottie enough so that she can follow?"

Opera must have been François's forte, because he spoke with the relaxed authority of someone familiar with its stories. "Lucia secretly marries the man she loves, an enemy to their family. When she later refuses to marry a man her family deems she should, her brother suspects what has happened. He forges a note from the secret husband, saying that he intends to marry another. Just as she signs the other marriage contract, the secret husband returns and, not understanding what has happened, leaves in a rage. Lucia goes mad and kills her new husband on their wedding night. In her state, she believes she is still married to her first love, deliriously believes she's gone to heaven, and dies. Awaiting his duel with her brother, the first love witnesses her lifeless body carried past him and hears that she called for him with her last dying breaths. He stabs himself to join her in heaven."

Why, of all operas, would Justine invite me to this one? The parallels between hers and Lucia's life caused Lottie discomfort even as François explained the story. But as she waited to alight from the carriage, she admonished herself for calling her friend's motives into question.

Don't be foolish, Lottie. Justine is not seeing the play with your heart. Appreciate this opportunity to spend time with your friend.

Following François and Isabelle, she and Justine made their way to the Theatre d'Orleans. Two arched openings on each side were flanked by tall Roman columns, making the opera house as imposing as it was elegant. Lottie had started telling Justine the story of Agnes praying her gown closed when Justine grabbed her elbow and discreetly pointed to several young men and women gathered near the door. "Look, Gabriel's here."

And if hearing that paralyzed Lottie, what she heard next made her want to run. "Who is that woman he just walked into the theatre with?"

CHAPTER NINETEEN

THE INTERIOR OF THE THEATRE D'ORLEANS contributed to the experience of the opera. Its sparkling ceiling, elevated floor—which, when covered, served as a ballroom floor as well—and imposing candlelit sconces lured even the jaded. At each side were special partitioned boxes, with another two tiers and a gallery above. The elegant ladies, many carrying nosegays, and gentlemen strolled through, as eager to be seen as to see.

The pit, or the "untamed," as Grand-mère called the men and women who stood to watch the performance, erupted with laughter and shoving as the spectators jostled for position before the opera started. A box too close meant the rancid odor of tobacco and too few cleanings of body or clothes wafting indiscriminately, along with the raucous noise, to the more refined patrons.

Three tiers of boxes formed a horseshoe facing the stage. The social hierarchy of the city played itself out in the location of the boxes. Placées sat in the third tier so their protectors, in the first or second tiers with their families, could stop by to visit during intermissions. Of course, well-placed screens maintained discretion, though no one needed to explain the traffic of men up and down the steps.

The aroma of freshly made coffee greeted patrons as they walked through the lobby, where many would, between acts, find themselves seeking refreshments of coffee, champagne, lemonade, and assorted sweets like pralines and fudge. Once seated in the Dumas family box on the second level near the front, Lottie fixed her eyes on the stage so as not to risk seeing Gabriel. It was likely that he would have been on the same level, though she didn't dare look up for fear that he would be seated above them. She was able to track the young men who hovered around the back of the boxes of some of the most eligible young women in the city. Seeing them prowl, Lottie felt relieved that at least her grandparents weren't subjecting her to that embarrassment.

The intensity of the play, the nagging suspicion of Justine's having invited her on this particular night, and not only seeing Gabriel but seeing him escorting a strikingly attractive woman extracted more of an emotional toll than Lottie had reserves to endure. Just as she did with Grand-mère, she herded her feelings into a tomb so she could promptly bury them. Keeping them alive proved pointless. Like Isabelle's toddlers, they bobbled around causing chaos and demanding attention. When feelings resurrected themselves, she simply held another funeral. And that's what she needed to do now with everything about Gabriel. They were so fresh, even the slightest wind could unearth them.

As soon as intermission started, Lottie stood. Between the tension of the play and the lingering image of Gabriel, she needed to move. A bit of walking outside would be refreshing. "Excuse me. I will be back shortly," she said, starting to leave the box.

"Wait one moment. I'll go with you." Justine swiped her sister's fan from her lap, lifted the cluster of curls perched on her left shoulder, and fanned her neck.

"If you are going into the cool air, why are you delaying Lottie by doing that?" Isabelle pointed to her fan.

"Because"—Justine handed her the fan—"I'm not going outside." She stood and swished her skirt forward to pass between Isabelle and François. "And please don't speak to me like I am one of your children."

Isabelle's mouth opened, but François spoke. "Be sure to return when you hear the chimes."

Justine pinched Lottie's elbow. "Stop trotting toward the entrance. You are not a horse. Remember, you are supposed to be seen."

"I don't want to be *seen* by Gabriel, so I would rather be outside, since he will probably be in the lobby."

Lottie snaked her way through an abundance of silks and velvets, cloying perfumes, and ungentlemanly stares to stand for a few moments outside the theatre, grateful for the cool air and for Gabriel not being outside. How many times before had they been to the theatre, knowing each other would be there and never seeing one another?

Tonight, of all nights.

The four-note chime sounded, signaling the end of the intermission. Lottie joined the others returning to their seats. And, just as she did that day at the girls' home, Lottie sensed Gabriel's presence before she saw him.

She summoned a smile, demanded it to perform, and started her own play. "Gabriel, what a surprise to see you here."

Dressed in his usual impeccable style, his coat outlining the spread of his shoulders, he broke his solemn expression with polite upturned lips. "And you," he said, his words so tender that Lottie stared at the floor until they passed through her. "I would like you to meet Nathalie Chaigneau. Nathalie, this is Charlotte LeClerc."

Again Lottie smiled, though this time it was made more difficult by the introduction to the captivating Mademoiselle Chaigneau of the patrician nose, the playful brown eyes, and the effortless grace. She wore an evening gown of the latest style in jacquard woven silk, deeply pointed at her small waist and with a neckline that grazed the better part of decency. No one would mistake the provocative swing of the skirt. Reserved, yet flirtatious.

Lottie forced the words, "Pleased to meet you."

"A pleasure to be introduced to you," Nathalie oozed and then glanced at Gabriel, who cleared his throat.

The chime saved them from the space of awkward silence.

"We must return to our seats," said Gabriel. "Good to see you, Lottie."

She felt her heart constrict, hearing her name wrapped in his voice, and all she could do was nod. Nathalie responded in kind, and Lottie watched them walk away. She saw Gabriel's broad hand pressed against Nathalie's bare back, his body leaned toward hers. Lottie imagined his touch and felt her skin ripple in response.

She watched until the crowd swallowed them.

FINALLY, I CAN GO HOME.

Until the third act, Lottie related to Lucia, the young woman duped into marrying another man while thinking her marriage to the love of her life had ended. But after the experience with Nathalie and Gabriel, she found herself grieving with Edgardo, the husband who came home only to find the woman he loved exchanging vows with another man, not knowing that her brother had forged a letter. Edgardo believed the deception was her choice, but by the time the betrayal and pain expressed in rage diminished, it was too late. Lucia was dead.

The despair of watching someone lead the life you wanted. That, Lottie understood.

Bundled into the carriage once again, the group carried the quiet of not yet ridding themselves of the carnage of the drama. It was Isabelle who broke through and asked if the girls wanted to stop at Vincent's before going home. She listed the options—"Brioche, pâtes, éclairs, meringue...." And when the temptation of food didn't lure them, Isabelle resorted to, "It is the place to be seen after performances."

Justine's eyes sparked with excitement, so Lottie spoke before she could. "Vincent's sounds good, but if you don't mind, I'm actually tired and would rather not be out any later."

"It's barely one o'clock," Justine whined. "We wouldn't have to stay very long."

"There's no point in going if we can't relax and enjoy ourselves," Isabelle said.

Lottie hated disappointing people. Some, like Grand-mère, proved nearly impossible to please. But she'd found she would rather keep the peace than start a war, so she preferred sacrificing what she wanted to make that happen. The problem tonight was she had been dishonest about the reason she didn't want to be at Vincent's. She feared Gabriel and Nathalie would be there, and she dreaded feeling trapped, as she had been during the intermission. If they were there, she would not only be trapped, but she'd be more miserable than she was even at this moment. But she didn't want to admit that to Justine, much less Isabelle and François.

The carriage had not yet moved, and Lottie knew Vincent's was too close for her to procrastinate making a decision. Her mind dashed back and forth between the going and the not going until each pulled so tightly it seemed her limbs ached. The notion that she and Justine might have fewer opportunities once she married weighed the heavier over her wanting to save herself from an encounter with Gabriel. Surely, with three friends surrounding her, she could survive his being there. *Stop being so selfish. Why should you be the reason everyone else is not enjoying the evening?*

Lottie squeezed Justine's hand. "How silly of me to think I couldn't stay awake long enough for a café au lait and an éclair."

"You are such a wonderful friend." Justine reached over and hugged her. "Isabelle?"

"If Lottie is certain she is not too tired, then we shall go."

———❦———

THE MURKY AMBER OF EARLY MORNING had not yet given way to the sun's rays when Lottie arrived home—where she wanted to be and wished she had been hours earlier. Even her gown appeared as exhausted as she felt, losing its elegance somewhere between the constant crushing of being seated and the remnants of powdered sugar lingering on the skirt.

Though she chatted merrily in the carriage on the return ride to her house, Lottie's conversation with herself was anything but merry. Once again she'd subjected herself to the very situation she wanted to avoid, and she had no one to blame but herself. Of course, moments after they were seated at Vincent's, Gabriel, Nathalie, and two other couples entered. Other than a weak smile of recognition, there had been no communication between them. But simply knowing that he was mere tables away, enjoying himself with someone else, disturbed her.

Agnes was carrying fresh coffee into the dining room when Lottie entered. "'Bout time you dragged yourself home. I suspect you must be having a good time, out so late."

"I'll have a better time when I am out of this dress." Lottie swiped at the small spots left by the sprinkles of sugar. "And it is going to need some cleaning in places."

Agnes placed the coffee on the sideboard, wiped her hands on her apron, and lifted Lottie's chin with her hand. "Honey, you don't look like a girl coming in from having fun. Whatsa matter?"

"Everything." She yanked off her gloves then twisted them in her hands. She really wanted to throw something. Something that would shatter into pieces on the floor, just like her heart.

CHAPTER TWENTY

T HE PARTY WAS FIVE DAYS away, and the frenzy of activity at the LeClerc house should have made the shutters rattle. Agnes, who'd never met a crisis she could not manage, became sharp-tongued and impatient. Grand-père ducked and dodged to avoid anyone female, and it seemed he elicited Abram's help in leaving early and arriving home late. Grand-mère remained exactly the same, as if her imperial attitude awaited this time and place.

Lottie devised as many excuses as possible to detach herself from the inevitable misery that awaited her on Saturday night. She slept, she read, she even pretended to work on her sampler. She learned from Penelope in *The Odyssey,* who wove by day and unwove by night to forestall her suitors' intentions to replace her husband, that she could avoid finishing her sampler. Except that, unlike the clever Penelope, she could prevent nothing.

After two days of watching her grandmother move furniture—that is, watching Grand-mère watching Abram move furniture—Lottie decided she needed a change of scenery. "I'm going to visit Justine," she announced to whoever might be listening, and left.

The two girls had not spent time together since the night of the opera. Before the party plans, being surrounded by the chaos of the Dumases' house provided a reprieve from the deafening silence of her own. Today, it would be a relief to be in someone else's confusion and know she didn't have to participate.

The shutters weren't opened, so Lottie knocked on the door. She picked up a wooden doll and a child's shoe on the top step and handed them to Madame Dumas when the woman opened the door.

"Lottie," she whispered, "the baby is sleeping, but please come in."

The Dumas family always seemed to have a sleeping baby, so much so that they were the only family Lottie knew that actually kept a tester baby bed in their study.

"Isabelle's oldest two aren't feeling well. No one else is home," she told Lottie as they tiptoed past Rosalie. The child slept on her stomach, noisily sucking her thumb, with her knees pushed up to her chest and petticoats and dress at full tilt. Her blond hair covered her head like a bonnet of curls.

"Justine should be home soon. She's…" Madame Dumas looked toward the ceiling and tapped her cheek as if that would expel the answer. After several taps, she shook her head in defeat, pulled out a dining room chair, and sat. "She's at a class, somewhere with someone. Who isn't you, apparently." She motioned for Lottie to sit, plucked a pair of boy's breeches out of a basket of jumbled clothes on the table, and pulled out the threaded needle in the waistband.

"No, I haven't been to many classes lately. I suppose with the party, Grand-mère's been too occupied to keep up with my schedule." Lottie didn't so much mind the break, figuring the classes would resume after the party.

Justine's mother attacked the rip in the pants. "I would think that your grandmother has a number of details to attend to," she said, snipping the thread loose and grabbing what appeared to be a petticoat from her basket. "You must be quite excited about Saturday night, yes?" There was the genetic tie she had with Isabelle, that way of making a question seem like an answer.

Lottie picked at imaginary lint on her new silk taffeta day dress, a dizzying tartan, and responded, "Of course." When she looked up, she found Madame Dumas staring at her with her head tilted and her mouth skewed to one side.

"Now, dear, that did not sound like an enthusiastic answer for a young lady on the verge of her coming-out party," she said. "When Isabelle had her debut—"

Then Justine shut the front door and called out, "I'm home!" and Rosalie responded with a howl.

"IF YOU HAD ARRIVED EVEN two minutes later, I would have been facing the Dumas interrogation," Lottie said.

"You don't need to spare my feelings by attempting to be funny. You most certainly would have been," said

Justine.

The two sat on the balcony off Justine's room, drinking lemonade and nibbling on brioche that Maisy, the cook, had brought them.

"I forgot how entertaining it could be to sit here," mused Lottie as she gazed over the black wrought-iron railing down to St. Louis Street. Wagons groaning with produce and swaying carriages competed for passage on the narrow street...the occasional vendor singing, "Oyster man, oyster man, git your fresh oysters"...water being sold from barrels in the street for those without cisterns.... "Doesn't the noise keep you awake at night?"

"No. In fact, I find it rather comforting. Sometimes quiet can be louder than noise."

Lottie pulled her capelet tighter, though she doubted it would help the chill she felt inside. "Maybe quiet simply means having nothing to say."

"Perhaps that would be true for someone else. Someone not sitting on my balcony pretending that her life is without complaint." Justine tore off a piece of the brioche and chewed.

It made Lottie laugh inside to think that only Justine would use eating as a way to test whether Lottie would answer. "It seems pointless to discuss a situation over which I have no control. You already know my feelings about this. I have never tried to hide those from you."

"Well, I suppose this is a beginning. But when are you going to share Gabriel's involvement in this?"

Lottie allowed the laugh she harbored to reveal itself.

"Involvement? Gabriel's involvement? Whatever do you mean?"

"Don't be foolish. Your faces glow like the gaslamps on the street at night when you see one another." Justine shook her head. "Though I do not understand why you allowed it to happen."

I allowed it to happen? Maybe she's right. But can you help who you fall in love with?

"Again, what is the point of talking? This"—Lottie swept her arm toward the street—"none of this will ever change."

"Exactly. It won't change. Neither the city nor the state will dismiss the law to accommodate you. So that means it's up to you. You are the one who needs to change."

"And how am I supposed to accomplish that? I can't simply toss my feelings into the Mississippi River." How much easier for Justine to have an opinion, having no one in her life she cared about as deeply as Lottie did for Gabriel.

"No, but you can drown them when you are faced with the impossibility…when the evidence is right there."

The image of Gabriel's hand on Nathalie's back surfaced. "Simply because your eyes see something, that does not mean your heart does," said Lottie, aware that her voice conveyed irritation. "It gives me cause to wonder, Justine, if you invited me to the opera knowing Gabriel would be there with Nathalie."

Justine finished her lemonade. "No, but if I thought it would result in your abandoning this impossible notion of yours, I would have."

THE DAYS GAVE THEMSELVES OVER to a soggy gray and the kind of stinging cold that kept children from complaining about wearing mittens, because they used them to warm their pink, chapped noses or revive their pale cheeks. Then there were the children who would have happily joined the grousing chorus had they gloves to complain about. Gabriel passed a number of mothers and their children, mostly the darker ones, who were probably headed to or from the French Market. While most house slaves wore better clothes than their plantation counterparts, especially since some owners felt their slaves' mode of dress reflected their own status, the plantation children's garb, if they had clothes at all, consisted of worn-thin homemade shirts, entirely too big or too small, and brogans.

Several times he wanted to shrug off his own coat and wrap it around the shoulders of a child whose arms weren't much thicker than twigs. But his two coats would have been quickly gone, and thirty times that many would have been insufficient. Alcee was right. Collecting gloves left at the café or from people who donated old ones was not going to be enough if they were going to clothe the children at the orphanages and the families in their reading classes. Of course, Alcee, for her own protection, knew nothing of those classes. But for the orphans, she volunteered to ask her classmates for old clothes. Gabriel told her he didn't want her to be perceived as a beggar. Alcee had looked up at him from her book and said, "If I am helping children, I do not care if others think I am begging. Would it be better for them to be cold?"

Gabriel entered the café and tugged off his own gloves, putting them in the pocket of his coat. He shook his head and thought how his younger sister's wisdom shamed his own at times.

"There you are."

Joseph's voice surprised Gabriel, who had arrived early and expected he would be there before the builder.

"Joseph." Gabriel nodded. "How did you—?"

Joseph held up a key, which he returned to his vest pocket. "Rosette told me to just use this to come in through the kitchen area. In case you weren't here yet."

Gabriel didn't hear an apologetic tone, and Joseph didn't offer the key. So, not only did his mother trust this man, but Joseph was confident she did so. "I see."

"Good. Then let's get started." He waved the rolled-up papers in his hand like a baton and walked in the direction of the kitchen. Gabriel followed him and listened while he pointed out areas where they could redesign the serving and cooking areas to be more efficient. Then Joseph walked around the seating area, showing Gabriel places he thought could be converted into counter spaces and where the seating area could be lengthened with awnings. He unrolled the papers on one of the tables. "Have a seat. I'd like to show you the plans I've designed."

On a long sheet of foolscap, Joseph had sketched the original area then overlaid another sheet showing the changes he suggested. "Everything is drawn to scale, so the proportions would be the same. Of course, we would do the changes in phases so as to disrupt the business as little as possible."

The designs evidenced Joseph's attention to detail as well as his precise measurings and drawings. Gabriel had not considered building structures, such as homes or smaller buildings, to involve much more than ordering lumber and construction materials. Studying the plans before him, his interest was in more than the benefit to the café or even his house. It intrigued him to envision these spaces and remodel and repurpose them—using skills not so unlike those he would use in engineering. "How did you come to learn this?"

Joseph leaned back on the stool and seemed puzzled. "I thought you had seen me here at the café watching how you and your mother worked, and—"

"No, that isn't what I meant. I know you have spent time here. How did you learn about designing?" Gabriel pointed to the plans on the table between them.

"Oh," Joseph said, the confusion on his face dissipating. "Construction." He rolled up the plans. "How much time do you have?"

"Until the first customer arrives and all night," Gabriel answered, his expression grim.

It was Saturday. The night of Lottie's birthday and coming-out party.

CHAPTER TWENTY-ONE

AGNES CARRIED MADAME OLYMPE'S CREATION into Lottie's room and transferred it to her bed as if the tulle was of thin sheets of glass instead of fabric.

"The dress weigh more than you. Guess they don't plan on you moving much." Agnes eyed the dress the way she eyed Henri when she'd find him lounging on one of the upholstered chairs in Lottie's bedroom.

"Maybe Grand-mère had Madame sew weights into the skirt. She knows how awfully excited I am about this soirée, and she feared I would float way." Lottie leaned against one of the bedposts, since she had already been too corseted to attempt sitting. She placed her hands around the waist of the black satin corset, and her fingertips almost met. "Agnes, this is unbearable, and the party is over an hour away."

"You wearing six petticoats, Miz Lottie, 'fore we even get you in that dress. Dey so stiff, your grandmother said your waist hafta be at seventeen inches."

"I should have dressed downstairs in the exact spot we will greet guests. Then I wouldn't need to move." Except for when she possibly fainted from lack of food or breath.

"Les' just get it over with," said Agnes, carrying the petticoats to Lottie.

Somehow they avoided disturbing the complicated hairdressing Lottie had sat still for that morning while the stylist twisted her hair into a pattern of braids and curls before finishing it off with a pair of diamond combs. While Agnes fastened the dozens of hooks and eyes from halfway between Lottie's shoulder blades to the end of her hips, Lottie held on to the bedpost, already feeling the weight of the gown.

The Lottie encased in this dress bore no resemblance to the sultry young woman in cranberry-red who'd attended the opera. Her face and neck had been lightened and softened with pure pearl powder, and her lips shimmered as if covered with the juice of strawberries.

Her grandmother and Madame Olympe had achieved their objective. Lottie could have stepped out of a castle, a princess down to her satin slippers. But though she may have looked like a princess, she felt a tower surrounding her everywhere she went.

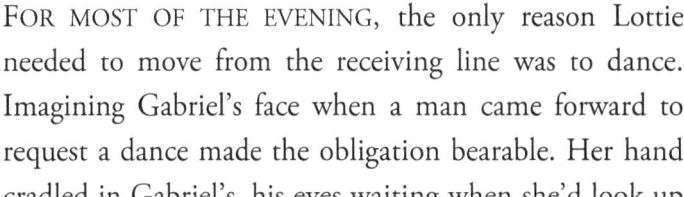

For most of the evening, the only reason Lottie needed to move from the receiving line was to dance. Imagining Gabriel's face when a man came forward to request a dance made the obligation bearable. Her hand cradled in Gabriel's, his eyes waiting when she'd look up at his face. What would it feel like to have his body close to hers as he led her across the floor?

She remembered the toe-smasher, the tight-hand-grabber, and the breath-offender. Rolling her eyes at Justine while a gentleman navigated her around the room would have disgraced generations of LeClercs, so Lottie devised an alternative. When dancing, she was a model of deportment, eyes downcast, sufficiently demur. When the dance ended, she and Justine would make eye contact and, depending on the partner, one or both would pinch the bridge of her nose. In a break between dances, she and Justine met over a tray of ginger cakes. Lottie could do no more than nibble a bite for fear her corset would pop.

"We'll have to devise another, more creative system of messaging when it's time for my party," said Justine as she finished her cake in a few bites.

Lottie shrugged. "By that time I will not need to concern myself with the idiosyncrasies of dance partners. I will already be married to the man my grandparents have selected for me."

Her first dance had been with a man, Lottie whispered to Justine, whose face was *une figure de pomme cuite* when he pretended to want to smile. So, when the young man whose face resembled a baked apple asked for a second dance, Lottie grew suspicious. The third request proved her right. Paul Bastion's detached, bored demeanor before, during, and after every dance actually comforted Lottie. His obvious and yet, unbeknownst to him, equal disinterest in the object of their parents' pursuit meant she would be saved from an emotional relationship. Grand-mère had, unwittingly, prepared her for marriage after all. Lottie knew how to conduct herself in that kind of relationship.

The day after the event, Lottie remembered jigsaw pieces of the party but couldn't put the entire puzzle together. The first piece was of her grandparents' countenances as they watched her, with Agnes's help, descend the stairs. Years faded from their faces, pushed away by whatever joy filled them as she moved toward them.

"I actually saw your grandmother smile more than once," Justine told her as the two perched on Lottie's bed.

"At me or in general?" Lottie's raised eyebrows as she sipped her café au lait signaled her disbelief. Justine's hesitation provided her answer. "If you had said at me, I would have thought you lied. Though I do appreciate your considering it to protect my feelings."

Justine gathered her apricot gown as she readied to leave. "I am sure we will remember even more tomorrow."

"Yes, we can talk about what food was served, since no morsel could make its way through the grip of my corset." Lottie's waist and hips still felt bruised from being restricted by fourteen long whalebones for hours.

She held the offender in front of her with both hands. "If my fate has already been decided, then I can rid myself of you." Maybe this article of clothing would make an appropriate donation to a prison.

Her back to the doorway of her room, Lottie heard her grandmother before she saw her.

"Are you leaving so soon, my dear?" Were it not for the molasses voice, Lottie might have been startled, thinking her grandmother could be addressing her.

"My parents haven't seen me since yesterday, and they should be home from church by now," Justine said. "And now that the party is over, Lottie and I will have more time together."

Grand-mère glanced at Lottie then back at Justine. "Well, perhaps you won't confine your visits to your classes."

This time it was the two girls who exchanged looks.

"What does that mean?" Whenever her grandmother dodged an answer, Lottie was suspicious.

"Charlotte, we can discuss this later, since it seems another friend awaits in the courtyard."

Justine squeezed the bridge of her nose, and Lottie instantly developed a coughing spasm that required holding her hands across her mouth.

"Then I really do need to leave, since my friend is already in demand. Those potential beaus of yours move *tout de suite*, Charlotte."

"Actually," said Grand-mère, entering the room so Justine could pass through the door, "it is not any of the gentlemen from last evening."

Lottie exhaled.

"In fact, I am not sure what reason Gabriel Girod has for being here."

Lottie heard Justine's footsteps as she headed down the stairs and out the door.

Grand-mère waited for an answer, while Lottie mentally followed Justine.

———

MADAME LECLERC WAS NOT THE WOMAN Gabriel expected to see as he walked through the courtyard.

Her expression reflected that she, too, was as surprised to see him. She closed the book she was reading then set it on the seat of the rocker after she rose to greet him.

"Gabriel, how can I help you?"

"Good afternoon, Madame LeClerc." He removed his hat and nodded dutifully, his mind searching for an appropriate and honest response without revealing too much. "I am visiting the girls' home this afternoon, and I stopped by to see Mademoiselle Charlotte."

She peered at him with curiosity. "So, would she be expecting you?"

He knew an answer in either direction forebode problems, but to appear intimidated would invite more questioning. "Perhaps."

She said, "I see," in a way that suggested she would rather not. "Please wait here." Madame LeClerc turned and left, not inviting him into her home.

Gabriel paced, alone, and waited for either Lottie or her grandmother to deliver a verdict. Abram and Agnes had Sunday off, so he could not depend on either of them for information.

His emotions wound through him like rope cords. For weeks, he had warned Lottie of the day coming when she couldn't depend on the predictability of her grandparents' absence on Sunday afternoons. Worse than their anger, Gabriel feared the consequences for Lottie. She couldn't be locked in her room any longer, but the few freedoms she did have would likely be eliminated. As he walked back and forth along the cobblestone paths, voices from Lottie's room drifted below, too indistinct for him to determine what they were saying. If they talked much longer, Gabriel would have to leave without her. The anxiety of their being late, and possibly endangering or disappointing the men and women waiting on them, took its toll on the hat brim he clenched and unclenched.

And always there was the torturous happiness of being with Lottie every Sunday. Even though they had reconciled themselves to the paths of their lives, Gabriel looked forward to the times their roads had to cross. How much longer they would be able to continue these visits depended on factors neither he nor Lottie could control. But the time they did spend together, he could hardly concentrate on teaching. He had to pull his eyes away from following the tilt of Lottie's head and the curve of her lips as she smiled at someone writing his or her own name for the first time. Gabriel could hardly smell lemons or almonds without thinking of her rushing through the gate to meet him, and he would fight to keep his breath steady when they walked together. It pained him to think that another man would feel the softness of her cheek against his hand. Yet he would endure whatever proved difficult to spend time with her.

He heard footsteps down the stairs, but it was Justine, not Lottie, who turned and walked through the hall toward him.

"What are you doing here? Lottie's grandmother looked quite perturbed," Justine said, her voice just above a whisper.

"Yes, I expect she would be."

"Has Lottie not stopped that orphan thing, whatever it is the two of you do? I thought she, well, with the party and…I just imagined she wouldn't continue."

She left unsaid, "being seen with you," but Gabriel understood, because he imagined the same. Justine didn't wait for an answer. "I need to be going. I hope…" She shook her head. "I don't know what I hope."

Minutes after Justine closed the front door behind her, Gabriel heard footsteps too light and too hurried to be Grand-mère's. Nervous excitement ripped through him as he waited for Lottie to turn the corner of the stairs.

Fastening her cape as she walked and, surprisingly, already wearing her bonnet, Lottie's eager smile was more than he had hoped for.

"Thank you for waiting. I didn't know if I would have to chase after you in the carriage," she said as she gathered the folds of her dress and stepped down to the courtyard path.

"Before we get too far, am I to assume you have been granted permission for this venture?" His weak attempt at Grand-mère's diction brought the intended grin to Lottie's face.

"Not at first. But I suggested that reaching the age of marriage should be sufficient for performing acts of kindness. And why would any family of a potential suitor think it untoward for me to be a charitable young woman?"

"That still does not explain why you are able to go with me." An answer Gabriel was certain he did not want but needed to know.

She looked down before responding. "I couldn't tell her the truth, of course, of why we go there. It's my fault, really, because I know you're going with me to protect me."

"Are you trying to protect *me* now?"

"I suppose. I don't like what I told her. But if it made going possible..." She looked at Gabriel. "I told her Abram and Agnes couldn't help, being as it is Sunday. And if I asked you to help with provisions, wouldn't that be the next best thing?"

CHAPTER TWENTY – TWO

"I'M CONCERNED ABOUT MOVING FORWARD. We asked the two of you to take over doing something dangerous." Sister Mary Catherine clutched her Bible as she spoke to Lottie and Gabriel after they finished the lessons. "How willing are you to continue?"

"I volunteered before you asked me," said Lottie. "And Gabriel—"

"Can speak for himself," he said. "You know I initially hesitated to participate in this, until I saw that Charlotte was not to be dissuaded. Sometimes she needs to be protected from herself." When he turned to look at her, Lottie understood how someone could melt during the winds of winter. "I understand your concerns, Sister, but teaching these men and women is a risk for all of us and for them. We're willing to continue."

Lottie nodded. "I couldn't tell the people who brave coming here, learning how to write their own names for the first time, that I wasn't coming back."

"Wait." Gabriel inched forward, his knees almost hitting Sister's desk. "Is this about Jacob and Thomas not being here this afternoon? Did something happen to them? Nobody said anything. But you know they do not withhold information in an effort to protect us." He shook his head in disbelief.

Please, God, let them be safe. Lottie pictured Jacob holding a quill for the first time, his fingers extended from his palms like pruned tree branches. He wrote with his left hand; the fingers on his right hand looked like they'd melted and hardened again without any attention to where they belonged. After Jacob told her that a wagon had run over his hand when he was younger, Lottie didn't ask. She had learned not to ask questions if she wasn't prepared for the answers.

His son Tom, thirteen, was eager and precocious. So much so that Lottie brought her copy of *Hamlet* for him. His excitement dissipated when Jacob forbade him to carry a book for fear of it being discovered. His disappointment was so great, it almost joined them in the room. Before they left, Lottie tore five pages from the book and handed them to him. "You can read it in installments," she'd told him.

Seeing Tom's face in her mind while he held those pages, Lottie almost couldn't breathe. "The play," she whispered. "Someone found the pages?" One of those questions...but she had to know the answer to this one. She wished she had her fan, but the only heat in the room was beneath her skin.

"I will answer that shortly." Sister Mary Catherine moved from her writing desk and closed the doors between their room and the front parlor. Lottie saw the pale, fearful eyes she felt in herself in the Sister's face. The nun slid her chair from behind her desk closer to where they sat. "We needed to know if you wanted to continue for two reasons. First, the other Sisters and I talked, prayed, and decided to move the lessons each week from our home to the girls' home. We've known for years that Madame Soniat, the benefactress, is sympathetic to our cause. She bought slaves in the past just so she could request a certificate of manumission to set them free. The court assessed the value of the slaves, she paid it, and they were issued their freedom."

"She bought the same slaves twice?" Gabriel asked the question Lottie was thinking.

"Sadly, yes, which is the reason she has not been able to free more than five slaves. When we explained what we were doing and why we needed her help, she readily agreed. So, we will meet here one more Sunday to explain to the others, and then you will be at the girls' home."

"Tom and Jacob—how is this related to their not being here today?" Lottie asked.

Sister shifted in the chair and blotted her face where the starched piece of fabric starting at her forehead edged it. "Have you heard about the Underground Railroad?"

"Underground? No. I'm certain I haven't," said Lottie. "Have you?" she asked Gabriel.

"I've heard of it, but it's difficult to know what is rumor. And since some free people of color own slaves themselves, we are not always trusted either."

"I know about it because I moved here from Boston five years ago," began Sister Mary Catherine. "The Underground Railroad is made up of secret routes and safe houses that slaves can use to escape to freedom. Most people this far south haven't heard of it, and very few slaves have even tried it. The distance to the North is so far, it makes the journey almost impossible without risk of getting captured."

"But Jacob and Tom are doing this?" Lottie didn't know which answer she wanted to hear.

"Jacob heard that his owner might sell Tom because he could get a good price for him at his age and build." The Sister fingered the large wooden rosary that served as a belt around her ample waist. "After being separated from Tom's mother and their two daughters a few years ago, he was desperate to do something to keep his son. I found out about a conductor, a person who helps them escape. He moved here years ago—"

"Sister, are you saying that this person is moving them all the way north?" Gabriel sounded shocked.

"No, no." She wiped her eyes, stood, and said, "They've been planning this for weeks. He brought them to a synagogue in the city where they can hide for now. From there they can go to Mexico, or he might try to get forged freedom papers for them."

"When will we know?" Half of Lottie danced with glee. The other half bit her nails. "Is this conductor person coming back to tell you what happened?"

Sister folded her arms so that they disappeared into

the full black crêpe sleeves of her habit. "I don't know. We may never know."

———∽∽∽———

WINTER IN NEW ORLEANS WAS a disagreeable child who, whenever he had one thing, wanted the other, and whose temper tantrums were marked by rivers of tears. Some days were bright and brisk, the wind like a whip that snapped flags and loose frock coats to attention. On other days the submissive sun forced the wearing of wools and muslins and velvets.

The discussion with Sister having delayed them, Lottie and Gabriel found themselves walking home on the brink of an evening plump with moisture, pushing its way through capes and skin and settling in bones. The indecisive sort of evening, when wearing a cape or not wearing one was equally uncomfortable. When it was too late for children and babies to play, and yet too early for adults contemplating an opera.

Gabriel's feet took measured steps on the banquette, but his head was somewhere between there and Mexico. He understood Jacob's anguish in contemplating someone he loved being wrenched away, and he could only imagine how much more wretched it was for that person to be his son. Casting a sideward glance at Lottie, he knew her mind to be as preoccupied as his. For one, she used her parasol at a time when the wind, not the already-sleeping sun, risked harm. And she made no attempt at conversation, about this afternoon or the weekend past. A weekend about which he wanted to know everything and nothing.

"It's the not knowing what's happened to them. That's the most difficult part, don't you think?"

So taken by the gray parrot in the upper window of the cottage they passed that screeched expressions in English Gabriel would be hesitant to say in any language, he barely heard Lottie's question.

"Do you mean not knowing where they are?"

She glanced up at her parasol as if seeing it for the first time, closed it, and pretended to stab him with it. "Were you listening to me?"

"Almost."

"If they're safe and free, it doesn't matter to me where they are. But we might never know the outcome and always be thinking 'What if?'" Lottie poked the tip of her parasol against the cobblestones. "I don't like hearing myself say this, but even when the worst happens, at least you don't have to wonder."

Gabriel stopped, and she followed suit. He didn't know what Lottie's response would be to what he was going to say. One thing he knew, though, and it had come to him this afternoon. Jacob and his son risked everything for their freedom—for their freedom to be together. Whatever the outcome, they would never regret not having tried.

He slowly lifted her chin until he saw her face. Instead of being startled by his touch, it was as if she yielded herself to it, not moving his hand even as they looked at each other. "Lottie, not knowing the outcome means there's always hope. Always."

She closed her eyes and nodded. But when she looked at him again, it was sadness he saw there, and it tugged at the corners of her lips.

Gabriel hesitated. Sadness? He hadn't expected sadness. But it didn't change what he needed to say. "I love—"

At the sound of the creaking and clattering of carriage wheels and horses' hooves, they both flinched. Lottie, instead of walking with him, stared at the ground and made a few backward and forward steps, all the while acting as if she had dropped something.

"What are you doing?"

But she didn't answer him, and he found himself echoing her movements, without any idea of what he was doing.

When the carriage passed them and was a distance off, Lottie straightened, and that's when Gabriel understood. If the curtains were open, the occupants would have seen only a girl wearing a bonnet and holding a parasol.

He reached out his hand, but she ignored him.

"It's late. I don't want my grandparents to worry. I need to be home. We cannot do this, Gabriel, remember?"

"Of course," he said, as if the past few minutes had not happened.

They walked to Lottie's house, jostling the awkward

silence between them.

Hope, Gabriel reminded himself. *You said it. Can you live it?*

CHAPTER TWENTY - THREE

"**Y**OU WILL BE GOING AGAIN next week?"
Lottie recognized Gabriel's café voice, the one he used when he asked customers what they wanted to order. She knew she was responsible for the shift in him, but she was glad. No, relieved. They could not allow themselves to plunge into that river of emotions. Too deep. Currents. Waves. Creatures. She wouldn't let it happen.

"Certainly." She closed the gate after she walked through. She needed him to leave soon, because she didn't know how much longer she could remain on shore when the river appeared so tempting. "Thank you."

He nodded, and they both turned home. In different directions.

Agnes was already lighting candles when Lottie found her in the dining room.

"I'd say look what the cat dragged in, but he at least show up during daylight." Agnes shaved wax from around the wick of one of the tapers in the silver candelabra on the sideboard.

"Are my grandparents home?" Lottie peeked under the napkin draped over the plate set alone on the table. Slices of chicken, wedges of tomatoes, and green beans. She pulled out one of the green beans and ate it before Agnes could shoo her away.

"No need to whisper. They went to the opera." Agnes stood the candelabra on the table near the place setting. "Jus' sit down and eat. Don't know why you stealing food off your own plate."

Until she started eating, Lottie hadn't realized how hungry she was. Between mouthfuls, she asked Agnes what had happened after she left.

"All I know is when me and Abram get back, you gone and your grandmother playing some kind of somethin' on that piano. She coulda woke the dead. But she jus' woke your grandfather, and he none too happy about that." She moved the platter of tomatoes and green beans within Lottie's reach on the table and went back to the sideboard.

"Do we have any bread? Lemonade?"

Agnes turned around, and the items Lottie had asked for were already in her hands. "Many years as I been feeding you, I knows what you gonna ask for."

Lottie pulled out a chair. "Please don't stand over there while I eat. Come sit down."

Agnes looked around as she slid into the chair. "Now you know I not suppost to be doing this."

"It's just the two of us. Besides, why can't I have dinner with someone who's known me almost my entire life?" She tore a piece of bread off the half loaf Agnes had set down. "Who made up these ridiculous rules?" She thought of Jacob and Tom, and heart pangs replaced her hunger pains.

"Miss Lottie, don't be saying them kind of things. White people can get in trouble for sounding like one them abullishonists."

She started to ask Agnes where she'd learned that word but then decided—like earlier today—there were some things she just didn't want answers to. "My grandparents haven't been to the opera in weeks. I'm glad they decided to attend, but it's still surprising."

"Your grandfather didn't want to go, but your grand-mère said they needed to go because somebody in this family had to be seen in the society, 'specially sence you out gallivanting with Gabriel. And just the day after your party. She worried what people think. Your grandfather weren't too happy."

"About my being with Gabriel or going to the opera?" Lottie left the uneaten bread on her plate and covered it with her napkin. As she did, she noticed the embroidered *LC* in the corner. The shaky, uneven first stitchings of a much younger Lottie. The one who wanted to surprise Grand-mère by embroidering her new linen napkins with the initials of their last name. She had sewn only two, one for each of her grandparents, and tiptoed into the dining room to place one on each of their plates. She waited in her bedroom where she ate, sometimes with Agnes, with the squirming anticipation of a child eager to see her grandmother's face when she thanked her for the surprise.

Lottie now traced the bumpy, zigzagged ebony stitches and heard in her memory the echo of Grand-mère's steps as they neared her room. Agnes had left for water, so Lottie sat alone at her small table. When she walked through the door, Grand-mère filled the room with her presence.

"Charlotte, did you sew these?" She held the napkins out to Lottie.

Excited that her grandmother came to thank her, Lottie nodded energetically. "Yes, Grand-mère. I did."

"Who gave you permission to do such a thing?"

Even now, Lottie remembered that imperious voice. The one that quieted her own. She had shrugged her shoulders, stared at the shamrocks that edged her plate, and twisted the folds of her gingham dress with her hands.

"Look at me when I speak to you."

She had raised her eyes and wished Agnes would hurry.

"Ne–ver, ne–ver," Grand-mère said, "presume to take anything that does not belong to you. These damask napkins are quite expensive. Now the set is useless unless I replace these."

Agnes then stood at the doorway, holding a pitcher of water, and looked from Lottie to her grandmother and back again. "Excuse me, Miz LeClerc," said Agnes as she stepped behind her into the room.

Lottie remembered Grand-mère's parting words of, "Do you understand?" and her handing the napkins to Agnes. "Perhaps you can find a use for these."

Agnes had saved her napkins all these years. How would she have known, today of all days, that this gesture would mean so much?

Lottie took the napkin from her plate and blotted her wet cheeks—tears cried for the little girl who failed to please who was important to her then, and for the young woman who failed to please the person most important to her now.

February 1841

Dear Mama and Papa,

Finally, I no longer live with the dread of the party. It is over. I know I resolved not to act selfishly or unkindly, and I promise I behaved properly.

The night of the party, Justine slept here, so that's why I didn't write. But even when I'm not writing on paper, I'm composing a letter in my head to you. I hope not to forget all that I wanted to share.

A week before the date, Grand-mère sent the notes for the party with Abram's brother, Elijah. The invitations were written on gilt-bordered papers, inserted in the same bordered envelopes, and closed with a small wax seal. He dressed quite nicely and completed the deliveries in two days' time.

I confess, Grand-mère fluttered around so that I did my best not to be in her way. She gathered mirrors and pins, combs, brushes, and hairpins for the ladies' dressing room, which was the spare bedroom upstairs. Then Justine's mother reminded her to include sewing supplies, perfume, and smelling salts. Grand-père suggested she might be in need of the salts herself before the night began. I don't believe she appreciates his humor as I do. Agnes coughs often when he jokes so as not to incite Grand-mère.

Agnes, Abram, Elijah, and Elijah's son Samuel spent the better part of the day carrying food from the kitchen into the house. Agnes created a magnificent centerpiece of pineapples, grapes, and trailing vines with soft, lavender-blue flowers. Gumbo, platters of fish, fruit dishes with pears and cherries and plums. Carafes of water and wine. Molded water ices for desserts—that's all I can remember. I don't think I ate more than a grape that night, for fear of ruining my white gown or being ill.

I did not expect to feel like a live statue for suitors' considerations. Much worse, though, I felt more like bait—the small fish Abram uses to catch the larger ones. Thrown into a river of hungry fish. Maybe sharks. Justine says I am too intractable. I think she learned that word at the deportment class she attended without me and she thought that word was more sophisticated than stubborn.

Of all the men who asked to dance with me that night, it seems Paul Bastion might be the man Grand-père and Grand-mère have decided upon. He was not as tall or as conversational as any of the other men. But having read The Ladies' Guide to True Politeness and Perfect Manners *by Miss Eliza Leslie (if he could, our deportment teacher would make Justine and I add it to our gumbo and consume it), I was relieved not to converse and risk my head being a "lumber-room."*

Later, I wondered if perhaps his demeanor might suggest he feels the same as I about this arrangement. If I knew that he did, I might— might—find a small bit of comfort in that.

I have heard that his family built an impressive home closer, actually, to the American section. They are quite wealthy, Justine tells me. I am not sure what constitutes "quite wealthy" as opposed to "wealthy," but by the way she emphasizes "quite," it must be significant.

There is so much more I want to write, but the events of today have exhausted me. I arrived home late this afternoon; maybe it was closer to early evening. Grand-mère and Grand-père are at the opera, and Agnes knows that when my candles burn this late, I must be writing my letters.

Until the next letter.

All my love,
Your Genevieve Charlotte

"MIZ LOTTIE, WAKE UP. YOU needs to wake up fast." Agnes alternately patted her face and shook her arm. "Your time be running out. Your grandmother on her way."

Lottie's eyes popped open at "grandmother." Between yawns, she asked Agnes where her grandmother was on her way to and why Agnes whispered instead of using her usual loud voice.

"You got two man problems, and I knows your grandmother 'bout to march up here and talk about one of them."

Gabriel? What could her grandmother have heard so soon? "Agnes, who are you talking about and why do you keep looking under my bed?"

"One of them problems ran in this house and is in yo room someplace." She peered under the bed again. "That cat gonna be the death of me yet."

Lottie put on the green robe Agnes must have placed on her bed and joined Agnes in the search for Henri. She heard pitiful mewing sounds coming from the shutters. She tried to draw the curtains open, but when the right side wouldn't move, she bent down and pushed the lumpy bulge.

"How did you get in there?" She reached underneath the yards of fabric puddling on the floor, and whatever part of Henri's body she latched onto, he did not appreciate it. With one angry yowl, he attempted to bolt, except that his back claws caught in the lining. "Agnes, hold the curtains." Lottie grabbed Henri while Agnes hurried over and extricated his claws from the fabric. Before Lottie could walk to the balcony with him, he bolted out the one open French door and followed his usual escape route off the balcony, the roof overhang, the lemon tree, and out the back.

"Are all men this much trouble?" Lottie mused as she examined the four fresh claw tracks Henri had left on the inside of her forearm. They had already started to welt, a thread of blood running down the middle of each.

Agnes dipped a hand towel in the water in Lottie's bowl and dabbed her arm. "Afraid you gonna find out soon, cuz your grandmother coming up here to tell you that man is coming for a visit."

Suddenly the burning sensation Lottie felt as the water met the open wound was far less painful than the one in her stomach.

———— ∽∽ ————

MISS LESLIE'S BEHAVIOR BOOK DID NOT address how a lady was supposed to hide the claw marks left by a cat in flight while in the presence of her possible future intended and grandparents.

Lottie wore a long-sleeved floral wool dress so the red welts branding her forearm could not be seen, but the fabric's fibers irritated them even more. She smiled what she hoped was demurely then practiced her downcast eyes and waited for some relief from this enforced torture. The few times she did glance at Paul Bastion, being careful not to lapse into impropriety, he appeared to be as uncomfortable as she felt. His expression, though, seemed to lend itself to furrows on his forehead and even along the top of his cheeks. He looked as if he might have been born squinting at the doctor who delivered him. He had arrived for what Grand-mère had said would be a brief visit before dinner. With barely enough time to ready herself for this visit, Lottie had neglected eating breakfast. Her empty stomach had not read Miss Leslie's guidebook. She hoped it would not announce itself during Monsieur Bastion's visit.

They sat in the parlor as if marking the ends of a square, the two women sitting diagonally across, as did the men. After their initial introductions, conversations floated and popped like bubbles in the silence. Lottie mentally reviewed the pitfalls to avoid as related during her deportment lessons: monomania, perpetual contradictions, arguing about politics or religion or finances, tattling, reminding others they were once poor or that you were not, asking gentlemen about their professions, and criticizing others. Whatever did a woman do without another woman friend, with whom she could ignore all these rules and speak freely? Yet even with Gabriel she did not censor herself with society's conventions. So were women not supposed to hold honest and comfortable talks with their husbands?

Lottie learned that Paul's parents and sisters were well, the weather was sometimes chill and sometimes warm, and the city seemed to be expanding. Other than expressing that she was pleased to meet Paul, which she surely was not, Lottie had not accomplished much more than discovering that each flower on her skirt had an uneven number of petals. Clearly not a topic Miss Leslie would find appropriate. But without being considered "vulgar," women were permitted to discuss music, books, or art as long as they did not assert themselves.

The conversation had fortunately progressed to the safe topic of William Shakespeare. Lottie remembered Grand-père laughing good-naturedly after she commented on a play they had finished reading. Surely her intended would have the same response. What harm could there be in providing a moment of levity?

Being careful to not let her eyes linger on their guest, Lottie said, "It appears to me that *The Tragedy of Romeo and Juliet* is one of William Shakespeare's gravest plays."

CHAPTER TWENTY - FOUR

G ABRIEL HELD ALCEE'S HAND TO STEADY her as she walked across the board placed over a particularly putrid drainage ditch clogged with the muck of dead mice and sewage. She pinched her nose with her other hand until they turned the corner, where even the soot-choked wind from the smokestacks of the riverboats provided relief.

Alcee covered her mouth with her handkerchief. "Yu mud do somedin."

"Please forgive me," he said with a small bow from the waist in his sister's direction. "I am not familiar with that language."

She removed the handkerchief to reveal a smirk. "You must do something about all this." Alcee waved her hand in the direction of the street. "Isn't this what engineers do? Solve these sorts of problems?"

"For now, it is your time to attend school, which is still a few blocks away, so you need to move those little feet of yours faster."

"Do not condescend," she said, turning up her face and folding her arms. Seconds later, she laughed. "I learned that word yesterday. But…" She paused, her face more serious. "It is not my little feet that are at fault. Do you see how I am dressed?" She sighed. "I should sew twenty pounds of lead into your frock coat. Then we would see whose feet are little."

"So what are your thoughts about Monsieur Joubert?" Gabriel trusted his sister to be forthright.

"Is that the reason you wanted to escort me to school? To find out more information about him?"

He should never doubt Alcee's ability to get to the point. That quality would serve her well as she grew older. "Not at first. But after Maman said she needed to leave early today to buy produce at the French Market, I thought it would be a good time for us to talk. Joseph seems to spend more and more time with our mother, so…"

"Maybe not as much as you think. He still has jobs to finish from wherever he moved from, so he comes and goes. He leaves for a few days at a time. Maman says she understands. I think she is…content." She nodded as if verifying the truth even to herself.

Gabriel thought about what his sister said—and then he thought something he wished he had not. "You don't think he might be married, do you?" He didn't know Joubert well enough to believe he would be capable of such a deception, but then that was the problem, wasn't it?

Alcee sidestepped a woman slinging water as she dipped her brush back and forth to scrub her stairs and doorway with red-brick dust. The woman paused as they walked by, her apron, calico dress bodice, and sleeves damp and coated with the red-orange ash. When she turned to wave at them and say, "*Bonjour, mes amis,*" her dark face glistened, and her smile was wide under her deep-set brown eyes.

They wished her a good day, and after they passed, Alcee said, "No. I think Monsieur Joubert is without a wife. He is far too appreciative of some things Maman does, like serve him his meals and coffee. Were he a husband, I think he would expect her to do those things. Or"—she poked Gabriel's shoulder—"he is a good actor. Like you."

"What do you mean?"

"It's not Maman who needs to put red-brick dust on her door to ward off curses. Perhaps you believe in the folktale and have considered sprinkling it on the LeClercs' doorstep."

They reached the front of her school, and Alcee—as usual—trailed behind the other students as they made their way to the tall paneled doors of the building. Her response confused Gabriel. From whom would the LeClercs need protection? "I still do not understand your point."

"Charlotte. I suspect you would like to protect her from Monsieur Bastion's visits."

SINCE LOTTIE HAD MENTIONED NOTHING about

Bastion visiting, Gabriel concluded that she either had chosen not to tell him or she hadn't known. Gabriel avoided the LeClerc house and, with the exception of seeing her on Sundays, steered clear of Lottie as well. Yet Rosette and Agnes still made time to see one another, so that had to be the source of Alcee's information. What more did they know that he did not?

Joseph's including him in the plans for the expansion of the café and their house had provided not only a welcome distraction but an opportunity to explore a field he had not considered before. For years, Gabriel had dreamed of Paris and engineering school, and then, for years, abandoned almost all hope of that possibility. He envisioned a time when he and his father might develop a relationship and eventually the future he had lost would be found again. But that brief experience after leaving the tailors', seeing Jean Noel with his white wife and son, sowed a seed of doubt of a happy reunion. A seed planted in a reality he could not deny.

Until recently, Gabriel's life path consisted of one road that led from home to the café and back to home again. He had committed himself to helping Rosette and Alcee, and, when they could travel without him, he would be free to find a path that diverged from theirs. Gabriel didn't resent Rosette and Alcee. They never demanded or insisted that he pack his ambitions into a storage crate. He had made that choice, just as he now had to choose to close off those forks in the road that led to Lottie and to Jean Noel.

Joseph Joubert, however, was not someone Gabriel would have expected to clear the wilderness and create something worth navigating. When they first met, Gabriel resigned him to a class not much higher than a common laborer. Until Joubert occupied the same seat in the corner of the café for days on end, he had thought of him only as someone hired to complete construction jobs. His constant presence around Rosette irritated him. Why would he think a woman of her beauty and intelligence would be interested in a man with no formal education, no status, no pedigree? And he continued to ask that until Lottie announced her party...when he realized he could substitute her name for his mother's and ask the same question about himself.

A humbling lesson in judging others, one God must have decided it was time for him to learn. Since then Gabriel spent time with Joseph, not just on the jobs at the café and their home, but at others in the city. Joseph asked for Gabriel's input, and when his ideas were not workable, he explained why. He brought him into homes, some Gabriel expected they would demolish for firewood, and showed him how to look beyond what was in front of him and imagine what could be. God taught Gabriel to not judge Joseph so Joseph could teach Gabriel how not to judge houses.

One day, he hoped soon, he would share that with Joseph. Today, though, they were laying out the new footprint for the café. Gabriel saw the towering stack of lumber but no workers and figured Joseph would be talking to Rosette. She had already started serving customers, so he helped her with a few tables. But there was still no sign of the builder. During a lull a few minutes later, Gabriel asked when he would be arriving.

"Roll up my sleeves, p'tit. You are much neater than I," she said. "As for Joseph, when his workers delivered the lumber this morning, one of them gave me this note."

He stopped and opened the paper, actually a billhead much like LeCroix's but with far less embellishment. Under Joseph's initials in the upper-right corner was printed Design, Build, Remodel. His handwriting was as precise and careful as his plans:

Dearest Rosette,

I trust that William has delivered this safely into your hands, and I beg your forgiveness for not being able to tell you the news in person. But the hour at which I received notice and the necessity for me to depart as soon as possible prevented me from doing so.

Please ask Gabriel to check the bills of lading at both the café and your home to make certain the lumber has arrived as per our orders. In the case of any discrepancies, he has my authority to contact the suppliers and remedy the situation as an agent of J and J Builders. Of course, if he is uncomfortable doing so, I will remedy the situation upon my return. I would hope to start the jobs as soon as possible.

I should be returning within a few days from your receipt of this note. As always, I look forward to our morning coffees and conversation.

Yours truly,
Joseph

Gabriel folded the note, handed it back to his mother, and rolled up her other sleeve. He wanted to speak carefully so as not to make Rosette defensive or unduly worried. But she spoke before he could mentally rehearse what he wanted to say.

"What bothers you?" She tied her pinstriped apron around her waist—probably one of the few women in the city whose aprons complemented her dresses—and waved to Reverend François as he strolled in after his morning Mass.

Gabriel talked while she poured cups of café au lait and he arranged beignets on a plate. "Does this happen often, these notes?" He spoke as if asking her whether she'd enjoyed an opera she'd just attended. And she responded in the same manner.

"No. This is the first one I've ever received," she said as she took the plate from him. "I'm bringing this to Père Antoine. Please ready some calas and beignets."

Gabriel knew the ebb and flow of customers prevented a serious conversation, though it seemed to be serious only to him. What cause would there be for a builder to leave quickly to attend to a job in another city, one that would mean days away? Perhaps Alcee wanting to believe that Joseph was not married swayed her perception of him around their mother, who herself reacted calmly to what Gabriel considered an obvious cause for suspicion.

Better to know now that Joseph Joubert was a *homme de paille*, a sham not to be trusted. His father, Jean Noel, had never pretended to deceive, and Gabriel had believed in him. He almost believed in Joubert. At least this was a familiar path and Gabriel already knew where it led and where it had to end.

———————

BY THE END OF THE DAY, Gabriel decided to confront Joseph Joubert before talking to his mother. He lacked any proof about Joseph leaving New Orleans because he had a family elsewhere, and Rosette would not tolerate an empty accusation. Nor should she. And with Alcee there, he especially was not going to open the discussion and chance that she would overhear.

When Alcee arrived at the café and asked Rosette about the construction, Rosette handed her Joseph's note. His sister shrugged and gave it back to Rosette, saying, "He would not go if he was not needed." She looked over her shoulder at Gabriel. "Don't you agree?" she asked, her eyes two dark bullets ready to fire should he not provide the answer she expected.

"Yes. Yes, I do," he said, nodding for emphasis. Gabriel needed to be civil now, so when they discovered the truth about Joseph later, his mother and sister would remember that he had done nothing to impugn the man's character.

Alcee rewarded him with a smile as Rosette smoothed her daughter's hair, tucking in stray pieces and readjusting her ivory combs. "Your hair reminds me of a chocolate-brown velvet gown I once wore to a ball. Sometimes, in the candlelight, it appeared to be sprinkled with gold dust. Like yours does in the sunlight." She kissed the top of Alcee's head. "Such a joy to be free of the tignon."

Gabriel watched his mother and sister and thought of Lottie as a young girl. She carried her eagerness like an offering yet was deprived of anyone with whom she could share it. Lottie had not experienced the generous affection demonstrated between Rosette and Alcee. What she would have given to be the object of her grandmother's affection.

CHAPTER TWENTY-FIVE

ALCEE AND ROSETTE WERE CARRYING COFFEE and a plate of éclairs from Vincent's into the dining room when Gabriel heard the iron knocker fall three times on their door. Only people who didn't know them well would enter that way, especially since the weather allowed the shutters and windows to be open.

"I will see who is here," said Gabriel. He opened the door and found Nathalie and Serafina—and a fiacre on the street outside the house. The women were too late had they intentions to attend that night's opera, but too early if their plans were to meet friends after.

"Good evening, Gabriel. Is Madame Girod home?" Nathalie's question was an unusual request.

"Gabriel." His mother's voice coming from behind him was an admonishment. "Have you not invited these ladies into our home?"

"Of course." He opened the door wide to accommodate their voluminous skirts and attempted not to appear on the outside like the six-year-old child he felt on the inside with his mother's address. As they entered, he realized they wore bonnets, Nathalie's with a long feather and Serafina's, a showy collection of smoky plumes, ribbons, and flowers, in place of their usual tignons. So, appearing in public in the city had not been their intended destination at all.

"Please, be seated," Rosette said. "If you would like to remove your capes, Alcee will be happy to place them in the cabinet."

Gabriel watched his sister's eyes brighten as first Nathalie presented her with a pale brown overcoat trimmed in the blue of her gown and then Serafina handed her a black velvet cape with ermine trim. Alcee rarely exhibited such extreme politeness. He had no doubt that each of the expensive capes would grace her body before hanging in the closet.

"Oh, and I'm sure you will excuse Alcee, as she will retire early tonight to be ready for school in the morning." Rosette's pronouncement caused Alcee a few wide-eyed blinks, but from previous veiled statements, she understood that it was her mother's way of telling her she would not be participating in the conversation. Gabriel suspected the capes might provide some solace as his sister said "Good night" and left for her bedroom.

Either out of the awkwardness of being the sole male in the room or the habit of serving during the day, Gabriel offered to bring in coffee and dessert, forgetting that outside of the home, men would always be the served, not the servers. But there was barely a flicker of surprise from the two young women, and Rosette thanked him as he left the parlor.

This visit to his mother had to be related to Paul Bastion being Serafina's protector. Why Nathalie accompanied her, Gabriel had no idea, but he was curious about what had happened to precipitate this visit. He carried the gold-and-cream coffee service into the parlor and set it on the ottoman near Rosette, who poured the coffee into cups.

Nathalie was talking when he entered, so Gabriel sat across from the women as if he had been there all along.

"…So after she explained what happened, I suggested she talk to you." Nathalie stopped to add a teaspoon of brown sugar to her coffee. "Serafina didn't think it would be appropriate to visit at this hour, but I assured her that Gabriel and I have known each other since he told me mud pies really did taste like chocolate. I didn't believe him, of course." Nathalie flicked her eyes in his direction. "But I knew that he would not mind if a friend visited with a friend in need."

Rosette slowly stirred her coffee. "And this need is?"

Without the ermine cape, the lime-green velvet dress, or the diamond-and-emerald earbobs and matching brooch, Serafina didn't seem much older than the girl sent to her room. She had looked at Nathalie when she spoke as if Nathalie had been reading a new ordinance passed by the city. But Rosette's voice seemed to lead her out of a fog. She set her coffee cup on the ottoman and started to speak when the eight o'clock cannon pounded the sky, notifying all in the city, especially slaves, of the beginning of curfew. Serafina smiled and said, "I suppose

I could not have asked for a better introduction."

"If you would prefer privacy, I understand," said Gabriel, almost forgetting that he had been an uninvited listener.

"In this city, very little is private for long, so I don't mind if you are here. Anyway, you are familiar with one of the parties involved. It is likely you would know this soon," she said. "Madame Girod, first let me thank you for this intrusion in your private time. I trust Nathalie, and when she reminded me that talking to you during the day is difficult because of your business, I agreed to come tonight."

"Sometimes Nathalie's pluckiness is a gift," Rosette said. "Had we not already met, this might have been uncomfortable. The first time we spoke, I didn't ask you this question. But now that you are back, I feel it is an important one. Why haven't you approached your mother with your concerns?"

"My mother is with her third protector. Not only does she send me away, telling me that I must learn to handle problems on my own, but she keeps me away so her protector does not see that she has an older daughter." Serafina looked away for a moment then continued. "I hope you understand my situation. My grandmother and I were quite close. When she died, I felt I lost a friend."

Hearing Serafina's story, Gabriel thought of Lottie. How having an attentive, concerned grandmother would delight her. Without Agnes, Lottie, like Serafina, would have no one. That Lottie had grown to be a compassionate and generous woman was almost incomprehensible… and another man being the beneficiary of that was infuriating.

"Paul's father, Emile, is interested in a prime parcel of land along the river. It has not ever been for sale, though he heard rumors that the owners may soon be interested. The owners met the Bastions at a party they both attended, and it was mentioned that their granddaughter would be making her debut, though late. You could probably surmise the rest. The land has now become the dowry, and when Paul marries Charlotte LeClerc, the land will be theirs."

Rosette turned to Gabriel. He understood that to react on his feelings would be an irreversible disaster.

Concern shadowed his mother's face. "This may sound harsh, Serafina, but did you not understand what it means to be a placée? It's one of the first lessons we learn. That the men who purchase houses, furniture, clothes, jewels, or provide maids and cooks will never be fully ours. All that is ever fully ours is our children. Eventually, your protector will court another woman, and you will be available for balls, the opera, late nights only. He will marry a white woman. Like he was always meant to do from the first night you met him."

"Except he is only marrying her for the land to be in the family."

Rosette shook her head in disbelief. "P'tit, have you not heard what I have tried to tell you? These marriages are hardly ever about anything but negotiation. Love is rarely an issue. Why do you think a man always goes back to his placée?"

"He told me he plans to leave her after the wedding. I would think she would want to know that."

"No, I don't think she would. But I do think he would say what he needs to say to make sure he has a warm house on Rue Ursulines," Gabriel said.

"Gabriel," Rosette said, "perhaps it is time for you to leave this conversation."

Gabriel walked away, hearing Serafina's hiccupping sobs, as Nathalie said, "She truly needs your advice, Madame Girod. She has discovered she is with child."

THE NEXT MORNING GABRIEL SMELLED fresh coffee and found a filled urn in the dining room. He leaned against the sideboard, warmed his hands around the cup, and stared at the cherry dining table where the shutters sifted the sun that, over time, had faded the once-gleaming wood.

New furniture had not made its way into the Girod house for years, although a few pieces of late had materialized from Tante Virgine's house—a walnut sewing cabinet, a cypress armoire, a wire safe for the back porch…. Virgine, his mother said, gave things away just to have an excuse to wear an elegant day dress and shop on Canal Street. Sometimes, items whose names she couldn't pronounce and, therefore, would not be able to impress others with found a home with the Girods. Like the cut-leaf silver centerpiece on the table, an *epergne* with a center vase and two trays that held flowers and fruit, or the two mirrored *girandole*s, ornate, branched sconces with pendants and festoons of cut crystal, that Gabriel now looked at in their dining room.

Tying her black-and-cream-toile tignon as she walked into the room, Rosette asked him to pour a cup for her before they left for the café. As Gabriel handed it to her, he said, "I want to apologize for what I said last night. I should not have said something so cruel."

"True. But then, I'm not sure why you stayed in the first place. Though it appeared Nathalie appreciated it, by the frequent glances in your direction." She put her cup on the table and tucked in the loose ends of the tignon. "Let's go. I let Alcee sleep, and Virgine is coming by to entertain her."

"I heard what Nathalie said, about Serafina being with child. Does Bastion know?" Gabriel ignored the remark about Nathalie. Rosette used to say she was "trouble waiting to happen," so he didn't think his mother was suggesting that he pursue the intention of those glances.

"I didn't ask her. It is not my business, nor yours. In fact, I'm not pleased to be this involved, but I understand she feels alone and needs someone to talk to about this. I'm going to tell you what I told her. Be patient. God has a plan, and He's not required to show it to you."

"I HEARD A PERSON CAN find the best coffee and calas in the city here."

Rosette almost poured powdered sugar on Gabriel's shoes when she heard Joseph Joubert's smoky voice as he strolled into the café. She handed Gabriel the canister and headed toward Joseph, her arms outstretched. "So, you have returned?"

He clasped her hands and bowed in what Gabriel deemed an exaggerated performance. "Yes. How could I stay away from all this?"

But when he spoke, he looked only at Rosette, whose cheeks reddened as if she had been bending over the open kettle, stirring sugar for pralines. She clearly did not react like a cautious woman, and Gabriel thought she trusted this man far too much and too soon. This uncharacteristic frivolous behavior from Rosette concerned him, especially since they all knew so little about Joubert. Gabriel had witnessed one painful and disappointing relationship; he would not allow another man to damage his mother again. To remind them they weren't alone, Gabriel walked over to hand them each a cup of coffee. "Welcome back, Monsieur Joubert," he said with a voice as cool as the coffee was hot.

"Thank you, Gabriel." Joseph lifted the cup and sniffed. "Ah, just as I remember. I've not had the pleasure of great coffee for days."

"Let me make you some fresh calas before the morning crowd arrives," Rosette chirped, fluttering off to the kitchen without waiting for an answer.

Gabriel started to follow her, but Joseph said, "Gabriel, wait. I've only been away a few days. Why have I lapsed into being 'Monsieur Joubert' again?"

"Habit, I suppose."

"Of course," he replied, with the same edge to his voice as Gabriel's—letting Gabriel know that Joseph didn't believe him any more than he expected Gabriel would believe Joseph. He finished his coffee then buttoned his frock coat. "I know Saturday is a busy day here, but I would like you to come with me this afternoon to look for more materials for the jobs. And that will allow us time to talk. Man to man."

"I would appreciate that opportunity," said Gabriel.

"Good. Then I—"

"Are you leaving?" Rosette appeared and handed Joseph a plate of sweet fried rice cakes under powdered sugar that looked like melted snow.

"Not until after I eat these," he said. "I need to check the progress of the two houses on Dauphine Street. The seasoned lumber was supposed to arrive from Florida this week. But I'll be back this afternoon. I'd like Gabriel to help me with some materials, if you think you can spare him."

Rosette smiled. "That won't be a problem," she said.

"Then we will see one another this afternoon," Joseph said.

CHAPTER TWENTY - SIX

A S THEY WENT DOWN DAUPHINE STREET, Joseph Joubert showed Gabriel two brick cottages with double chimneys and kitchens with upper galleries that were almost finished.

"I wanted to show you the facade on these cottages. It's called *floche*. The plaster is scored to resemble stone, and then it can be painted with a washed-out red to make it decorative. I thought about doing this on the addition to your mother's house. What do you think?"

"I think it's impressive, but she needs to see this herself. That's not a decision I want to make for her. Can you imagine her coming home to an exterior she detests?"

Joseph laughed. "I understand. She'd start tearing it down with her bare hands. Or tearing us down."

Inside one of the houses, Joseph pointed out the cypress pilaster-style mantel with a faux marble treatment, the tongue-and-groove wood ceiling, and the intricate cornices in the main rooms. "I know Rosette respects your opinion, so I thought it would be important for you to see all this before I discussed it with her. Showing you a design on paper isn't the same as seeing the final product. I want the people I build for to trust the quality of my work."

Before getting in the cab, Joseph was stopped by one of the men with a question about a wrought-iron fence. While they spoke, Gabriel examined the hand-crafted corbels waiting to be added to the ceiling. He had faith in the quality of the builder's construction. It was evident in his attention to detail in door moldings and carved ceiling medallions, those finishing touches that set a house apart from ordinary. Gabriel wanted to have the same faith in the quality of the man his mother obviously cared about.

"I have one more place to stop. Do you still have time?" Joseph headed down Dauphine.

"Sure. Rosette isn't expecting me back until she closes."

"Good, because I suspect you didn't agree to this just to look at a few houses. Am I correct? And if so, then be honest with me."

Gabriel wondered if Joseph truly meant what he said. There was only one way to find out. "Are you married?"

"Whoa, stop," Joseph pulled the reins. "Married? You think I am married?"

"I do not know that you aren't. You leave suddenly for days, sometimes longer, and return unexpectedly. This has happened a number of times, and you've only lived here two years, and she's known you for only a few months. It is cause for suspicion."

"Marriage? I never thought of that." He looked like a man who'd had a new idea dock in his mind like a ship on the river. "Of all the things someone might conjecture about my comings and goings, I had not considered that possibility."

"Well, no one in my family did either. Except me. I'm old enough to remember my father leaving. My mother is one of the strongest women I know, but after he left, there were nights she cried herself to sleep. If this is going to end the same way, I do not want it to start."

Joseph shook his head back and forth, mumbling. Whatever conversation he was having with himself, he seemed to be losing. Still holding the reins, his elbows resting on his knees, he said, "If she knew we were sitting in the middle of New Orleans talking about her, she'd be home making voodoo dolls."

Maybe Joseph knew Rosette better than Gabriel thought, because he wasn't going to debate that one.

"I'm not married, and you're too late for not wanting it to start. I care about your mother. And I respect her. And to explain the comings and goings, well, if you've ever made promises to people, then you know how it feels if you have to disappoint them. I didn't want them to feel that way. That's going to have to be enough for now. I think the reins are going to freeze in my gloves, and I'm about to be late for my appointment."

"I WILL STAB EACH OF my fingers with this needle if I

must sit inside one more hour." Lottie pushed the needle through the new sampler she had started after being bored with the other. If Grand-mère fussed, then she would fuss. Soon Lottie would be married, so what could she do? In fact, this arrangement had the effect of bestowing a power upon Lottie that only the pouting and whining daughters of the dreadfully rich had.

Grand-mère, of late, had been daringly close, however begrudgingly, to what one might call kindness. Lottie's not wanting to marry Paul, no one cared a whit about. But if Paul chose to walk away from Lottie because of her uncivil language or compulsion to twirl her hair and raise her skirts above her ankles, *that* Grand-mère cared about. And though Lottie wouldn't destroy her grandparents in such a way, her grandmother didn't doubt that she was capable.

The drama of it all was sufficient to amuse Lottie most days, but not today. Winter had decided to be an unbearable brat, and it hurled wind and cold and sometimes rain that hit bare skin like pins. For days, she had been confined to the house, not attending any of her lessons—according to her grandmother—because of the ferocious weather. Not visiting Justine. And facing the worrisome possibility of not being able to go to the orphanage tomorrow.

"Lottie, my girl, if General Jackson knew you stabbed that well, he would have recruited you for the Battle of New Orleans."

"I wasn't born yet, PaPa," said Lottie, who grinned at

her grandfather standing in the doorway of the parlor and looking at her over his spectacles as if he were surveying land. She had spent so little time with him because of the "girl things," as he called all the party preparations, she'd forgotten how calming it felt to be around him. Not like Grand-mère, who required constant vigilance to assure she couldn't break through Lottie's barrier.

"Maybe 'Old Hickory' was born too soon, p'tit."

"He managed a victory without me," she said. "But a little battle right now would be welcome." She secured her needle in the sampler and tossed it onto the settee next to her. "I understand how prison could make a person crazy. You know there is an entire world just beyond a wall, but you can only reach it in your mind."

Grand-père slipped his gold pocket watch out of his vest pocket. "I have time," he said as he snapped the watch closed, "to wander in the bookshop on Camp Street. Then I can go to my office, where a young lady might choose to read or, if she is not opposed to a brief walk, find herself in Barriere's, the leading store on Royal Street, where she can browse through all the *nouveautés*. Assuming there is a young lady here who would meet those qualifications of loving new merchandise like books, fancy things, and her grandfather."

"Oh, PaPa, you have saved my life!" Lottie jumped up and reached her arms around him, the familiar smell of pipe tobacco making her six again, waiting for him to lift her off the ground. Every night it was the same secret, but for as long as he could gather her up in his arms, she'd cup her hands around his ear and whisper, "Lottie loves you." Their little ritual ended when Grand-mère decided Lottie was too old for this and that she needed to conduct herself like a young lady. Lottie didn't tell her grandmother, of course, but one night she told Agnes that if being a young lady meant not hugging Grand-père, then she never wanted to be one. And now she was one, and her occasions to hug him waned, and in months, they wouldn't even live in the same house. Where had all those days gone?

He tugged one of her curls. "Your grandmother is taking a nap, so I need to tell Agnes you'll be with me. Hurry. Go fetch all your girl things. Abram and I will wait for you in the carriage."

Lottie could not remember the last time she'd moved so quickly wearing six petticoats and a wool gown with layers of ruffles.

"What a surprise that you selected only one book today. I expected not to see the bottom half of your face, for all that you'd be carrying." Grand-père opened the door to his office and followed Lottie in.

Actually, Lottie wanted more books, but if she was to be the wife of wealthy Paul Bastion, then why spend Grand-père's money when she could spend his? She set the package on one of the side tables in the viewing room and removed her cape, hanging it, along with her bonnet and muff, in the armoire in Grand-père's office.

"I don't have as much time to read now. I'm certain that, later, I will be making more visits to the shop." She kept her voice light, not wanting to weigh her words with the resignation and frustration from which they originated. Since the day he told her about the coming-out party, the two of them had not had one conversation about the suitors there, Paul, or her future. But Lottie did not want to have that discussion today. She wanted this day to be colored scenes painted for the magic projector, so that years from today, she could shine the pictures on the wall and always remember it.

Large black leather portfolios of houses, house plans, and maps crowded the visitors' table where clients and prospective clients looked to sell or buy or build. Before they understood how their lives had already been charted, she, Justine, Gabriel, and sometimes André would pore over the books, picking Faubourgs and land and houses on sale for prices they couldn't comprehend. Grand-père also sold and bought land for businesses, though that wasn't of much interest to them then—or now.

Grand-père walked out of his office, dusting the sleeves of his frock coat. "After all these years, you would think I would have learned to wear a coat at least the same shade of silver as the dust, instead of blacks and browns."

Lottie flipped pages in the Faubourg-Marigny portfo-lio. "But you look so distinguished in those dark colors."

"Is that your kind way of telling me that a gray coat and my silver hair might make me look like a riverboat gambler?"

"I doubt Père François would allow you to look like a gambler and still attend Mass. Certainly Grand-mère would not." She closed the portfolio. "When your appointment comes, I'll go to Barriere's for another change of scenery. I won't be there long. Unless you need me to be."

"No, no. Come and go as you please. I suspect my client will be here at least an hour. He's already looked at the properties for sale, so today we're meeting to determine the ones he wants to purchase. We were scheduled to meet last week, but he was called away on other business. I've tried to keep the weekends free of work, but sometimes in this business you have to be available if you intend to sell."

It sounded as if he was apologizing, though Lottie had no idea why he felt he should.

He glanced at his watch again; then he pointed to the door. "There he is. Joseph Joubert."

Lottie looked out the long windows at the front of the office just as her grandfather said, "Isn't that Gabriel following him?"

CHAPTER TWENTY - SEVEN

J OSEPH JOUBERT AND LOUIS LECLERC started their meeting, delighted that the two young people with them could entertain one another. Lottie acted equally pleased, while Gabriel did his best to avoid eye contact with her.

The two men went into her grandfather's office, and Lottie wished they could have taken the awkwardness between her and Gabriel with them and shut the door.

"I didn't expect you would be here. Though, until Joseph stopped, I did not know I would be, for that matter," said Gabriel.

"Grand-père saved me from boredom and brought me to the bookstore. He told me he had an appointment, but had he told me the name, I would not have known who he was. Or that you would be with him." She didn't want Gabriel to think he was the reason for her being at the office.

"Joseph is designing and building additions to our house and the café. I've been working with him."

"Oh, I see," said Lottie.

Pretending to be transfixed by a map of the Garden

District, Lottie sat at the table and hoped she could outwait Gabriel. After ten times of visually tracing her finger up and down St. Charles, she'd almost conceded when he said, "You always won the breath-holding games."

"Except for the time I passed out." She let her eyes rest on his face.

"Oh, I disagree. That was most definitely a win. André and I proclaimed you champion. Remember, we looked for laurel to make you a wreath just like the Greeks would be awarded."

She laughed. "The wreath. I didn't forget the wreath for days. None of us did. Our first lesson in identifying poison ivy."

He stood behind her, reached his arm over her shoulder, and pointed at the map. "Garden District?"

His sleeve grazed her neck, and at that moment she was grateful to be an expert breath-holder. She nodded.

"I think Monsieur Joubert might be talking to your father about land there. The Americans, he said, are attempting to outdo one another in who can construct the most pretentious house."

Sitting in her grandfather's office and struggling to limit their dialogue to unimportant topics was more painful than jabbing herself with her sewing needle. "I planned to walk to Barriere's while I waited for Grand-père, since I expected to be waiting alone. Would you care to join me? We could go to Woodlief's on Chartres Street, if you'd prefer. I don't have a particular reason for shopping, so either is fine."

"Let's start at one, then if time permits, we can walk to the other," Gabriel said.

If only he knew that, given different circumstances, she was willing to walk right into his life.

STROLLING DOWN EXCHANGE ALLEY, LOTTIE wanted to share with Gabriel how much she detested the visit from Paul Bastion and how she dreaded the ones that would be forthcoming. But to mention his name would be insensitive, and she had demonstrated her capacity for that last week. Lottie didn't really need Gabriel to say the words to know he loved her. It was easier—for her—if he didn't. Words spoken aloud were irretrievable. Voices gave them form. She was grateful for the wagon that had passed that day, else she might have had to find a way to stop him herself.

On Sundays before they met, she had time to construct an emotional barrier, to convince herself that since what they wanted was impossible, she needed to be protected behind a wall of politeness. Today, the surprise attack of his appearance lowered her defenses and her vulnerability. She sensed it in him as well.

"I want to apologize for how I acted toward you last week on the way home," Lottie said.

His eyes scanned her face, but he said nothing.

So, he wasn't going to make this easy for her.

"If the carriage hadn't passed to interrupt you, I—I

was scared… am scared. Because this can go nowhere. And if I let you say those words, they will echo in my heart for the rest of my life."

She blotted her eyes with one gloved hand and felt Gabriel's hand entwine itself in her other.

A trio passed, too intensely and loudly arguing about their food bill at Antoine's to be attentive to Lottie and Gabriel. When the three young men turned out of the alley, Gabriel lifted his arm, bringing Lottie's hand to his lips.

She didn't object and might have offered her other hand to have the experience again except that, with his kiss still lingering on her hand, Gabriel tugged her toward him. "I hardly need to tell you how I feel about you. It's in my eyes from the moment I see your face. Your beautiful face," he whispered.

His hands held her waist, and she saw such longing in his eyes that she closed her own, for fear that he would see the same in hers. If he did not kiss her, she would never know what she missed. And if he did, she would always know.

He didn't give her time to think about the slow heat that rose from where his fingertips pressed into her, that made her heart race as if it could outrun the very warmth it craved, or the fire he created when he kissed first one eye, then the other. His lips…his lips gently kissed their way down the curve of her cheek, and when she felt them on her mouth, everything in her begged to melt into this one moment.

But where could they go from here?

She had barely time to feel his mouth on hers when she leaned away. "I can't, Gabriel. I can't."

THE SUNDAY SERVICE ENDED AND, as usual, Grand-mère hurried from the pew to reach the church doors ahead of Père François. He stationed himself there to greet his congregation as they went forth to their houses, their placées, the gambling hall, the racetrack, or one of the guzzle shops along the river. And, as usual, the reverend appeared as if he had bloomed from between a crowd of his parishioners to smile at Lottie's grandmother as she left.

Lottie saw the shine in his eyes and wondered if this had become a game for him, this making sure she didn't escape without seeing him. Grand-mère wore her disdain like expensive perfume, and he diluted it every time they made eye contact.

"Lottie, Lottie." Justine bounced at the bottom of the stairs, waving her hand.

Lottie tapped her grandfather on the shoulder and pointed in her friend's direction. "I'm going to talk to Justine. I won't be long."

He reached back to pat her hand. "Take your time."

Lottie squeezed between the Bourgeois twins, who, at fifteen, still dressed identically, except that Eulalie's curls were on the left side of her face and Eleanor's were on the right side. Passage through was complicated by their matching blue, green, and white plaid skirts creating a twelve-foot-wide swath of fabric blocking her path. Lottie had almost cleared their blockage when one of them stopped her. "Charlotte LeClerc, we heard that a suitor came calling." It sounded like Eulalie sang instead of spoke.

"Yes, but just once. Last week. Thank you for inquiring. I am meeting a friend." She waved to Justine, who offered proof by waving back.

Eleanor leaned close to Lottie. "Mama says he's rich enough to have two women." The two girls smiled as if they'd dispensed communication from a heavenly body.

"Then I must make certain to ask Madame Bourgeois to explain what she means." Lottie waited for the girls to react to what she said, which they did with their *O*-shaped mouths, and then she smiled until her cheeks pinched the corners of her eyes and made it down the steps to hug her friend.

"I haven't seen you in weeks!" declared Justine, who didn't move her hands from Lottie's shoulders after their hug. "My mother said you can join us for dinner. We're eating early because Isabelle and the brats are there. Please join us. Please."

"You're starting to sound like one of Isabelle's brats," Lottie teased. "Of course I want to come." She looked over the thinning crowd of churchgoers. Her grandmother was one of three women today who, in the gray morning of winter, opened her parasol. "There they are," Lottie said to Justine as she motioned for her to follow.

She made her way through the crowd, smiling sweetly at Madame Bourgeois for the benefit of her daughters, until she reached the tasseled gold silk parasol with her grandmother underneath.

Lottie waited for her to finish her conversation with Madame Adolphe. "Grandmother, I wanted you to know that I will be having an early lunch with Justine and her family. I'll be home before leaving for the orphanage this afternoon." She kissed her grandmother and grandfather, Justine rattled a hello and good-bye in the same sentence, and they trailed after the assortment of Dumases heading home.

"We look like our own Carnival organization, don't we?" Justine and Lottie walked side by side, arms locked together. "And you no longer need to request permission?"

"No. Apparently permission is not required now that I've conceded to their selecting the man with whom I will spend the rest of my life."

THE DUMAS MEN PLUS ISABELLE'S HUSBAND FRANÇOIS retired to the library after dinner with their cigars, espressos, and opinions. Justine's mother, Isabelle, Justine, and Lottie moved into the parlor, where Ruth, the Dumases' maid, carried in a coffee service. Ruth's parents had been given as a wedding gift to Justine's father from his parents. Neither Monsieur Dumas or Ruth's parents realized how the newest Madame Dumas quietly abhorred slavery. She and Ruth's parents became friends, and they raised their families right alongside one another.

Ruth's husband, Laurent, was a slave from a nearby plantation who helped his owner sell vegetables in the French Market. The two of them met there, and when they decided they were in love, Madame Dumas sent her husband with enough cash to buy Laurent from the Greywoods. Isabelle inherited her mother's color-blind compassion. Justine and her father, who thought anyone born with black skin was supposed to be a slave, kept their opinions to themselves while they were home. They just asked Isabelle and her mother to do the same in public, as Monsieur Dumas said, "I sure don't want the good people of this city to think I'm living with abolitionists."

Lottie had learned years ago not to be surprised where she might find the servants—Madame refused to call them house slaves—in the Dumas house.

"Ruthie, here, let me help you with that." Isabelle relieved her of the broad silver tray and set it on the piano bench. Lottie knew Ruthie was with child, but without the tray in front of her, she was able to realize how close the woman was to actually having the child.

"Mother," Isabelle said, "Ruthie should not be carrying so much weight when she is this close to being delivered."

"Perhaps she will listen to you, because I've said the same to her and she insists she is capable."

"Let me see your ankles, Ruthie."

"Miz Isabelle, you wants me to lift up my skirt?"

"Gracious, Ruthie, do you see any men in this room? We all have ankles." Isabelle turned to her mother. "This is exactly the reason more women need to be doctors."

Madame Dumas eyed her. "Isabelle, I never forbid you to attend medical school."

"Do we have to start this discussion of women's rights, or their lack of?" Justine handed Lottie a cup of coffee. "Ruthie, please show Isabelle your ankles, or she'll be the one lifting your skirt."

Ruthie stared at the ceiling, as if to shield herself from the embarrassment of knowing all those eyes were examining her bare skin, and gingerly picked up the folds of fabric covering her feet.

"Oh dear." Justine's mother covered her mouth with her hand.

Someone not knowing Ruthie was with child would have thought her deprived of ankles at birth, they were so swollen.

"You need to rest. Stay off your feet for the rest of the day. Wait." Isabelle turned to her mother. "Why is she here? This is Sunday. She's not supposed to be working."

Madame Dumas's spoon lazily made its way around her coffee cup. "Tell her, Ruthie." Her voice had as much energy as her spoon.

"Where I'm going to go like this? Jus' soon work and pass the time. Dis child already ain't stayin' still. Least if

I'm doing, it's quiet in there." She pointed to her round belly. "And sometimes a break from everybody is a welcome thing."

"That, I understand." Isabelle smiled and clasped Ruthie's hand. "Now, go lay down."

"Oh, and Ruthie, make yourself a plate. We have plenty left. And tell your mother to see me when she returns, and I'll give her the rest," said Madame Dumas.

Justine rolled her eyes as Ruthie left. "My stars. One day I am going to return home to find that Ruth's entire family has moved into our home."

"Mother will be sure to marry you off before then. Right, Mother?"

Madame Dumas gave Justine a wide-eyed nod. "Absolutely."

"Well, good, then. Best for all of us," Justine answered, sounding offended. She looked at her mother's and sister's grins. "You are not at all amusing."

Isabelle poured herself coffee and refilled her mother's cup. "Speaking of marriage, Charlotte, how are things since your debut?"

Lottie opened her mouth to reply, but Justine's voice erupted. "Haven't you heard? Paul Bastion is visiting."

"He's only been once, Justine." Lottie wished she had missed the flicker of communication when Isabelle and her mother made eye contact. That silent exchange became a loud warning. She looked back and forth between the two. "What? What do you know?"

"What did I miss?" Justine eyed all three of them.

"Nothing yet," said Lottie. "I want to know."

Isabelle stared at her mother, who seemed to blink more than nod her agreement, then turned to Lottie. "Keep in mind that men gossip, probably more than women. They call it an exchange of ideas—"

"Get to the point, Isabelle. Lottie doesn't want to hear your diatribe about men," Justine's mother said in that soft but firm Dumas way.

"François was told that Paul keeps a placée. A young placée. Sixteen, maybe seventeen years old."

Lottie felt her lungs unwind. "That's the news? It's no secret that Creole men are protectors for women."

She had the briefest moment of time to appreciate the irony of being relieved that her intended had a mistress before Isabelle said, "That's not all the news. She is with child."

The coffee cup shivered in Lottie's hand. "Does he know?"

"Yes. Yes, he does. And it is said that he is proud and happy."

CHAPTER TWENTY – EIGHT

L OTTIE CONSIDERED THE NOXIOUS GUTTERS in summer, swollen with rotting animal carcasses, the slop of chamber pots, and the dirt and trash of every passerby the most repugnant aspect of living in the city…until Isabelle revealed what she had heard about Paul Bastion. By comparison, the gutters were troughs of intensely sweet-smelling gardenias and exotic violets.

The plaçage relationship did not shock her, but she had nurtured a degree of hope that he would, like many protectors after marriage, gift his placée *pour prendre congé*—he would leave the woman and it would be over. How vexing to be told that she would marry a man who had another woman carrying his child. Surely this information had not been shared with her grandparents? Yet another one of those questions to which she really did not want to know the answer. She had expected more from them in selecting a man who would be her husband. That young Creole men had placées who would have children was a given, but to have to compete with a baby as a new bride was humiliating.

Had someone else told her about Paul's placée and

his child, she hoped she could have forced herself to faint at that moment; then words would not be necessary. She appreciated that people who cared about her were the ones who told her what almost everyone in New Orleans must have already known about Paul. Otherwise, why would the Bourgeois twins have passed that remark about him and two women? Of all the gossips! A pair of girls who together didn't have enough sense to pick out different gowns.

She was relieved to have the orphanage as a reason to leave the Dumas house early. The parlor fireplace did little to appease the cold ripples that danced up and down her back. The women tried to comfort her, but some hurts just had to work themselves out, like knots. Agnes had told her, "You try make 'em go away, pullin' and tuggin'. Ain't gonna do you no good. Just make it worst. Just works on 'em little bit at a time." Madame Dumas hugged Lottie before she left, a hug that pressed her so close, she felt as if she'd grown another body. She rubbed Lottie's back in circles when they hugged, just like she did with her own daughters. Lottie closed her eyes and drifted for a small moment. *This is how my mother would have hugged me.*

After they released one another, Madame Dumas still clutched her shoulders. "Lottie, have you asked your grandparents why Paul Bastion?"

Lottie shook her head. "No, ma'am."

"You need to ask them. Don't be the last person to know."

SHE FOUND HER GRANDPARENTS IN the library. Grand-mère and a hill of mending competed for space on the small settee, which had been moved from its usual place and was now closer to the tall windows. At first glance, Lottie thought her grandfather was reading a book, until she stepped into the room and saw the cover. It was a book, but it was one of his ledger books where he kept records of his business and his clients' accounts.

They both looked up when she entered the room. Her grandfather smiled and closed his ledger. "Did you enjoy yourself, p'tit?"

Lottie hesitated. Should she broach the question about Paul now? Soon Gabriel would be here, and she did not want the lingering feelings of that conversation to follow her the remainder of the day. Knowing the reason for their decision would not change the making of it, so waiting for the answer would not change the substance of it. Were she to plan the possibility of misery, she did not want it to be today.

"Yes, Grand-père, very much so. Being at the Dumas house is always enlightening."

"Are you still intending to visit that orphanage with Gabriel Girod?" Grand-mère picked up a ruffled petticoat and examined it.

Lottie could have substituted "to pick a field of cotton" as her intention and the sound of her grandmother's voice would not have changed. "Of course. As the future wife of a wealthy man, would I not want to appear concerned about the less fortunate?"

Her grandmother managed a "Hmpf," and continued stitching.

Grand-père quickly reopened his ledger, and he briefly cut his eyes in his wife's direction. His pursed lips were a sure sign of his attempt to stifle the smile that threatened his lips.

"I'm going upstairs to refresh myself and rest a bit," Lottie said and left the study.

PARTLY TO CHEER HERSELF, LOTTIE selected a bright turquoise-blue gown belted at the waist with a gold buckle and bands of white-lace ruffles and tucked fabric that ran from the waist to the hemline. A pair of soft blue gloves and a black cape with blue bows to match her bonnet finished her outfit. She pulled her curls to the back, and after seeing her pale cheeks in the mirror, she pinched them to draw some color into her face. If only pinching her eyes would brighten them.

Lottie gathered the gloves, bonnets, and underpinnings she planned to carry with her today. She didn't find her grandparents in the library or anywhere else downstairs, so she assumed they were napping. She located the basket of food she was to take with them— Agnes had filled it before leaving this morning—and waited for Gabriel in the rocker on the gallery. Since their encounter the day before, Lottie had wished she could have forbidden herself to think of him. It might have been easier to forbid herself to breathe. She couldn't control the way she felt when Gabriel neared her any more than the earth could control the moon's tug on its waters. And when his lips touched her fingertips, Romeo's words to Juliet, "let lips do what hands do," never became more alive than they did at that moment.

But what did Gabriel know that she did? Or, worse, that she didn't? Paul would be visiting again tomorrow, and just the thought of sitting in the same room with him repulsed her. If they could spend their married lives in different rooms, which might be likely considering the situation with his placée, then Lottie could tolerate him. Unlike the man who walked through the courtyard so tall that, should they be close enough, she could hear his heartbeat. He sidestepped where Abram had been in the process of placing new bricks along the flower ledge, and when his face lifted, Lottie's skin warmed with the sight of his dark eyes focused on her and his lips slowly responding with a smile.

She met him before he reached the gallery, thankful for the cold wind that would account for the blush on her face. "Agnes prepared this. She must have intended for you to carry it, because it's quite heavy."

He relieved her of the basket of breads, rice, and yams. "Good to see you," Gabriel said.

"And you." How was it that his reply could leave her both sad and happy?

They walked in silence for some time.

"At least you don't need to be concerned that I will hold your hand on the way," Gabriel said.

Lottie stared straight ahead, else her disappointment be obvious. "No, I'm not concerned," she responded, employing her best matter-of-fact voice.

"That is not at all what I meant. I'm holding Agnes's basket in one hand and books in the other. I don't have a hand to spare."

"Oh, I hadn't considered that."

"Probably because you haven't looked at me since you turned this over to me"—he held up the food—"when we met. Does that mean you woke up a different person today than the one I was with yesterday?"

Like horses terrified by an unexpected noise, thoughts of yesterday, this morning, tomorrow, the rest of her life trampled over her. A different person? How would she know? She heard the thundering hooves, but she couldn't stop them. She blurted, "Am I different? That would suggest I knew myself as the same person. It doesn't matter, because everything I might have thought I was is crushed under the weight of what everyone else wants me to be."

"Stop. Come here." Gabriel stepped into an alcove between two houses and set the basket and books on the ground.

When he reached to place his hands on Lottie's shoulders, she took a step back. "Please, don't. Don't touch me," she whispered.

"I can't believe you said that to me. Do you think me

capable of hurting you?"

"Yes. You hurt me every time you touch me. Every time, it reminds me of what I won't have. What I cannot have," she said. "The person I am with you will not survive the future other people have charted for me. Yet I don't want to be that other person when we are together."

"I don't want you to be her either." He turned and nodded to the couple that passed slowly, their curiosity evident in their unapologetic stares. "We can't continue having these discussions in alleys."

Lottie did find some humor in that. "Where we talk will not change the *what*. It will not change who we are in this world."

"And that's exactly why," he said as he picked up the basket and books again, "we need to. Being in this world doesn't mean we need to be of it."

"All we need is our own underground railroad," said Lottie.

⁓⁓⁓

CLEMENT STARED AT THE SHEET of foolscap in front of him with the wonder of a child on Christmas Day.

"Clement," he said as if meeting himself for the first time. "Miz Lottie, I's most fifty, and I never think I write my own name."

Lottie turned away lest Clement see her squeeze her eyes together to forestall tears. These men and women struggling to learn, knowing it could mean their lives, humbled her. One day, leaving after the lessons, Gabriel had remarked, "I'm a grandparent and a parent away from sitting on the other side of the table in that room." Lottie didn't grasp the enormity of that statement until today. And she would never know it in the way Gabriel felt it.

Clement, Anna, and Percy practiced their names one more time before they had to leave. Across the room, three men and Gabriel sat in a circle holding Bibles and taking turns reading a line from the Gospel of Matthew. When they finished, each man would tear out a page and take it with him. At first, Sister Mary Catherine was appalled to discover Gabriel ripping Bibles apart. But when he explained that one thin sheet was easy to carry, easy to hide, and easy to dispose of if necessary, she quickly changed her mind. "I think God would certainly approve of sending His Word out, even if it means one page at a time," said Sister.

Anna, who finished writing her name first, leaned over, tapped Lottie's arm. "I needs a favor. Can you help?" she whispered. "I needs some writin'." Why was she being so secretive about wanting something written? Whatever it was, helping her by putting words on paper was easy. "What do you need me to write?" Lottie pulled two sheets of paper from the stack in front of her.

Clement and Percy looked up from their papers to one another and then to Anna. She stared back at them, and they went right back to their writing.

"Miz Lottie, you need not raise the dead when you

talk." She closed her eyes as if she could see what Lottie needed to write. "Here what you say: 'Marcus and Jeremiah gots their tickets.'"

Lottie omitted the *s* and would explain that to Anna at another lesson. She printed the sentence neatly, folded the paper in fours, and handed it to Anna.

Anna pushed her hand back, "No, Miz Lottie, I needs you to gets it somewhere."

Whatever Lottie's expression was at that point, it amused Anna, who patted her hand and said, "It be fine. I trust you."

She glanced at the two men across from them, who must have written their names five times by then but diligently kept printing. "What is it?"

"All you gotta do is put it in the collection box at the Cathlik church."

Lottie felt herself breathe again. "Oh, Anna, that is easily handled."

"No. It gotta be there tonight, else it won't need to be there at all."

CHAPTER TWENTY - NINE

"WHEN ARE WE GOING TO TALK?" Gabriel was going to use guilt to hold Lottie to the gate and pray it would work. He did not know how much longer he could look into her eyes, chart her cheekbones and her lips, and not want to feel her soft cheeks brush against the palms of his hands as he gently brought her face to meet his.

Then again, he understood that reality with Lottie might never exist, because the only way they could be together would require them to be apart from everyone they knew. People who loved one another should not have to abandon the people who loved them. But all of it was supposition without his knowing Lottie's feelings and resolve, neither of which appeared to be important as he waited for her answer.

She tapped one hand on the basket and kept an eye on her house as if she expected someone to walk out. "I don't know. Do we need to decide right now? Grand-mère barely tolerates these trips to the homes each Sunday. The idea of us sitting alone somewhere, for all the city to see, would be such a severe violation of social etiquette that the marriage contract might be jeopardized. I'm surprised no one has reported us being in Woodlief's together."

"Together? There were at least a dozen other people in the shop. We were all 'together,' for that matter. Are you suggesting we breached social etiquette merely by being in the same place at the same time?"

"You know my grandmother would not see it that way." Lottie continued to fidget.

"You have been distracted since we left the home. Why?"

"This day...you have no idea." Lottie tried to explain. "I promise I will find a way and a time for us to talk."

Gabriel left, but Lottie's behavior continued to concern him.

***

LOTTIE HURRIED INSIDE, HOPING AGNES OR ABRAM would be able to accompany her to the church that night. The longer she spoke to Gabriel, the more difficult it became not to tell him about the favor Anna asked of her. If she included him, he would have wanted to walk with her. And if that happened, her grandmother would want the reason she and Gabriel needed to be at the church, together, and on and on and on.

She didn't see Agnes or her grandparents, but she heard music coming from the parlor. Removing her cape, gloves, and bonnet and leaving them on the dining table, she inched open the concealed doors between the two rooms. Her grandmother sat at the pianoforte and either ignored or did not hear the doors scraping open, because she continued playing. Grand-père played marble solitaire at the game table and quietly motioned Lottie over. He pulled out the chair next to him from the table and continued playing. He was four marbles away from winning and having just one single stone at the center of the mahogany board.

The three of them resembled a colored sketch in the *Lady's Book* by Louis Godey. Lottie marveled finding them looking so…so content. She had not seen her grandmother at the pianoforte for a long time. Maybe this was what she did when Lottie wasn't here. But why? With her eyes closed and her fingers moving on the keys, her grandmother's severe features softened. Like she did in the dressmaker's shop, Lottie glimpsed her not as a grandmother, but as a woman. But she braced herself for the inevitable crack in the facade. When the song ended, so would the emotions of the woman who played it.

When her grandmother played the last note, Lottie followed her grandfather's lead and applauded, with gentility, of course.

"That was lovely," her grandfather said. "And look"—he pointed to the board—"I have successfully completed my game." He stood and bowed. "Please, no ovation."

"You should play more often. Grand-père was right. It was beautiful," Lottie told her.

"Thank you, Charlotte," her grandmother said, and a smile almost broke through. "How was your visit?"

If Lottie could have squirmed as she sat in the upholstered chair, ten yards of fabric and four petticoats swelling over her, her grandparents might have witnessed her body shift. She couldn't reveal what she and Gabriel did in addition to being with the children, because she truly would be risking lives. But, still, she felt uncomfortable accounting for only half the time she and Gabriel were there.

"It's rewarding. Every week we're able to read to the children and play games with them, and they are truly appreciative of our time there." As she spoke, she realized not only that Grand-mère never asked, but she was hearing her own words for the first time. "At first, I thought I went to help them because I—we—had the means to provide food and clothes. Now, I think we're helping each other. When I look at those little girls, I know I could have been one of them except for the two of you. Having sapphire ear bobs or new gowns every season or a summer home can't buy a family or faith."

"Genevieve Charlotte, I do believe you've matured into a strong young woman right before our eyes." Grand-père kissed Lottie's forehead. "You are a treasure."

"Thank you, PaPa," Lottie whispered. Tonight's letter to her parents would preserve this time for the rest of her life.

Lottie thought about this morning and Madame Dumas telling her to ask her grandparents about Paul.

But she could not spoil this rare moment she had with them. Paul was not going to disappear before tomorrow. She could ask them before his visit. It would provide new information for her to think about while the four of them sweltered in silence.

Anna's note—that was her priority. Her grandparents decided to walk along the levee after supper. She needed Agnes or Abram to walk with her to the church. Lottie headed to their living quarters. *Please be home. Please be home. Please be home.* She knocked as she opened the door, already knowing she would find two empty rooms, rooms so small that raising the latch would have stirred Agnes. Sections of the whitewashed plaster peeled away from the four walls, leaving exposed red bricks like sores around the room. A mint-green chenille spread stretched across Lottie's castoff bed pushed against the far wall. The broken leg had been replaced with small boards nailed together and propped underneath to level the mattress. Opposite the bed was the small cypress armoire Lottie had had as a child. The only other furniture was a cane rocker, and next to it was a basket with quilting squares. Agnes called the other room their "necessary" room, because in it was a small fireplace used for warmth and for cooking, a two-burner stove, and their stand-up tub.

A stone's throw away, the LeClercs' home had four times as many rooms as people who lived there. All that space wasted because, as Lottie was told, slaves did not sleep in the same house as their owners. "It's just not proper," her grandmother insisted any time Lottie would ask. The answer never changed. One day, still young enough to wear her dresses well above her ankles, Lottie raised her voice and declared, "It's stupid." It was another night of no supper. Grand-mère refused to allow her granddaughter to be known as uncultured.

Lottie closed the door to their living quarters and laughed inwardly at the possibility of asking for Agnes and Abram as her wedding presents. With her new husband's money, she could buy their freedom and they could live in a house she could pay Monsieur Joubert to build. That would make for a lively discussion at Paul's next visit.

As she walked through the courtyard, it occurred to Lottie that her grandparents' leaving before Agnes arrived home actually worked out better for her delivering Anna's note. After returning from their levee stroll, Lottie could casually mention having gone to the church. So, now her prayer was for Agnes and Abram to arrive later, to want what she did not want before. It was times like these when Lottie wondered how man was made in God's image. Could God really be confused about what He should be praying for?

LOTTIE HAD STARTED READING *MANSFIELD PARK,* which she'd bought the week before with her grandfather, when her grandparents left. They invited her to join them, but she declined, telling them she was anxious to read the novel because she had heard so much about it. It was Gabriel who'd told her Alcee was reading it and he questioned whether she should, so, in truth, Lottie *had* been told a great deal about it. It just happened to be all from one person.

She didn't intend to lose herself in the book, but merely to distract herself from incessantly checking for any sign of Agnes. But then she discovered that Fanny, too, was essentially an orphan, cast off by her parents and living as a burden to her relatives. Lottie found herself reluctant to leave Fanny with her heartless aunt. Unlike Lottie, Fanny did not have a version of Agnes, someone who could comfort her. *Thank You, God, for my always being able to rely on Agnes. And I really want not to have a different prayer tomorrow, so would You send her home soon?*

Agnes and Abram arrived an entire chapter later, and when Lottie spotted them walking through the porte cochère, she gathered her dress well above her ankles and dashed out to meet them.

"Thank goodness you're home," she said and threw her arms around Agnes. "You too, Abram," she added as she released Agnes.

"Why you so happy I home?"

Agnes's suspicion shot right through those narrowed dark eyes of hers. She detected dishonesty like Henri detected milk, and neither one of them would discontinue their search until they found what they wanted.

"Because I need to go to the church, my grandparents are strolling along the levee, I can't go alone even though I am perfectly capable of it, so I need you to come with me."

"She talking faster den the wind kin blow," Agnes said to Abram. "Lemme go put this down, and I be back."

"I got it. You go now 'fore it gets too late. Dem gaslamps be hanging soon," said Abram as he took the bundle of what appeared to be clothes from Agnes.

"Your grandparents know you going to the church? And fo' what are you going? En you had better go inside for what-all you need. Out here, nothin' coverin' your arms."

Lottie gathered her cape, making sure Anna's note was still inside the pocket, her bonnet, and her gloves, and went to meet Agnes without one good excuse for why she needed to go.

"Why is we going to that church if you comin' out here with nothin'?"

Lottie contemplated that the same mouth she'd used for prayers earlier should not be the one to use for lies. But she also had a responsibility to Anna and the two people whose names were on that paper. "I have something to place in the collection box. A friend asked me, and I promised I would do it for her."

"And your grandmother don't say you kin do this tomorrow?"

Agnes was not making this easy.

"Well, no. But I can't do it tomorrow. And I know

Grand-mère would not mind, as long as I did not go alone."

"I know sure's my feet on this banquette, parts of this story missing somewhere. 'Less you got gold in that pocket, don't see why we gotta go now." She performed one of her extravagant Agnes sighs and followed it with mumblings.

Lottie walked to the central door of the cathedral, already feeling the weight of her promise lighten. She pulled the handle. Locked. She tried the other door. Locked. She tried the first door again. Locked. She pulled both handles. Still locked.

"Don't know why you 'spect church to be open at almost dark," said Agnes.

A rising tide of panic roiled through Lottie's body. "Not now, Agnes. Please. Not now." She buried her face in her hands, felt the warmth of her own breath, and willed herself to stay calm. The lives of two people, perhaps more, depended on her. Why didn't Anna ask Gabriel to do this? Why hadn't *she* asked Gabriel?

"Somebody coming to help, honey," Agnes said as she patted Lottie's arm.

Lottie looked up, and Agnes pointed behind her.

Gabriel asked, "What are you doing?"

"You don't have to ask me as if I'm attempting to trespass," snapped Lottie.

"It appears that way to people passing by," he said. "Good evening, Agnes."

That was when Lottie saw the stunning young woman from the opera waiting by the lamppost near the street. "What are you doing? How did you know I was here?"

"If you are that angry to find me here, I can easily leave. I didn't know you were here until Nathalie and I left the café. And until we came closer, I didn't realize the person shaking the church doors was you." He took a step backward. "It seemed someone might need help. If I'm mistaken, I apologize." He nodded toward Agnes. "Good to see you."

"Wait. I am sorry," Lottie said. "I promised someone I would place something in the church collection box. It must go in tonight."

Gabriel appeared confused. "Tonight? Why does—"

"Because it does. So can you help or not?"

"Father lives behind the cathedral. We might find him there."

As much as she wanted to, Lottie did not ignore Nathalie as she passed. Although Nathalie would not have been surprised to not be greeted by Lottie. Generally, white women did not recognize free women of color on the street. But Lottie gave her a polite smile. Gabriel told Nathalie, "Please, if you don't mind, wait. I will be back shortly."

Agnes stayed with Nathalie.

As they walked around the cathedral, Gabriel said, "What is this about, really? No one needs to donate to the collection box that desperately."

Lottie hesitated, then removed the folded note from

the pocket of her cape and showed it to him. "Anna said if this wasn't in by tonight, tomorrow would be too late."

He scanned the paper. "Why didn't you ask me to do this?"

"To place a sheet of paper in a collection box did not seem so difficult or dangerous a task at the time. Besides," said Lottie, taking the note back, "you obviously already had plans." After seeing Gabriel tonight, Lottie decided their expected talk might veer in a different direction.

"If you are referring to Nathalie, she was not a 'plan,'" he said. "She happened to be in the café when I went there after leaving you this afternoon."

Happened to be? However limited Lottie's personal romantic experience, she'd read a sufficient number of books to know that for women like Nathalie, coincidence required thoughtful planning.

They turned the corner onto Orleans Street, and Father François's sudden appearance saved Lottie from responding.

"Good evening, Father," said Gabriel. "May we ask a favor of you?"

The priest appeared frail in the folds of his long brown cassock, which was bound with a thick cord around his waist. His long nose and thin white hair and face narrowing to the point of his chin might have been severe except for his warm eyes and easy smile. "Yes, of course." He glanced from Gabriel to Lottie and back to Gabriel. "But I am on my way to visit a family whose child is ill. Depending on the nature of your favor, we may need to meet tomorrow."

Gabriel started to explain. "The favor is not for the two of us, except that—"

"I promised someone I would place something in the collection box, and the cathedral is locked," Lottie blurted. "I apologize for interrupting, but we do not want to delay your visit."

"Your understanding is appreciated. I am happy to help. If you would just give me what you needed to place, I will be sure that it is done."

Lottie's hand closed over the note. "But I promised I would do it myself."

Father François looked more amused than annoyed. "I can be trusted with your friend's donation."

"It's...it's not exactly a donation, and it has to be there tonight."

"In that case, you must trust me." He waited as a couple strolled by, exchanged greetings, and walked on. "I am not a stranger to these unusual donations."

Lottie looked at Gabriel. "Yes. I trust him," he told her.

Her hand trembled as she drew the note out of her pocket and placed it in Father's outstretched hand. He closed his fingers over the paper and tucked it into one of the folds of his cassock. Two lives. Lottie shuddered. *Oh, please God, let me not have trusted in vain.*

"I open the collection box daily. That paper was meant for me," said Father François. He clasped her still-shaking hands. "You do not need to fear. They will be safe."

CHAPTER THIRTY

L OTTIE CAME DOWN TO BREAKFAST and waited for one of her grandparents to question her about the night before, since they had arrived home first. The sour expression on her grandmother's face when she saw them concerned Lottie more for Agnes than for herself.

After announcing "Good morning" in her cheeriest of voices, Lottie poured herself coffee from the breakfront and took her seat at the table. She filled her bowl with grits and made a small crater in the middle, which she filled with a pat of molded butter that melted into a creamy yellow pool. She stirred the melted butter into her grits and added a slice of ham to her plate.

"We were quite surprised not to find you home last night after you declined our invitation to join us on the levee," said her grandmother, who looked at her husband and then at her granddaughter after the declaration.

She didn't ask the "where" question, which meant she had probably already spoken to Agnes. Lottie was sure Agnes would have told her grandmother the truth; she just wasn't sure how much of it. But years of being the subject of Grand-mère's inquisitions had taught her how to play this game. Lottie cut her ham and said, with the matter-of-factness of Madame Dumas, "Oh, I'm sure that did come as a surprise," and continued to eat.

Grand-père coughed several times into his napkin, and Grand-mère's coffee cup stopped, for a moment, midway to the saucer.

Her grandmother cleared her throat. "Charlotte, whatever do you mean?"

"Paul will be here again tonight, so it's obvious who the clear choice is. I want to know why. Why Paul Bastion? And please, please be honest with me. This city is too small to keep secrets."

"I don't know how you expect us to address this question when your grandfather and I have not been given time to discuss it."

The message Grand-mère transmitted was as loud as a steamboat's whistle. She didn't want Lottie to know the answer, or at least there was part of it she wanted to protect, but she couldn't without speaking to Grand-père first.

"Are you telling me that my grandparents have selected someone without knowing why? Or do you mean you cannot tell me without speaking to one another first?" Lottie's feigned astonishment signaled that she didn't believe her own questions.

"Marie, she has a right to know. The first people she should hear it from is us, not from gossip. Certainly not from Paul himself."

"I still do not believe this is the time. It is only Paul's

second visit. There may not be more, and then whatever the reason, it is no longer even significant."

"We both know, short of a miracle, one part of that will not change. I am going to tell her," Grand-père said.

He explained about the financial panic in 1837, how land prices had become inflated, people bought on speculation, and the bottom fell out. "People all over the country suffered, so we weren't the only ones hit hard by this. Your grandmother and I lost a significant amount of money, but we managed to hold onto this house and certain comforts to which we had become accustomed. Having a real-estate business was a nightmare. Land was overvalued and then, after the panic, wasn't worth half as much, but people borrowed on the inflated price."

"So even if you sold the property, you still owed the bank?"

"Exactly. Over the past four years, we found ways to muddle through. Then the yellow fever hit the city, and we had to climb out of that hole."

"Grand-père, I truly do not mean to be disrespectful, but I'm not understanding how Paul or his family is important."

"Sometimes your grandfather finds it difficult to simply state the facts. The truth is, we are on the verge of losing almost everything. Even Agnes and Abram. We have mortgaged our home and sold every piece of land except for one. It is a large swath of riverfront property. By the grace of God, we have been able to keep it."

"But you spent so much money on gowns and my

party. Why didn't you just tell me then?"

"We saved some money by having you share some of your classes; then we finally had to discontinue them. But a family with our background must have their daughter or, in our case, granddaughter, make a debut."

Grand-père continued, "Girls bring a dowry into the marriage, most often cash. That would not be possible for your grandmother and me. All we own is that one piece of land, and it would only be valuable to a person who truly wanted it. As your dowry, it would be a gift to the man marrying you. But we need a portion of that money to pull ourselves out of trouble.

"So, why Paul? His family wants that land for warehouses for their cotton, and they have shipbuilding plans. Other families were interested, but not nearly to the extent of the Bastions. The weekend of the plantation party, his father agreed to an option to buy the land, for which he has already paid. Then, as part of the wedding settlement, he will purchase the land and I will retain a sufficient share so as not to lose our home."

Lottie gave herself time to assemble the pieces of information into a frame, and when she did, the picture shocked her. All these weeks, she had tried to create meaning, understanding, from the wrong picture. She had been looking at herself. But it wasn't about her. It was about a piece of riverfront property. She couldn't help but laugh at her own foolishness and naïveté. What a *couillonne.*

HENRI ARRIVED, UNANNOUNCED AS USUAL, for Paul Bastion's second visit. Paul entered through the front door. Henri found a sliver of space to squeeze through in the open French doors of the dining room, and they both entered the parlor at the same time. Henri wasted no time in finding the woman he came to see and conquered thirteen yards and five feet of crimson velvet to claim her.

Paul cut a wide circle around Lottie on his way to the corner of the room and stared at the cat like he were a carcass. Henri seemed to understand and returned the glare then yawned before settling into his lounging position. Lottie suspected Paul would have yawned as well, given the opportunity.

Her grandparents were not yet in the room, so Lottie was unsure of the protocol in this situation. She had no recollection of Miss Leslie having a chapter on lap cats and courting etiquette, but she was certain it would be improper to abandon her guest in the parlor. She was equally certain that Grand-mère's expression when she entered would be one she hoped she could burn into her brain and access whenever she needed to laugh.

"Is it yours? The cat?" Paul's tone clearly indicated he hoped not, as he brushed the sleeves of his black frockcoat.

"No. I don't think he belongs to anyone in particular. He simply shows up," Lottie said, scratching behind

Henri's ears. "Sometimes he follows Madame Margaret Haguarty, the milk lady." But Paul had lost eye contact after the word "no."

"Good. I do not understand why anyone would want an animal in the house. It is entirely unsanitary."

Lottie wanted to say that not every animal in a house was four-legged but settled instead for, "I see." She heard a rustling of skirts and knew that her grandparents, entering from the dining room, would only see Paul and the waterfall of curls Agnes had arranged at the back of Lottie's head.

The polite greetings ended, and Lottie prepared her brain to imprint her grandmother's expression when she saw Henri in her lap, who was now amusing himself by batting the lace on Lottie's cuffs when she moved her hands.

She was horrified. Loud gasp, hand over mouth, wide-eyed horrified. And episodes of chalk-white and strawberry-red flushing from her neck to her forehead.

"Charlotte, what is that creature… You must dispose of it immediately." Grand-mère turned to Paul and covered him with effusive apologies before turning back to Lottie. "How did it—never mind. Please." She waved her closed fan toward the back of the house. "Deliver it outside. Then have Agnes bring you fresh water for your hands."

Grand-père guided her to a chair. "You look flushed. Calm yourself."

"I waited for you so as not to be rude to Monsieur

Bastion by leaving him solitary in the parlor. Of course I never intended for Henri to join us this afternoon," said Lottie. She gently untangled her lace from Henri's claws, else Grand-mère would need a fainting couch. Cradling Henri in her arms, she excused herself and walked to the gallery. "Thank you for making this more bearable," she whispered, gently setting him down outside.

Agnes came from the kitchen, looked at Henri, then at Lottie, and said just low enough for Lottie to hear, "Now, you got to tell me that story later. Your grandmother done passed out?"

Lottie laughed. "No, unless she did after I left."

"Come on. Let Agnes get all those Henri hairs off this gown. Then I'll bring in the tea and coffee."

"Take care of everything else," Lottie said, sweeping her palms over the lap of her skirt. "Perfect." She actually appreciated learning that Paul cared more about their land than he did about her. It freed her from attempting to win his favor. She knew what he thought of her. Nothing.

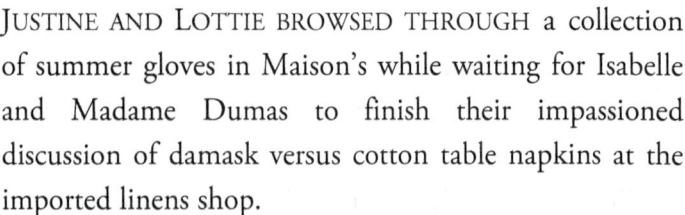

JUSTINE AND LOTTIE BROWSED THROUGH a collection of summer gloves in Maison's while waiting for Isabelle and Madame Dumas to finish their impassioned discussion of damask versus cotton table napkins at the imported linens shop.

"Why didn't you ask about Paul's placée? I thought that would be most important," Justine said as she held up a pair of delicate white-lace gloves.

"Lovely." Lottie slipped her hand into one. It would have fit had her fingers been one knuckle shorter. She handed the glove back to Justine. "I almost asked. But Grand-mère has taught me well. If they do know, then what cause do they have for not revealing it?" Lottie shrugged her shoulders. "So I will hold it. I don't doubt the time will come when it might be useful."

"Red gloves, Justine? You will terrify your nieces and nephew, who will think your hands are bleeding." Isabelle and her mother appeared, with Ruthie's husband Laurent following and holding an assortment of boxes.

"In that case, I may indeed want to have a pair," Justine said, turning her hands as if waving. "What do you think, Mother?"

"I think you and your sister behave like children, those red gloves are dreadful, people will think you a classless American wearing them, and Laurent is taking these packages home. Do you have any?"

"No. Lottie and I have nothing to add to your burden, Laurent."

Tall and muscular, Laurent's dark-honey skin, Romanesque nose, and square chin were not what people reacted to the first time they met him. His eyes were undeniably blue and an untold story. He never explained, and no one ever asked.

Laurent, probably not much older than Justine, responded, "Why, thank you, Miz Justine."

"Why do you always speak that way to her?" Isabelle

asked.

"Because she expects me to. I daresay it makes her more comfort-able than my white voice."

"You're probably right," Isabelle said. "Mother and I want to take the girls to Antoine's for lunch. Would you pick us up from there in about two hours?"

"Certainly. And please forgive me, Mademoiselle LeClerc, for not greeting you sooner. I will see you ladies in two hours."

As they left Maison's, Justine said to Lottie, "And that's exactly why you and Gabriel Girod need to abandon this idea that you could have a life together. Goodness, in whose world would you expect your children to live? He seems to spend more time with Nathalie. That's the talk the two of you need to have. You just need to let him go."

Lottie concentrated on Madame Dumas's braided hair as she walked in front of them, afraid that if she looked at Justine, she might share with her exactly how she felt. She remembered what Laurent had said about Justine's expectations. Another lesson learned. "Thank you for your advice," she said.

Justine smiled. "I just want to help."

CHAPTER THIRTY-ONE

"ROSETTE WANTS THESE AWNINGS TO COME out from the building on three sides, but I think we're going to have to remeasure that space next to the banquette. It doesn't seem wide enough to accommodate what she wants. What do you think?" Joseph showed Gabriel the plans for the café addition and the drawing of the original footprint.

"I marked off the property lines yesterday, and I think I have an idea that might work," said Gabriel. He and Joseph met to discuss a few changes his mother wanted to make, though Joseph warned him to expect changes to the changes. "It's one part of this business that can keep a man awake at night. Just when you think you've nailed it down, up it comes again." The more time Gabriel spent with Joseph, the more he admired and respected him. Since the day he accompanied Joseph to the LeClercs' real-estate office, Gabriel had been impressed with his honesty.

Joseph seemed to value Gabriel's opinion, telling him he had a good eye for detail and design. He began to include Gabriel in more of his work, but Gabriel's first responsibility was to Rosette and he didn't want to leave her, even when she assured him she'd be fine on her own. Recently, one of those "fine on her own" days proved to be busier than she had anticipated. But that day resulted in an outcome none of them anticipated.

Nathalie and Serafina were there for breakfast, and when Nathalie saw that Rosette could not handle her many customers, she put an apron over her new ecru velvet-and-silk gown, waited on customers, and worked in the kitchen frying or making coffee or warming milk or washing dishes. Her disarming personality compensated for what she didn't know. When a table of six asked what they owed, Rosette said she cringed when she heard Nathalie say, "I have no idea. Why don't you just pay what you think you should?" When she brought the money to Rosette, they had paid almost three times what Rosette would have charged. Nathalie said, "That means your prices are too low."

By the end of the day, Nathalie's feet throbbed and so did the three fingers she'd burned because, she explained, the only time she'd been around fire was to warm her hands. She joked that her dress was like giraffe skin because of the dark, scattered coffee splotches. And where there wasn't coffee, there were patches and trails of powdered sugar. She refused to allow Rosette to pay her, but wanted to know when she could work again.

The evening Gabriel saw Lottie attempting to get into the cathedral, he and Rosette and Nathalie had met and set up a schedule that would free him to work more with Joseph. Nathalie still refused to be paid. "I don't need the money, and if you pay me, then it's"—she wrinkled her nose—"a job. I don't want a job. Could you take the money you would pay me and give it away? I'd feel so much better if you did."

The next day, Joseph joined the Girods for dinner. Gabriel told him and Rosette that Nathalie was the person he would have least expected to solve his problem.

"When God means for something to happen, He finds a way," Rosette said…except that she was staring at Joseph and not Gabriel.

Gabriel wanted to ask if it meant that, if there was no way for something to happen, was that a sign God didn't mean it to?

"UNTIL I STARTED WORKING WITH YOU, a hardware store would never have been a place in which I would choose to spend time. But each shelf is one surprise after another," remarked Gabriel as he picked through an assortment of latches, strap hinges, and pulls with handles at Armstrong's Hardware.

"You might need to consider investing in a set of work clothes even for the days we aren't at the job sites. Most of the stores do not cater to gentlemen dressed in their morning frock coats," Joseph said, pointing to the accumulation of dust on the sleeves and vest of Gabriel's coat.

"Old habits do not break easily. Your advice is well-taken, and I am certain Rosette will appreciate not having to beat my coats as if they are rugs."

Joseph purchased five dozen hooks to secure batten doors and the same number of wrought-iron double ram's horn hinges for French and paneled doors. He wrote down the address of the job site for the delivery and handed it to Armstrong. "Could you make sure these are delivered by tomorrow?"

"Of course, Monsieur Joubert." Armstrong whistled to a younger version of himself perched on a barrel and cleaning his fingernails with a knife. "William, come get this order ready."

His son folded the knife closed with one hand and slid off the barrel with the speed of thick molasses. "If I had hair, half this weight, and all my teeth, I wouldn't be holding down a barrel waiting for the next whistle. Guess it's my fault for not making my son work as hard to feed himself as I had to." He handed Joseph the invoice. "Don't let that happen to him," he said, pointing to Gabriel. Joseph just smiled and nodded.

As they left the store, Gabriel said, "You didn't correct Armstrong when he mistook me for your son."

"No, I didn't mind him thinking that at all. Though he must be wondering how you came to be so light with me as your father," Joseph said. "Wait. Gabriel. I just realized how that must have sounded. I didn't mean to suggest any disrespect to your father. Or to you. I shouldn't assume."

"No one has ever recognized me, mistaken or not, for

anyone's son before today." So that was the feeling he'd missed all those years. Gabriel wanted to resent Jean Noel for having deprived him of a father–son relationship. But sons of placées, even when their fathers had no other biological children, were rarely acknowledged. Joseph had given him what his own father could not. Recognition.

GABRIEL AND JOSEPH STOPPED SAWING when they saw Nathalie step behind the kitchen and move to where they were framing the addition. A shower of fine white dust covered almost every part of her gown that her apron didn't.

"Have you checked the powdered-sugar expenses since she started working for your mother?" Joseph smiled and shook his head.

"No. Rosette said anyone who wonders what it means to beat the devil out of something needs to watch Nathalie with a shaker and a plate of beignets," said Gabriel. "She said she hates to spoil her fun, and it entertains the customers."

"You two are laughing at me, aren't you?" Since Nathalie laughed herself when she asked them, the men figured they were safe in agreeing with her. "Customers haven't complained about the new prices. They think that little mountain of sugar is lagniappe. Just you wait."

"Did you need to tell us something?" Gabriel asked, knowing she would not have bothered them outside otherwise.

"Oh, yes. Gabriel, you have visitors. Charlotte and her friend, the one who talks constantly—Justine. Yes. Do you want them to meet you out here?"

"Tell them I'll be right in."

"I already did. They're having coffee." She winked and went back inside.

Joseph wiped his face with his handkerchief. "Some man is going to have his hands full, taking care of her."

"And it's not going to be me," Gabriel said as he rolled down his sleeves and cuffed them at the wrist.

"Does she know that?" Joseph wiped sawdust off his shirt and brown cotton work pants.

"Why wouldn't she? I didn't think it was ever an issue," said Gabriel. He had always considered Nathalie a friend. Their discussions and actions had never ventured beyond that relationship.

"I wouldn't be too sure," Joseph warned. "I might as well take a break while you do. I'm sure your mother misses me."

Gabriel saw Lottie in one of those unguarded moments before she knew he was in the room. Her hair had been tightly drawn back on each side of her face but released in a thick sea of curls that flowed past the nape of her neck. The teardrop emerald hanging from her pearl choker nestled itself in the hollow of her throat. He outlined her face with his eyes and in that moment knew he could not watch her become the wife of Paul Bastion. She scanned the café, and when her eyes found him, his heart shattered.

He threaded his way through the tables, pausing to greet a regular customer or friend as he went. When he reached Lottie and Justine, he first apologized for and then explained his disheveled appearance. "I did not expect company," he said, "but I am glad you are here."

"Justine and I planned to spend time this evening strolling along the levee since the winter has not seemed nearly so angry the past few days. Agnes and Abram will be with us, of course. I thought, if you were free—"

"Sometimes I do not know why she bumbles when you are around. Or maybe I do. She is trying to tell you that the two of you could meet and have that talk. I'm only going to lend legitimacy to the event. That, and to avoid being asked to do Ruthie's chores since she is so ready to deliver that child she needs help to stand once she's seated. I'm even being told to flatten my own mattress and fill my own pitcher for my bedroom and help with meals. My mother and Isabelle are going to ruin that girl if they continue to treat her as if she is white."

In the time Justine took to realize what she had said and to whom, Gabriel had moved past speechless. "Yes, what an outrage, to treat a slave as if she is human."

He left after he told Lottie that if he finished in time, he would meet her in the evening. But for the Justines of society, he and Lottie might have a chance at the life they wanted.

GABRIEL PUSHED THE SAW THROUGH the boards with a vengeance as he repeated to Joseph what Justine had told him and Lottie.

"I know you've met your share of Justines through the years, and you already know you've not met the last. We may detest what she says, but she's at least letting you know what she thinks. As far as I'm concerned, the people who think it and never say it are sometimes more dangerous. Most of them already know that the Bible says we're all God's creation. Sometimes I wish the verse would have ended with 'we're just different colors.'" Joseph handed Gabriel a hammer and took over sawing. "But Justine isn't really the person we ought to be talking about. What are you going to do about Lottie?"

"Lottie? How do you know anything about Lottie?"

"The day we went to her grandfather's office, the two of you laid eyes on each other like you'd just seen water after being in the desert for weeks. I started paying attention after that. Same way nobody had to tell you how I feel about Rosette." Joseph stopped, got a long nail, placed it into the opening he'd already cut so it wouldn't close in on his saw, and went back to cutting the wood. "You don't have many options, though I'm sure you figured that out already."

"One thing I've figured out is, it's one thing to swing a hammer. Making the nail go in straight is another."

"Practice. It's all practice. Stop focusing on the

hammer; focus on the nail head. That's why you're getting all those sideways swings. I'm surprised you haven't flattened a few fingers," Joseph observed.

"Maybe that's my problem with Lottie too—the wrong focus. It's not enough just to want to be together. If we're serious, then we both know it can't happen here. And that's what we have to focus on. But I don't know what she's willing to do to make that happen."

"Lottie may not either. Sometimes people learn what they're willing to sacrifice only when life doesn't require it of them anymore. If you're lucky, she won't be one of those people."

CHAPTER THIRTY - TWO

A NEW ORLEANS EVENING SUN coaxed people out of their houses to revel in the gift of a mild winter day. Some families abandoned strolling in favor of watching their chubby-legged children run in wide circles, in the hopes that they would fall fast asleep once they reached home. Mothers with the foresight to wear fewer petticoats and dresses more ready to be cut down than worn found it possible to arrange themselves appropriately and sit on the hard, dry ground. When a steamboat blasted its giant trumpet and belched inky, smoky notes, the delighted children celebrated with a symphony of squeals, giggles, and applause. Later, carried onward by the wind, a sprinkling of soot rested on collars and capes and gowns.

The scent in the fresh air depended on the number of ships and their cargo. Hogsheads of sugar and tobacco, molasses and flour, and so many bales of cotton they seemed as endless as the Mississippi River waited to be loaded or had been off-loaded. Lottie breathed in pineapple-fragrant air as far down as her corset would allow. She envied the little girls who bent and stretched so effortlessly, their soft bodies not held prisoner by laces and whalebones. Even Alcee, whom Gabriel had invited along, rarely bothered with uncomfortable underpinnings. But looking at her as she walked with Justine ahead of them, Lottie could see the woman in Alcee pushing out the little girl.

"She is truly repentant. I know she wants to apologize," said Lottie about Justine's remark at the café. "And one day, one of us might need to grant forgiveness before we seek it."

"You're beginning to sound like Rosette, which is not conducive to what I want to say. I intended to talk to Justine later. Anything about Agnes, Abram, or Alcee we need to address?"

"Nothing," she said. "But I want to talk to you first." Lottie wished she had pockets so he wouldn't see her fidgeting with her hands. She intertwined her fingers and her hands bounced with the movement of her skirt as she walked. A long stretch of ground lay ahead, so she would have time to finish. "I'm not exactly sure when it happened—when I crossed from 'Gabriel as friend' to 'Gabriel as more than friend.' I do know there was one day in particular when I could no longer ignore or deny those feelings. When you smiled, all I could think about was what your lips would feel like on my forehead, my cheeks, my own lips. How it would feel to stand so close to you and be held so tightly and be kissed so deeply. I feared you could read my mind. And I feared you couldn't."

Justine stopped and pointed ahead. "Alcee and I are going to get a lemonade. Would you like one?"

They both said no, and when they closed the distance between the two girls, Alcee whispered she could convince Abram and Agnes to stay with them. "You two keep walking and don't turn around."

"That sounds dire, Alcee. Biblically dire," Lottie whispered back.

Lottie and Gabriel continued to walk and were only steps away when Alcee let out a high-pitched mewl. "Justine, I have to stop. My ankle must be shattered." Then, within moments, "Agnes, how could you leave me...."

"We missed her first theatrical performance in front of an audience," Gabriel said. "You were talking about my lips on yours." He smiled.

Lottie sidestepped a low spot but her voluminous skirt did not, and the weight of it started to pull her to the ground. She emitted a noise that sounded more like Isabelle's child, but Gabriel's arm encircled her waist and his other hand held her arm before she fully embarrassed herself by tumbling down the levee.

"You did that on purpose, didn't you?" he whispered in her ear before he released her.

Lottie smiled. "No. But I would be happy if you wanted an encore."

"Continue," Gabriel said.

If only I did not have to. She wished the memories of this day would end here. "Before and even after my party, I allowed myself the luxury of imagining a life with you. Each possibility ended in having to leave the city. That terrified me, until I thought of a life without you. That is when I knew I had the courage to leave."

"That is exactly what I came to tell you," he said.

His fingertips on her face were like feathers, moving from her eyes to her cheeks to her chin. He kissed her forehead. He was so close, she felt him breathe. And with every ounce of strength she could pull from her heart, she placed her hand on his lips. "Stop. I wasn't finished."

She explained everything her grandparents had told her, what they would lose if the marriage didn't happen. "I can't walk away, knowing what the consequences would be for them. You wouldn't want to be with me, because I wouldn't want to be with myself."

"I…I can't believe you are telling me that you will marry a man you don't love so your grandparents can sell a piece of land and make money from it. From you."

"Why does that surprise you? Look at the marriages among my friends. Plantations, business partners, cash, stocks…they are arranged mergers. And my grandparents are not earning a profit. I am making it possible for them to keep their home," Lottie said. "What would happen to Agnes and Abram if they couldn't?"

"So, that is it, then?"

"You have been making a sacrifice for your family ever since you chose not to go to Paris to stay here and help your mother. I at least thought you would understand that much."

"Except that the decision to choose Paris never happened for me in the way that it was meant. What I sacrificed was an immediate education, and it was fully my decision. Rosette supported me either way. It's not the same, Lottie."

"I'm sorry. I'm so sorry. But they are my grandparents. They raised me, and now they need me."

"I'm sorry too. You know about his other marriage, don't you? And that she is with child?" Gabriel's tone was harsh, unfamiliar.

"If I had not known before, that was a cruel way to tell me."

Gabriel stopped out of hearing range of everyone waiting for them. "Please do not expect me to understand that the woman I love will marry a man whom she does not love and who probably does not love her. Bartering herself for a piece of land." He looked at her, the sadness in his eyes belying the coldness in his voice. "I do not want you to come with me on Sunday. Or any Sunday thereafter. I hope you understand."

"HONEY CHILE, YOU NEED TO WAKE up."

Lottie heard the scrape of the draperies, which meant her room would be pulsing with sunshine and, when Agnes opened her French doors, cold. Still, she didn't move. She didn't even remember how she came to be in bed. Gabriel walking away and Agnes's voice, but nothing in between.

"You already missed breakfast, and if you get up now, you might make it to lunch. If you don't fall over all dis you left on the floor before you git out of your room."

Agnes must have been hanging her clothes, judging by the creaking of the armoire doors.

"What you want to wear today? How 'bout dis yellow one? Brighten you up."

"Please leave me alone, Agnes. I am not getting up, and I am not wearing that horrid yellow dress. And when I do wake up, I will find my scissors and make yellow shreds of it." Lottie felt the mattress tilt. Agnes sat close enough to unpin the mess of curls at the back of Lottie's head. When she had freed every curl, Agnes finger-combed Lottie's hair, stretching it across the other pillow.

Her hand felt tender and soft and kind. Lottie didn't want to feel that. She wanted to stay empty.

She rolled toward Agnes, placed her head in her lap, and shook the bed with her sobs.

"You go on and cry. You feel better getting it out. But you just remember, Genevieve Charlotte, Jesus always got a way."

"SORRY I'M LATE." GABRIEL REMOVED his hat, gloves, and coat. Then he walked outside, grabbed the hammer and a nail, and came back in. Still holding everything he'd taken off, he pounded a nail into the wall then took the hammer back outside. Reentering the café, he shoved his gloves into his coat then hung his coat with his hat over it on the nail he'd just hammered.

Rosette and Nathalie watched him as if he were a one-man play and they stood waiting for the second act. Gabriel poured his own coffee and sat on the stool, and the two women still looked at him as if he had gone bald overnight. "What?"

"I'm not sure. You look familiar, but you aren't acting familiar. You're so far away, you might as well be with André in Paris," Rosette said, not taking her eyes off him.

"Interesting you said that about André. I've been thinking maybe I need to finally do that. Go to Paris for school, that is."

Nathalie tied on her apron. "I'm going to find something to do in there," she announced and pointed to the café. "You two may continue your conversation without me."

"You've been thinking about this? For how long?" Rosette took out the flour, sugar, eggs, and spices she needed to make the calas, setting everything down as if a noise might frighten Gabriel away. She found the basket she had brought from home. She had cooked the rice yesterday and left it out overnight so that it would be cold today.

"I grew up thinking about it, remember? Then it didn't happen. And I thought I needed to stay here to help you, which I did. But you have Joseph and Nathalie now. So I'd feel better about leaving."

"And when do you plan for this leaving to happen?" Rosette worked the rice with her hands to break up any clumps then started adding all the dry ingredients.

"I don't have any definite plans yet. There's a great deal to consider: which school, the tuition, the cost of getting there, finding a place to live, a job…. I need to write André and get as many questions answered as possible."

"Certainly." She added the eggs and vanilla and started mixing. She handed Gabriel a few grains of rice she'd kept out of the mix. "Here, test that oil for me."

Gabriel dropped a grain of rice in the hot oil, but it floated lazily to the top instead of popping right up and starting to sizzle. "Not yet. Maybe another minute or two."

"I need to ask Nathalie about coming in tomorrow. Would you please watch over the oil for just a minute?"

"Yes. I will call you when it's ready."

The conversation with Rosette had gone so much better than he'd expected. He heard the caution, maybe skepticism, in her voice. He understood how surprising this announcement was to her. It was to him as well.

Gabriel dropped in another grain of rice. Almost the right temperature. Like Rosette, he had learned that being impatient and rushing the oil produced calas that no one would purchase, much less eat.

He had awoken early this morning. After yesterday's talk on the levee, he knew his life had to change. He could not live in the city when Charlotte LeClerc would become Madame Bastion. But he determined that leaving New Orleans had to be about what he wanted, not what he wanted to run away from. For over fifteen years, he'd awakened in the same garçonnière, gazed out the same window to see the same rooftops, looked over the same courtyard, and looked over the same life. It occurred to him this morning, when he was capable of more rational thought, that what had happened with Charlotte forced him to examine his life just when he needed to. Perhaps, in its own way, it was a blessing.

Gabriel dropped in the next grain, and it burst through to the top with just the right sizzle.

When it was ready, it was obvious. He just had to wait for that one right moment.

CHAPTER THIRTY-THREE

March 1841

Dear Mama and Papa,

I have not written for days, and I am loath to write now, because I do not want to compose with my own hand how wretchedly miserable I am.

Though I cooperated with all that my grandparents asked of me in the coming-out party, I allowed myself to nurture the dream of being with Gabriel. How very, very childish.

It must be sufficient, for today, for me to reveal that there is no longer a future for me with Gabriel. I contemplated the possibilities, recognizing what having a life with Gabriel would mean. What we would both be required to sacrifice. I wonder now if I would have been as willing to leave if you were here instead of Grand-mère and Grand-père. Could I have endured, knowing the disappointment I would have caused you?

But it matters not now. My grandparents need me to do what generations have done before me.

Why did I ever think I could escape what was expected of me as the daughter of a wealthy Creole family whose name and status mattered in the city?

Oh, what I would give to be poor.

My love and affection,
Genevieve Charlotte

———

LOTTIE TOLERATED PAUL'S THIRD VISIT. As validation of his utter disregard for her he displayed not a whit of consternation observing the shell of the woman soon to be his wife. If he noted that the dull-eyed, slack-faced young woman who arranged herself in the upholstered chair seemed to be different, it was not obvious in the careful examination of his fingernails or the continued straightening of his ascot.

Before his sentence with her expired, he invited her and her grandparents to attend the opera with the Bastion family, who had a box at the opulent St. Charles theatre. The invitation was quite a coup for her grandmother, who was among the last of her friends to claim having viewed the lavishly appointed theatre. Grand-mère prated on about the chandelier, which even enticed Lottie to divert her attention long enough to hear its description. Made of over twenty-three thousand crystal prisms, the twelve-foot-high, thirty-foot-wide chandelier was lit by almost two hundred gas jets. Little wonder why the St. Charles cost over 350,000 dollars to construct.

The discussion of Paul's placée or her being with child no longer held any significance. Being a protector made him like most rich Creole men his age, so his having a left-handed marriage shocked no one. With Gabriel out of her life, Lottie now hoped that he wouldn't dismiss his placée, when she did become Paul's wife. It would relieve her of the burden of expecting or providing an emotional attachment. And perhaps a physical one as well.

After Paul finally escaped, Lottie picked up *Mansfield Park,* opened the French doors of her bedroom, and sat outside to read. The same marchande who'd asked her to purchase a nosegay passed on the street, except this afternoon her tray held food, perhaps figs or nougats or the popcorn made with brown sugar. Only a few people traipsed back and forth. Most were probably napping or recovering from their afternoon meal. The Carnival days were approaching, though, and revelers leaving early, coming home late, and in all manner of inebriation and exhaustion would litter the streets.

Lottie opened her novel to read about the loathsome Henry Crawford's relentless pursuit of Fanny and was vexed by the arrogance of a man who sought to entertain himself by manipulating a woman's affection and pretending to care about her. Was Paul's one admirable quality his honesty in not pretending to care for Lottie? Or, perhaps, was that more evidence of his selfishness? She commended Fanny for refusing Mr. Crawford, as incomprehensible as the choice was to Fanny's relations, and choosing instead to marry for love. Lottie closed the book with a sigh, wishing her own story could turn out as happily as Fanny's.

In the coming weeks, after Paul's father and her grandfather negotiated the marriage contract, the formal engagement would be announced, which meant Paul could visit whenever he wanted. Lottie didn't expect that to be often.

She didn't want to think about anything or anyone beyond that.

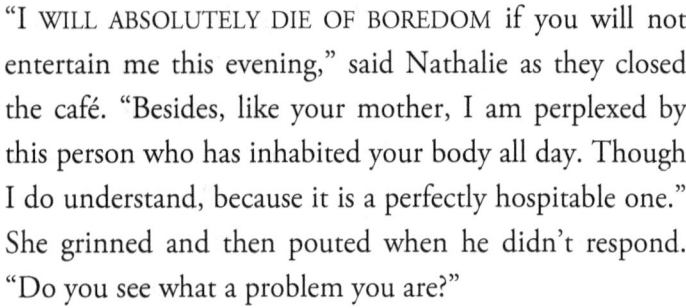

"I WILL ABSOLUTELY DIE OF BOREDOM if you will not entertain me this evening," said Nathalie as they closed the café. "Besides, like your mother, I am perplexed by this person who has inhabited your body all day. Though I do understand, because it is a perfectly hospitable one." She grinned and then pouted when he didn't respond. "Do you see what a problem you are?"

Nathalie almost always amused Gabriel, as she did now, but she required a great deal of attention. She was not the person anyone would think to invite for a quiet stroll. A woman unafraid to express and sometimes demand what she wanted both terrified and outraged most men and even some women. Having known her since they were both too young to realize they straddled the world they lived in, Gabriel found her harmless. And he admired her determination, though she loved her mother, not to subject herself to quadroon balls, where she would be ogled by men and ultimately signed over to one who promised to care for her. Nathalie was her father's daughter from his placée. His wife gave him sons. He refused to allow his only daughter to be parceled out on a dance floor. Fortunately for him and his daughter, he made money in the sugar industry faster than she could spend it. And that wealth enabled her to flaunt the conventions of society that expected so much and yet so little from women.

"Can you postpone your death by one day?" He asked for no other reason than to put more time between his pain and the person he hoped he could be: the person who had learned to live without Lottie. Gabriel didn't want Nathalie knocking down new walls.

He set the last stool on top of the table so the floors could be mopped when Rosette opened in the morning. She had left early to pick up Alcee to be home in time to meet Joseph, who wanted to stake out the footprint for the addition to the house.

"What if we just go to Lafayette Square? It's not far, it's a lovely evening, and you need the company of someone with a sense of humor."

Nathalie waited for his response. Her brown eyes, wide in anticipation, a delicate smile… She was beautiful. And yet, she wasn't Charlotte. But perhaps that, too, could change.

"You win. Let me not be responsible for your demise."

LAFAYETTE SQUARE IN THE EARLY EVENING hummed with children and their nannies, both relishing a few more precious minutes of playtime but for entirely different reasons. With the hanging of the gaslamps and the dusky glow of the moon, the humming ceased and the tempo ebbed and flowed based on the intensity of the latest political discussions, the scattered lone musician playing to the stars, and the couples who either whispered or softly squabbled.

"I don't want to talk about it," Gabriel told Nathalie, though she had not broached the subject of Lottie at all. He didn't want it lingering like an unwelcomed guest in the corners of their conversations.

"Well, I'm not going to ask anything specifically about her. But I do want to tell you a story that my mother shared this past weekend.

Nathalie told him that her mother, her two aunts, and her grandmother went to Antoine's for lunch on Saturday. One of her aunts pointed to a nearby table and said that one of the young women there reminded her of someone who once lived near her. "In fact," Nathalie said, "my mother said Tante Louise used the words 'startling' about how much they resembled each another. My aunt told them she hadn't seen the woman for years and heard rumors that she'd left the country, then rumors she'd died. She never found out for sure, but she would recognize Mignon anywhere."

Gabriel continued to gaze vacantly.

"She was pointing to Charlotte," Nathalie said.

Gabriel shrugged. "Yes, that is an interesting story."

Nathalie tugged on the sleeve of his frock coat. "I'm not sure you're understanding what is truly interesting about this story. My tante Louise is not white. Neither was Mignon. They were both placées."

———— ❧ ————

GABRIEL SLAMMED THE FRONT DOOR, the tremor pitching a ceramic vase from the mantel to the floor, which landed on the carpet next to the framed portrait of his grandmother that had slid down the wall.

Rosette, her back to him, screamed for Joseph. Gabriel heard the hard scraping of wood against wood as Joseph pushed away from the table. His mother spun around, her hands cupped over her mouth. Shifting his eyes to the dining room, Gabriel saw a flash of relief on Joseph's face as he realized who had walked into the house.

"Tell me. Tell me what you know about Lottie's mother." The words came out in huffs of breath. He had run the entire way home. He hadn't bothered to rent a hansom cab. He could outrun one, and he did.

"What happened?" She looked him over as if expecting to find an open wound. "You need to calm yourself. Sit." She patted the chair's back and called to Joseph to bring Gabriel something to drink.

"I don't want to sit. I don't want to drink." He

pulled off his frock coat and tossed it onto the sofa. Sweat still trickled down his back despite the cool night air. "I want the truth, and I know you have it. I can see it in your eyes."

Joseph handed him a glass, but Gabriel shook his head. "No, thank you. Not yet." His mother had shown no confusion and no denial.

"Not now, Gabriel. Please, not now." Her voice was so low that he had to step closer to hear her. She was on the verge of crying. He heard it in her voice and saw it in her eyes, but he didn't care. She could tell him through the tears.

"It has to be now. I didn't run here for you to tell me later." Gabriel raised his voice with each word. Joseph moved a step in. She moved two steps back. Chess. They were playing a human game of chess.

"You don't understand. I can't."

He hung his head. His hands were still clenched. He felt that if he opened them, his blood would stream out through his fingers and puddle at his feet. Nothing in his brain made sense. Then came the slow drag of a chair again and a voice.

"Because of me. Because I'm here."

Serafina stood near Joseph, biting her lower lip, her head moving from Gabriel to his mother.

Another pawn.

GABRIEL SAT, FINALLY, WIPED HIS FACE AND NECK with

his ascot, and pushed the wet fringes of his hair off his forehead. He finished the orange water Joseph had prepared. Serafina, Joseph, Gabriel, even Alcee, who had dashed into the dining room, she told them later, because she thought a tree had fallen on the house— Rosette told them all.

"Her name was Mignon DuFossat. I don't need to describe her… just imagine Lottie's face. Mignon and her mother had moved to the neighborhood sometime during the months I was pregnant, and since I spent almost all my time off my feet, we didn't meet until after Gabriel was born." She paused to look at her son. "You were actually the reason we met," she said softly. "In addition to having more servants than I thought I needed, Jean Noel insisted on my having a nursemaid. She wanted to do everything for Gabriel. I almost had to beg to tend to my own child."

"Jean Noel was leaving one day, and I had bundled Gabriel for the stroller, intending to walk after he was gone. Zulime, the nursemaid, tried to walk out the door with the baby, and I wanted to strike her." An assortment of soft laughter interrupted her. "No, really I did. I called Jean Noel's name—he'd only taken a few steps— and told him I wanted to stroll my own child and Zulime wasn't allowing it. Not knowing what a wench she had been the previous week, he told me he didn't see any harm in letting her do that. It all ended with Zulime leaving with your father."

"Good for you," Joseph said, and he clapped a few

times as if she had just won a prize fight.

Rosette rewarded him with a smile. She continued, "In the meantime, Mignon heard the noise and came outside, and when I walked by her house, she introduced herself. Fawned over Gabriel, and became a fast friend after that. She hadn't attended a ball yet, but she always had this notion that when she did, she would find someone she loved. I explained it didn't work that way. She insisted it could. The first ball was a disaster. She caused all sorts of trouble when a man she didn't like approached her mother. I think she turned over a table. Of course, he left. Her mother warned her if there was no contract at the second ball, she would sign her over to the asylum."

"Asylum? The insane asylum? Her mother didn't mean that, did she?" Alcee asked.

"I wouldn't doubt it, but it didn't matter. She met Charles LeClerc that night, and they were besotted with one another. We didn't see each other as much after he built her house, but we still met enough for me to know he wasn't a man she had to learn to love. I didn't think it possible for her to be prettier than she already was, but if you could have seen her face when he walked into a room…like someone lit a thousand candles at one time. And when he looked at her…" She paused, as if she had to bring herself back from decades ago. "You almost had to turn away because you felt like an intruder.

"They wanted to marry. I don't need to say much more than the LeClercs thought him crazy, told him to come back when he was brought to his senses. They went to Paris, and they married there. Mignon and I exchanged a few letters, but you know how long it all takes. I had written her to tell her that her mother had died of the fever, and a few days later a letter came from her saying they were coming home. They wanted their daughter to meet her grandparents. She asked if I would meet them when they landed. They wanted to stay here, not just arrive unannounced on the LeClercs' doorstep. Charles planned to go there first."

She looked at Gabriel, breathed deeply, and continued. "They didn't know how bad the yellow fever was, and by the time I knew they were coming, it was too late to tell them. That year was so awful. Dead bodies everywhere. They couldn't bury them fast enough. People tied stones to corpses and threw them into the river. Businesses were closed. Some of the more rank bodies were set on fire. If you went outside, ashes fell like black snow. The morning after they arrived, Charles complained of cramps. By the time we were able to find Dr. Clapp and have him come to the house, Charles's hands and feet had already turned blue. Yet he would sweat and sweat. He wanted to see his parents. Dr. Clapp said only if he wanted to kill them should he go to them. He died that night. Mignon and I were terrified for our children. I knew Virgine was leaving to go to her protector's house across the lake. She took Gabriel and Lottie with her. Mignon was so distraught, we had to pull her arms off Lottie. She covered her in kisses. Hours later she was still crying. Charles dead. Her daughter gone. She cried so much, she could barely breathe. At least that's what I thought. She asked for paper and a quill. That's when I knew. Mignon, of course, did as well. Charles's body was not yet out of the house, and she was dying too."

Joseph handed her his handkerchief. Rosette dried her face, gathered herself, and began again.

"She wrote a letter to Charlotte, and she made me promise not to give it to her until it was time. I remember screaming at her, 'No. You give it to her. Get well. I don't want to have to deliver this letter.' She smiled. Can you believe it? She smiled at me. I told her I would raise Lottie if she wanted me to. She shook her head. Told me to bring Lottie to Charles's parents. 'Explain what happened. Tell them Charles and I loved each other, we were happy, but we wanted Lottie to know her family.' And then she told me and told me and told me. She wanted to make sure I understood, and she made me promise that I would do what she asked me to do. She said, 'Tell the LeClercs they are to raise Lottie as if she is white. She'll be able to pass. The rest is up to them.' I kept that promise."

CHAPTER THIRTY - FOUR

"WHY HAVEN'T YOU GIVEN HER the letter? Her mother's letter? This changes everything. You can't withhold this from her." Gabriel paced, circling the dining room table.

"You're assuming the letter tells the whole story. I'm doing exactly what she asked me to do. She said I would know the right time. I don't think this is it," Rosette said.

"She's about to marry a man she doesn't love. A man who would not marry her if he knew about her mother. I don't understand what else you need. What if 'not the right time' turns into 'too late'?"

"This is my decision to make. A friend and her husband died in my house within a day of each other. And don't forget that had Mignon accepted my offer, Lottie would be like a sister."

"I can forget that," said Alcee.

"I'm going to escort Serafina back to her house," said Joseph, who turned to Serafina and noted, "It doesn't seem they know we are still here anyway. I'll return, and they will probably not even realize I left."

"May I join you? They don't need me either," said Alcee.

"Wait!" Rosette stood as if about to call a meeting to order. "I never intended for Mignon's story to be told this way. Please, please respect that and do not say anything. At least for now."

Alcee, Joseph, and Serafina all nodded their acceptance and left.

Rosette stopped Gabriel mid-circle. "You are going to have to trust me. I have carried this for eighteen years. I am not going to risk ruining someone's life. Do you understand?"

"Would it matter? I understand. I don't like it, but I understand."

"It's not the final piece of rice. Not yet," Rosette said as she hugged her son.

―――✦―――

GABRIEL FELL ASLEEP, BUT HE found it impossible to stay asleep. He created one scenario after another, but tonight they all ended the same way. He and Lottie could share a life together.

When he woke in that hazy time between night and day, he decided to dress and go to the café early. He could surprise Rosette, and perhaps even Joseph, by nailing a few boards together without the nail pointing east or west or getting bent on top. Years of education, and yet he struggled with a hammer and nail. He found leftover French bread wrapped in a towel on the dining room table. Gabriel tore off a sizable chunk to eat along the way.

He had forgotten what it was like to witness the city waking up. Not that he could see much from his room when he'd wake up early to study. But he could see enough that the lights from the candles of the early risers tracked their movements through their houses. Other times, like this morning, he would see a few lights extinguished from those staying too late at Vincent's or the gambling house or the guzzle shops. The last ones presented the most trouble, with their sloppy walking and penchant for disposing of their stomach contents wherever and whenever necessary.

He had time to walk past his father's office, though he knew the man wouldn't be there. Jean Noel probably didn't arrive until after his servants brought home breakfast or the makings of it from the French Market. With the exception of returning home from the clothiers that day, Gabriel avoided the street as much as possible. Never during the day could he simply stand in front to peer through the plate-glass window inscribed with Mounier and Hart, whether people recognized him as Jean Noel's son or not. Gabriel didn't know if his own father would recognize the man he had become. This morning, when he reached his father's door, it wasn't Jean Noel that came to mind. It was Joseph Joubert. In the brief time he'd known Joseph, the man brought him on jobs, showed him the particulars of drafting, and included him in his business at every opportunity. He had been honest with Gabriel when Gabriel confronted him about being away. He adored Alcee, and he loved his mother. What more could Gabriel ask for in a father? Nothing.

Jean Noel would have always been half a father, but Gabriel didn't want just half a relationship. It wasn't as if his father never cared about him. He remembered times his father read to him, played kickball with him…even paid for his new wardrobe several weeks ago. If Rosette had not asked him to leave, would he have been able to be two fathers? Jean Noel respected his mother's wish, and for that, he respected his father. Gabriel could let go now.

Closer to the river, he could hear the whistles of the incoming boats sounding as if they needed to wake up, their usual robust blarings now long groans. As the sun raised the thick, moist velvet curtain of darkness, figures that seemed like shadows emerged from doorways and carriages. The servants headed to the French Market; dock workers and merchants moved through the city. And this particular morning, Gabriel was one of them, and he prayed he would not wake and find it all a dream.

He did surprise Rosette when she arrived at the café that morning. His frock coat, folded in half, made a pillow of sorts over his crossed arms, and he was sound asleep.

"HAVE YOU CONTACTED ANDRÉ YET?" Nathalie was

counting the inventory of plates and cups so they could place an order for more when the addition was ready.

Gabriel scraped a new cone of sugar into several little hills of granules. "André?"

"Remember, yesterday you were forging a trail to Paris, leaving the city behind?" She stuck the pencil into a fold of her tignon.

"Yes, I remember that." He already sounded defensive.

"You had another change of heart overnight?"

He returned the cone to the sugar box and handed Nathalie the key. "And if I did? You seem upset. Is it because I may stay here? Or is it because I may not?"

"Did what I tell you yesterday have anything to do with your sudden reversal?"

He hesitated, and for Nathalie that was as good as a response. She narrowed her eyes and stared. He wondered if she might be trying to read his mind. "What are you thinking?"

"That you're hiding something." She wagged a finger at him. "You know I'll find out. I always do."

Gabriel wanted to tell her that he hoped she did find out, because that would mean he would be with Lottie.

GABRIEL COULD NOT RECALL A TIME when he had seen his mother this angry.

He walked into the house that evening to find a bawling Serafina on the sofa and his mother walking back and forth, her fingertips pressed against her temples and her face mottled. A barrage of unfamiliar French expressions, which meant they must have been highly volatile, filled every space she entered.

"Eighteen years. You have just destroyed eighteen years. People's lives are at stake here. What were you thinking?"

Tonight Gabriel made sure to close the door without shaking the walls. "What happened?"

Between his mother's rants and Serafina's hiccupping sobs, he pieced the story together. And after he did, he understood his mother's fury.

Thinking she would help the process along, Serafina had told Paul the truth about Lottie's mother.

"Why would he choose to marry a free woman of color when he already has me? I thought he would be so angry that he would call off the wedding," Serafina said.

But he didn't.

What he did tell her was that his intentions for the property he would get in the dowry had nothing to do with the warehouse his father wanted to build. He had to have that property because he spent too many nights at the racetrack and the gambling halls—and he wanted to build his own. Even a Bastion did not have unlimited privileges when it came to debt. He said the wedding might not even be soon enough, but he had some money in the bank. "I asked him why he needed money if he had some already. He told me his slaves were his money in the bank."

Now it was Gabriel's turn to seethe. This lying, manipulative man was to marry Lottie?

Serafina gulped some air. "But he said he loves me. That he's only going through with this wedding for that land. He promised me he's going to take care of me and his child."

"I want you to look at me when I say this so you will remember." Rosette leaned toward Serafina and placed her hand on the woman's arm. "If you believe that Paul Bastion has any intention of following through with what he says, then you are truly a couillonne. You and your child deserve more than this selfish—and that's the kindest word I can use to describe him right now—man."

"I thought I was going to make it easier for everyone. I am not stupid. I know Paul, and once he settles his debts, he will be back in my house." Serafina refused to believe otherwise.

"Well, if he is, then keep him there. No one else wants him," said Rosette as she opened the door for Serafina. "Your carriage is here."

After seeing her out, Rosette sat, her hands trembling as she reached for her coffee cup. She managed a sip by holding it with both hands.

"Where are Joseph and Alcee?"

"I sent your sister to her room. If I strangled Serafina, I didn't want a witness."

Gabriel smiled. His mother did not.

"I don't care that Alcee heard, but I didn't want

Serafina to have a set of eyes that might show sympathy. As for Joseph, he had a meeting with clients. He said he would stop by tomorrow," Rosette said.

"I have heard people say 'I am at a loss,' and until now, I did not understand how someone could have nothing to say. What she did…" Gabriel sat, his head in his hands.

Rosette set her coffee cup on the saucer without it clattering. She arranged her dress on the sofa, pulling the folds, smoothing. She was thinking, somehow working out the problem as she set everything around her in order. He had watched this so many times over the years that when he saw her begin the ritual, he waited.

She folded one hand over the other on her lap. "This is what we are going to do. Tomorrow morning, you will go to Monsieur LeClerc's office and tell him you need to speak to him privately. You will tell him what you know about how Paul plans to use the land and why. I promise you, the LeClercs do not want their legacy to be that they were the family who sold prime real estate for a gambling hall."

"You said 'we.' What are you going to do?"

"I will pray."

CHAPTER THIRTY - FIVE

ROSETTE WAS RIGHT ABOUT LOUIS LECLERC.

At first, he thought Gabriel wanted to discuss Joseph Joubert's properties. Then, when Gabriel explained he was there to discuss information he had heard about Paul Bastion, Monsieur LeClerc closed the door to his office. After Gabriel told him about Paul's gambling debts and his real intentions with the property, he ran his fingers over the top of his head and stared at the wall behind Gabriel.

Then, as if he had just realized he wasn't alone in his office, Monsieur LeClerc grabbed the arms of his chair, stood, and reached his hand to shake Gabriel's. "Thank you. Thank you very much. I trust this information will stay between us."

"Absolutely, sir." As long as "us" included Serafina, Rosette, Gabriel, and, likely, Alcee.

Lottie's grandfather opened the door. "I don't know how to repay you for this. I am very grateful."

Gabriel smiled. "We'll think of something."

JUSTINE PROMISED LOTTIE SHE'D BE over after her Spanish lesson. Or maybe it was her art lesson. Her lessons required more and more of her time, so much so that Lottie told her she would start her own lessons and Justine could then schedule a time with her.

Justine was almost fifteen minutes late. Lottie threw herself across her bed. Is this what her life was going to be like as the bored wife of a wealthy man? So little to do that a friend's being late was a tragedy? She missed the life where she cared about other people. The children at the homes, the men and women she and Gabriel taught. Maybe Paul would let her build a home for orphans. She could name it after her parents. And then they would live happily ever after just like the fairy tales promised.

"Lottie? I'm here. Where are you?"

"I'm coming!" Lottie scrambled off her bed and practically trotted downstairs. "What took you so long?" She hugged Justine before she even had a chance to take off her cape and bonnet.

"Gracious, Lottie. It hasn't been that long since we've seen one another." Justine pulled off her gloves. "Let's see. Oh, I remember, that evening—"

"Don't say it. If I don't hear it, I won't think about it."

"Even I know that's not true. You probably hear it in your own brain a dozen times a day." Justine sniffed and pretended to squeeze her nose shut. "What is that horrid smell? It's so bad it's even in my mouth."

Lottie sniffed. "I must be getting used to it. I think

312

it's hair and linen. Agnes is teaching someone how to press clothes. Apparently there's a big demand for slaves who can do that. People even pay them. Well, probably not everyone. It's so much harder than I thought. And you have to be careful, else things burn and catch fire, and then there are ashes everywhere."

"I don't need another lesson. Please tell me Agnes made coffee." She pulled Lottie toward the dining room.

"Not only that, but she made these little cakes, petits fours, and they're covered in icing. If I have a cook, I've decided I'll have her make extra desserts and I'll bring them to Agnes."

"Well, perhaps it's best you don't start counting on cooks. Let's get our coffee and cakes, and then I must catch you up on what I've heard about Paul." Justine sampled one of the petits fours. "These are very good."

"Are these just rumors? Honestly, I can't handle much more."

"Isabelle said François told her, and the last information he told her was right. You know my sister wouldn't tolerate gossip. She insists that if two reliable sources agree, then it's not gossip."

"Who's the second person?" Lottie reached for a petit four before Justine swallowed the plate whole.

"I don't know. You can ask Isabelle the next time you see her. All she told me was Paul likes to gamble, but he hasn't been winning. He owes so much money that he told someone he may have to sell a slave or two."

Lottie placed her half-eaten petit four on her plate.

She felt as if her stomach had turned inside out. She was about to be violently ill at the thought of this despicable man touching her.

"And," Justine had more, "because I knew you would want to know, I asked Ruthie if she knew who worked for him. She told me there's a family—the son may be seventeen or eighteen, and their daughter is ten. She's already heard he might sell them together or separately. It just depends on the offers."

GABRIEL AND JOSEPH WERE FRAMING the exterior walls of the café addition when Nathalie walked over and asked to talk to Gabriel.

"Go on," said Joseph. "I can use a break." He wiped his face and arms and went inside.

"I don't want to talk in the café. Can we walk across the street to the park?" Nathalie ducked out of the way of a carriage.

"Yes, but what did you do with the old Nathalie when you inhabited her body? Did the voodoo curse finally work?" Gabriel dried his face, rolled down his sleeves, and picked up his vest that was hanging on a nail where he was framing.

"Not today, Gabriel," she snapped and opened her parasol.

"When you are this serious, I feel a problem about to happen." He helped her cross the boards laid over the foul gutters then unlatched the gate to enter the park.

With the exception of a few nursemaids and an occasional reveler lost on the way home, the area was empty. The broad spans of St. Augustine grass had become squares of mostly mud sprinkled with patches of dry winter grass.

"I'm afraid it already happened. I'm here because Serafina asked me to come. She didn't think you or your mother could stand the sight of her, much less have her in your home."

"She told you?" It sounded like an accusation, not a question.

"Of course she told me. We've been friends for years. Now, before you become spitting angry, keep in mind that I am the one who gave you the information that just might get you the life you want. She said for me to tell you that Paul and Monsieur LeClerc had a meeting. Lottie's grandfather, as you know, because you're likely the one who told him, knows about Paul using the land for a gambling hall. He wanted Paul and his father to sign a contract stating that it wouldn't happen or else he wouldn't sell him the land. Paul laughed and told Monsieur LeClerc that if he didn't go through with the agreement, he would take an ad in *The Bee* if necessary, but he would make sure the entire city knew that Charlotte was not white. After he told her himself."

Gabriel's anger could have fueled a ship. "This man is evil. He's using a man's granddaughter as bait to blackmail him. And that's just part of it. You said Serafina's your friend. Aren't you afraid for her and her child?"

"Not anymore. This wasn't the only news he gave her. Paul told her that if he's going to be with a free woman of color, no matter which direction he chose, he'd rather have one who isn't with child."

AFTER JUSTINE LEFT, LOTTIE WALKED outside to find Agnes. She was consoling her "student," a young woman close to Lottie's age. Taller than Agnes and stick-thin, everything on her seemed long—her face, her neck, her legs and arms, even her fingers. From a few feet away, she resembled a spider that suddenly found itself on two legs. When she bent to heat the iron and moved back again, she moved like she was underwater. A pile of fabric near Agnes's feet showed scorch marks, but Agnes continued to gently pat her back, saying, "Gonna be all right, gonna be all right."

Lottie hated to interrupt but she didn't want to wait. The one napkin on the board was taking an extraordinarily long time. She stood back a respectful distance and waved Agnes over when she caught her eye. "How much longer will you be working with her?"

"Let's see. 'Fore she's good? Be a while. Couple months," said Agnes, still watching her as she spoke.

"No, Agnes. Today. Now. When will you be finished?"

"Why? What you need?" A suspicious scowl was overtaking her face.

"I need to go to the church, just for a little while."

Agnes shook her head. "I don't even want to know why you needs to go to church so much lately. But if I tells you I can't go with you and somethin' happens, Jesus gonna be none too happy. Lemme tell Suellen she kin rest a bit. I be inside to git you."

"Thank you, Agnes," Lottie said as she hugged her. "What am I going to do without you?"

"I don't want to know that either," she said.

Lottie figured Père François had to be involved somehow in these underground dealings, and if she could get word to him about Paul's slaves, then he could help. There was still information she didn't know, like when Paul planned to do anything or even the names of the people in the family he wanted to separate. She would have to figure out a way to get that information and soon. Going to Paul's house was out of the question, and they weren't going to see one another until the opera in two days.

"You ready?" Agnes walked to the front door with a basket on her arm.

"What's that for?"

"I might see something along the way I want. Never you mind. I'm going, ain't I?" Agnes opened the door and waited while Lottie's six-foot-wide flowered-muslin dress pushed through a four-foot-wide doorway.

❧

THIS TIME LOTTIE DIDN'T NEED to rattle the doors of the cathedral. She stepped into the alcove and let her eyes adjust from the glaring sun to the dim light. A few people were scattered about. Some were on the kneelers with bowed heads. The others, she noticed as she quietly walked past, sat with their rosary beads, their lips moving in silent prayer.

Not seeing Father François at the altar, Lottie suddenly realized she had assumed he would be in the church, and she had no idea where to find him if he wasn't. She remembered Gabriel saying he lived behind the cathedral, and she hoped she could find the place. Agnes was in the last pew, kneeling and praying, probably with one eye open to track her. Lottie sat in the first pew, scanning the front of the church and the alcoves nearby. Still no sign of Father. She couldn't sit here all day. Actually, she could. It was Agnes who couldn't. Lottie thought she might be able to convince Agnes of that if she needed to do so.

She pushed her fifteen yards of fabric off the pew and on to the kneeler. This had to work. *Show me, please, how to save this family.* Except Paul couldn't know she was involved. She had to protect her grandparents. Without that sale, they would lose everything. As long as they had the money they needed, she would deal with the rest later. *God, Agnes said You always find a way.*

Lottie didn't know how long she knelt there, only that she could feel the seams of her petticoats pushing into her knees. She looked up when she heard doors opening and closing. The confessional. Father François had been there. It had looked like a large closet, and she had not even noticed it. He passed close enough for her to reach out and tug the sleeve of his cassock.

"Father," she whispered, "I need to speak to you. It's important."

He looked at her, she could tell, not remembering her.

"I gave you the note for the collection box."

"Ah, yes." He scanned the church then told her to meet him in the confessional, as there was no one else waiting.

She stood, and Agnes had her in her sights just as Lottie had hoped. She pointed to the confessional. If Agnes had looked up and not seen her, the church might have become a great deal less solemn. Agnes nodded and smiled, probably thinking Lottie was making her confession. She'd explain later.

Father François entered through one door and Lottie the other. He sat in his space; she knelt in hers. Only the outline of his profile could be seen through the small woven cane screen separating them.

"How can I help you?" he said softly.

Lottie explained enough for him to know that a family was about to be torn apart and sold to pay a gambling debt. "I thought, Father, if you contacted the person you pass the notes on to, this family could be helped."

"Without more information, I can do little."

"What do you need?" It shouldn't be that difficult to find out their names. The challenge would be knowing

Paul's plan. Maybe she needed to leave that part up to God.

"There is another way," Father said. "Many of the slaves congregate in Congo Square on Sunday. Can you get word to them to look for a gentleman wearing a red-and-black cravat? They need to be there by noon. I will tell the gentleman to be prepared to meet a man, his wife, a son, and a daughter. Correct?"

Lottie nodded then realized he couldn't see her doing that. "Yes, Father. Thank you. Bless you."

"Please make sure they know they cannot be late, for there is a schedule. And if they cannot be there or you cannot contact them, you must tell me as soon as possible. Four other people might be waiting to take their place."

"Yes, Father. I understand. Thank you."

"God be with you and with them."

Lottie wanted to run down the aisle to Agnes, she felt so relieved. She had no idea how she would pass the information on to the family, but she trusted that all she had to do was trust.

CHAPTER THIRTY - SIX

THAT NIGHT AS SHE LAY in bed, Lottie considered how to make this plan work. Earlier, she thought she had the problem solved. She would write a note and find someone to pass it on. But it was unlikely they would be able to read, and she couldn't take that chance. Lottie would eventually be invited to the Bastion home, but not until after the formal engagement. Ruthie had heard rumors, and she might know them, but her baby could be delivered any day and Lottie refused to risk involving her. As much as she might have liked to have an excuse to talk to him, she didn't think Gabriel would know Paul's slaves.

There was only one person who truly knew Paul Bastion well enough to know the answer. Paul's placée. But could she be trusted? Lottie didn't know who she was, how to find her, or what she even looked like. Gabriel knew about her, but that didn't mean he knew her. And then she realized the answer. Of course. Justine. She could ask Isabelle. The Dumas family was a shrimp net that information flowed through. All the little shrimp escaped, but not the big ones. And Paul was like one of those huge crabs trapped in the net, in the wrong place at the wrong time.

The next morning, Lottie scrambled out of bed. She had to be at the Dumases' early, before Justine set off on another one of those lessons or lunch or whatever she occupied her days with lately. By the time Agnes came to wake her, Lottie was dressed and ready to leave.

"Where you going? Ain't nothing happenin' dis early dat you gotta git to except breakfast down the stairs."

"I am just going to Justine's house, and I do not need you to chaperone me four houses away. I will be back soon." Lottie headed out the door before Agnes or her grandparents could find a reason why she shouldn't.

LOTTIE WAS POURING HERSELF A CUP of coffee when her grandparents came in for breakfast.

"My, you seem quite energetic this morning, my p'tit. You must be feeling better," her grandfather said as he came over to pour his own cup. He kissed her on the top of her head. "It's good to see you smile."

She kissed him on the cheek. "Yes, and it is going to be a wonderful day."

Her plan was coming together. When she had knocked on the Dumases' door, Isabelle opened it. As God would have it, Ruthie was in labor and Isabelle had come to help. Lottie didn't elaborate. She asked Isabelle if she could find out the name of Paul's placée and where she lived. Isabelle didn't flinch when Lottie said she needed the information today. And she didn't ask questions. "I have no idea when this baby will decide to let go of Ruthie, so can you come back after lunch? François will be home then, and he's not yet left for the office. He can track this information down between now and then. Men gossip too, but their gossip is always much more reliable."

By lunch, Ruthie had a son who overcame the indignity of being delivered of his mother when he learned that the same body that housed him could also feed him. Isabelle was his self-declared grandmother, already quibbling about his name. Ruthie wanted Isaac because it reminded her of Isabelle's name. Isabelle thought he should be Laurent Junior. Madame Dumas settled the argument. "Laurent, when you decide on a name for your son, and we hope it is soon, please inform us."

And not long after that, François came home with the name Sera-fina Lividaus and an address.

LOTTIE SELECTED A MUTED-GREEN POLISHED cotton gown with velvet cuffs on the long sleeves and panels in the skirt, only slightly off the shoulders and absent the fripperies she detested that cluttered and ruined dresses. If she flaunted herself, she seemed desperate. If she showed up in a dowdy gown, she appeared unmannered. She wanted Serafina to be attentive to what she said, not what she wore.

Who could she trust to deliver her there? Suellen and

cooking occupied Agnes. Abram was the only logical choice because, though she loved Justine, she talked too much and couldn't be trusted. She wouldn't need to stay long. Serafina was going to help or not, and Lottie knew the risk was high that she might confess everything to Paul to win his favor. She knew not to underestimate the education, etiquette, or insight of a placée. But if Serafina possessed all those things and Paul did not show her a different face, which she doubted he would because he lacked the discipline to do so, then in her heart Serafina knew who he really was.

Usually, early evening marked the time to enjoy being outdoors, so Lottie had time. Her grandparents had been invited to play cards. She found Abram, asked him to take her, and told him that what she had to do was so important, she couldn't tell him, and she needed him not to say anything either. "I'm not saying you will never be able to talk about this. Just not until the time is right."

She checked her hair in the mirror. Her pearl studs were simple but elegant. Her gold cross fell perfectly above the top of her gown. Lottie was ready to meet her future husband's mistress.

Once in the carriage, Lottie questioned what she was doing, but only long enough to convince herself she'd made the right decision. The closed curtains, the cool quiet, and the gentle sway of the wagon with the clip-clopping of the horses' hooves against the cobblestones almost rocked her to sleep. Some time later, the slight jolt told Lottie they'd arrived. She peeked around the curtain to see the house. The Creole cottage had been painted a celery green. Lottie congratulated herself on her gown selection.

Abram opened the door and helped her down, though by the time Lottie lifted the wrought-iron knocker, she believed she left her stomach in the carriage.

———✺———

THE HOME, AS LOTTIE EXPECTED, was beautifully and elegantly furnished. To Serafina's credit, she politely welcomed her in and asked the maid to bring tea.

At first, the two women emotionally circled one another like two contenders who were each promised, by the same person, to win the battle against one another. They discovered they had nothing to fight over if Paul was the prize, because neither one of them wanted him.

Serafina was an attractive young woman who wanted to make a life for herself and the child. It saddened Lottie that she might have to raise her child alone with precarious finances. But she was resilient.

Paul himself had told Serafina about selling the slaves, so Lottie explained the plan to her. Where they needed to be, when, and to look for the red-and-black cravat. Serafina wrote the information in an elegant script on a small sheet of paper. "I promise to burn this after my housemaid Clarisse carries the information to them. But if I neglect one detail, it could be tragic."

"I suppose we could appreciate that our mutual dis-like of the same man is ultimately going to save four lives," said Lottie as she rose to leave.

Serafina clasped Lottie's hand in hers. "Yes, and it will save our lives as well."

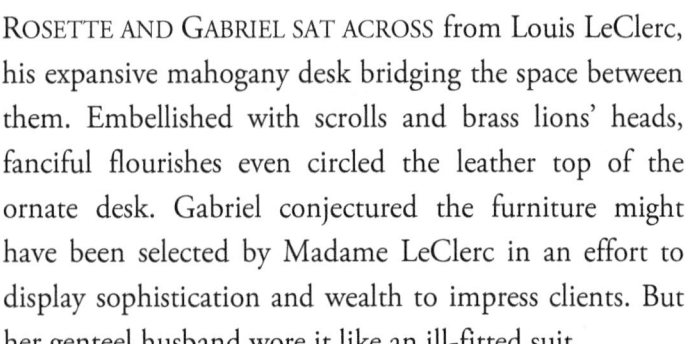

ROSETTE AND GABRIEL SAT ACROSS from Louis LeClerc, his expansive mahogany desk bridging the space between them. Embellished with scrolls and brass lions' heads, fanciful flourishes even circled the leather top of the ornate desk. Gabriel conjectured the furniture might have been selected by Madame LeClerc in an effort to display sophistication and wealth to impress clients. But her genteel husband wore it like an ill-fitted suit.

Perhaps, though, Monsieur LeClerc's shiftings in his chair and clasping and reclasping of his hands more reflected the discomfort of the impending conversation than the ostentation of his surroundings.

"Monsieur LeClerc," said Rosette, "you probably already know why I am here."

"Please call me Louis. And, yes, we both knew this day would come," he replied. "I had not expected it to come this way."

"I understand. I cannot imagine how difficult this must be for you." Rosette's warm voice appeared to diffuse the tension etched across Monsieur LeClerc's features.

His solemn face cracked just the hint of a smile before it retreated into sadness again. "It is not nearly as difficult as hearing your granddaughter say that she will marry a man she does not care about, when there is one she does." His eyes went to Gabriel. "And that she is marrying him to save us from financial ruin. Then, to turn around and have that very man attempt to blackmail me…it makes what we need to do seem easy in comparison."

"I am sorry, sir, about what you stand to lose. But I am happy knowing what you stand to gain," said Gabriel.

"As well as you, *oui*?" He looked first at Rosette, then at Gabriel.

Gabriel nodded. "I hope."

"Another day for that discussion," said Rosette, patting Gabriel's hand. "I know none of us are certain how this will unfold, but I do want to be the one to give the letter to Charlotte."

"Of course. That is as it should be," Louis said. "The rest…" He paused, cleared his throat, and looked at Rosette. "…will be in God's hands."

"Yes, yes, it will," said Rosette. "As it always has been." She stood, reaching her hand out to Monsieur LeClerc, whose eyes seemed to be focused someplace only he could see. She held his hand between her own gloved ones. "You have raised your granddaughter well."

"I wish I could have been more of a grandfather to her. Perhaps soon I will have that opportunity."

As he and Rosette left the office, Gabriel turned and saw Lottie's grandfather quickly brush the tears away from his eyes then open a ledger on his desk and begin to work.

CHAPTER THIRTY - SEVEN

PAUL ARRIVED AT THE LeClercs' without his parents. "They asked me to give you their deepest apologies. My grandmother in Atlanta has taken ill, and we just received word this afternoon. Arrangements are being made for them to leave tonight."

Lottie's grandparents murmured their sympathies, though neither one of them seemed bothered at all to go to the opera without the elder Bastions. Wearing a creamy yellow gown edged in satin and paneled with hand-embroidered flowers in a thread a few shades darker, Lottie felt airy as her dress. Agnes told her it was a summer gown and she shouldn't wear it, but Lottie didn't care. Slowly, she was giving herself permission to be self-reliant. And the stronger she felt about that, the less her grandmother's judgments or Paul's detachment mattered.

"Aren't you wearing a cape?" Her grandmother handed her a black cape trimmed with fur at the hem and neck.

Lottie handed it to Agnes. "No, thank you. I'm ready."

At intermission, an associate of Paul's wandered over from where he and his family were sitting several boxes away. Arnstead, whose evening frock coat had likely been more comfortable quite a number of meals ago, must not have thought Lottie had anything above her neck, because his eyes didn't once land there when Paul introduced her.

"And so this is the fair Mademoiselle LeClerc." He kissed her hand, and Lottie felt as if a garden snake crawled up her back. She wished now she had followed her grandparents for refreshments. The abundance of gas jets, while they made for a stunning display on everything that could sparkle, created heat that reminded Lottie of their outdoor kitchen. She had forgotten her fan, which deprived her of cooling herself and of something to fiddle with while she pretended to both delight in Paul's company and ignore his conversation as women were supposed to do.

She stood for a moment to ease the weight of sixteen yards of fabric in her lap and heard Paul tell Arnstead he was glad his parents had decided to leave tonight so his plans didn't need to change. His friend said something unintelligible—more than likely unintelligent as well—but it ended with "…them darkies won't suspect anything on a Saturday night."

Lottie was the only one in the box not laughing. Her mind raced, but her body refused to move. She had to get word to Père François to send someone to warn them. Where would they go? The church. Surely he would allow them to stay there. Serafina? No, she was too far away. But they couldn't just leave, a black family wandering the streets of New Orleans on a Saturday night. She prayed her knees would not collapse under her from their incessant shaking. *Smile sweetly, Lottie.* "Excuse me, Monsieurs. May I just pass my little self along here? I am in dire need of fresh air."

"The air is hardly ever fresh here," said Paul. "Isn't intermission almost over?"

"Why, no. I have buckets of time to find some refreshments and maybe just a spot of air." All those weeks of little conversation were an advantage. Paul didn't seem confused by her cloyingly sweet and vapid dialogue. That's who he thought he would be marrying. "You gentlemen just carry on. I am sure you have so many important things to talk about, they would probably bore me to tears."

"Probably? Not probably, certain. Certain to bore you to tears," said Arnstead, and he and Paul shared yet another laugh at her expense.

"I won't be long." She would have to remind herself to play that innocent game with Alcee, but now she had to make her way to Père François.

She made it through the flock of people without seeing her grandparents. Several couples still strolled outside, so she walked as far as they walked to the end of the building and then stopped. She peered around as if she waited for someone, and when the couples wound their way back into the building, she stepped into the darkness where the hanging gaslamps wouldn't drape her body in a hazy, gold light.

A hire passed and she almost flagged it, but she had not brought her clutch. They were not known for providing free service even if the passenger wore Victorian lace. She had two blocks and then had to cross Canal Street. Young ladies pitter-pattering down St. Charles Avenue were not often seen, especially at night. Without a chaperone. The social etiquette sins became too numerous to count. By the time she picked up her skirts over her ankles so she could move faster, Lottie considered how she might spend the rest of her life as a social outcast.

Canal Street didn't have a canal, but it had mud, rocks, and unmentionable things, and she had stepped on or in them all. She had forgotten how wide the street was, and by the time she reached the other side, her corset refused to allow her more breaths. A few people asked if she needed help, and she gave a polite no because they wouldn't want the real answer. Lottie's side ached, and her shoes were useless. If she could break out of the prison of this corset, she might be able to make it. She could see the spires of the cathedral from where she was, their white tops piercing the night air. If only they were as close as they appeared.

Intermission had long been over. She wondered what Paul was doing or thinking. Lottie gasped, bent over the little she could, held her sides, and kept repeating, "I forgot. I forgot. I forgot." So concerned with assuring herself that Paul would not be alarmed by her being gone, she had forgotten about her grandparents. They would be concerned if she did not appear within a reasonable length of time. Which meant they would look for her, which meant so would Paul. She had to get this information to Father before Paul found her, or else she might as well have stayed in the theatre.

She hurried through one more block but had to breathe again before she could go on. If she had worn long sleeves, she could have wiped her face on them. What did it matter? She picked up her lovely, delicately embroidered skirt and blotted her wet face.

"Don't I know you?"

She looked up into the eyes of a tall and truly dark man. Lottie was too tired to be frightened, and his eyes were too kind to be someone who wanted to cause her harm. He moved into the light so she could see him, and his face did seem so familiar. The voice—she remembered the voice.

"You were with Gabriel at my grandfather's office. I'm Charlotte LeClerc."

"Joseph Joubert. I thought so." He paused. "You look, if you don't mind me saying so, a bit ragged. I'm not used to seeing the daughters of wealthy Creole men roaming the streets at night. Is there somewhere I can take you?"

She smiled. "I have information I need to give someone, and I'm afraid I might not get there...so I probably need to start walking again...."

"Do you think I might be able to help?"

"Can you run a few blocks carrying me?"

He looked her over. "Maybe. How many blocks?"

She heard the clattering of carriage wheels and looked behind her. "Oh no. Oh no." Paul was two short blocks away.

Lottie's chest tightened. Her breaths came fast and shallow. If she couldn't talk to Father, four people's lives would be ripped apart. She was still too far away. Lottie looked at the man gaining on her and the one in front of her.

She grabbed Joseph's arm. "I'm not going to have time to repeat this, and I'm trusting you because you're Gabriel's friend. Find Père François. Tell him somebody has to get to the people tonight. The Mazants. They're slaves of Paul Bastion. Please. Please. Please." She wiped her eyes. "They have to be safe. They have no one."

She knew Paul was close. In a too-loud voice, Joseph said, "It was so very nice to meet you again, Mademoiselle LeClerc. I do hope you get to feeling better. Who knows? Might all be gone by tomorrow."

"Charlotte? What is going on? Why are you with that man?" Paul demanded.

As Joseph Jobert turned to leave, the gaslamp illuminated his face and chest. The man wore a cravat. A black-and-red cravat.

Charlotte did what any self-respecting Southern girl would do when faced with something for which there is no reasonable or believable reply.

She utterly, completely, and willingly fainted.

CHAPTER THIRTY - EIGHT

WHEN SHE OPENED HER EYES, Paul was holding her, so she knew she had not died...or at least she hoped not. Because if she had died and Paul held her, then she doubted she would be in heaven.

Her head felt as if it went in one direction and her body in another. She saw her grandparents across from her and realized she was in the carriage.

Grand-père leaned over. "Lottie, we are going home."

Lottie nodded. Joseph. The cravat. When he walked away, she'd heard Agnes's voice saying, "God always finds a way." And she had just witnessed it. She remembered thinking how tired she was and how she couldn't feel her legs and how if she just let this spinning in her head alone, it would stop.

Her gown was ruined. Another rework for the orphan home. She peeked at what was left of her shoes. They could be thrown into the fireplace. Serafina. Did she throw the paper away?

"Lottie, who was that man you were talking to?" Paul said the word *man* as if he really meant *boy* but did not want to show the hand of prejudice yet.

"A friend."

Her grandmother stared out the window. Grand-père stared at Paul.

"Why were you talking to this friend, if you insist on calling him that, blocks away from the opera, unchaperoned? Had you planned to meet him there?"

"Paul, Lottie can face your questions later. Her grandmother and I just want her to rest."

"As someone who intends to marry her, I think I have the right to question a young woman who ran away from the opera to meet a black man on the street like a—"

"Don't. I will not allow you to speak to my granddaughter in such a tone or to suggest calling her something so offensive." Grand-père's entire body seemed cast in iron.

Lottie heard Paul, but nothing he said was of any importance to her. He lied, he was dishonest, and he used people. She might have to marry him, but she didn't have to love or like him.

The carriage turned in and stopped in front of the stable. Paul watched Abram and Lottie's grandfather help her to the ground. Lottie's legs cooperated, but her chest and sides felt bruised from the corset, and even small breaths were uncomfortable. Paul stood directly in front of her, making it difficult for her to move around him. "Please let me by," Lottie said.

"I'll let you by, but first you must remember your obligation to me and my family not to behave in a way that brings shame on all of us. Your actions were reprehensible. I have no idea how I will repair the embarrassing damage you caused to the Bastion name. If your cavorting tonight was your attempt to force my hand in calling off this wedding, you have wasted your time. This wedding will happen."

"And if it doesn't?" Lottie wanted to face the worst now.

"Don't think I do not know about you and that man and what the two of you did on Sundays." This time her grandparents' eyes were fixed on her.

Lottie waited for him to tell her.

"Teaching slaves to read and write. We can drag all those smart slaves to the post and chop off their fingers, and you and that man can spend time in jail. So think about that when you want to walk away from me."

"My name is Gabriel. Gabriel Girod." He stepped around Paul and stood next to Lottie. She did not know how or why Gabriel materialized, but she decided not to question her good fortune. "Do, please, report us. Will you drag the good Sisters to the post? The ones who have no recollection of anything you would be talking about?"

Paul sputtered.

"And"—Gabriel looked down at Lottie—"don't ever speak to or about Charlotte that way."

"Do you think I'm afraid of you?" Paul laughed.

Gabriel held Lottie's arm and helped her balance. Lottie knew her swaying was more from the fact that Gabriel held her than from whatever the fall may have rearranged in her head.

"No, no, I don't," said Gabriel.

Paul scoffed.

"But I have very protective friends who manage to be exactly where I might need them, even in the middle of the night."

AGNES INSISTED THAT LOTTIE SETTLE on the reclining couch Abram carried into the parlor. "I knows you already fainted, but you gonna put yourself in that couch right now."

Since Gabriel continued to hold on to her and she had no intention of moving away from him, Lottie allowed herself to be steered in that direction. Agnes shooed him away. "You go on. I don't want you standing here whilst I'm taking off Miz Lottie's shoes."

"I would not think of being so improper, Agnes," Gabriel answered as if she had offended him. He squeezed Lottie's hand. "I'm glad you're home," he said before he walked away.

Agnes unlaced Lottie's silk boots, warning her not to move. "You can't be showing those ankles. You just let Agnes take off these good-for-nothing shoes."

Lottie smiled, amused by Agnes's concern for her modesty after her adventures. Now that she wasn't standing, Lottie felt the stinging burn in the soles of her feet, like walking barefooted on cobblestones during the heat of August.

"I don't know if these gonna ever look the same." Agnes held them up, examining them the way she did eggplant at the French Market. "I be right back with some fresh coffee."

"Could you bring some cakes too?" Lottie's stomach was having its own adventure, and she hoped food might quiet it.

Resting against the back of the couch relieved some of the pressure of the corset, but so did the disappearance of Paul and knowing he would arrive home with his slaves absent, wondering why the buyer had taken the whole family. By the time he realized what really happened, they would be safely away. The man in the cravat, Joseph Joubert—she wanted to tell Gabriel, but he seemed to have disappeared.

"Should we send Abram for Dr. Clapp?" Lottie couldn't determine if Grand-père, sitting across from her, directed the question to Grand-mère or to her.

"I'm much better. Just tired, really. I don't need Dr. Clapp." Lottie felt uncomfortable about the way they looked at her. She watched Abram light more candles around the room and thought of the brightness of the gaslamps tonight in the opera house. The opera house. Of course. Her grandparents had not questioned her in front of Paul, but no doubt they waited for her to provide some explanation. But did they know Paul's real intention? Surely not. Her grandfather despised the gambling halls, the people they attracted, and the despair they caused families. And if he did know, then the

LeClercs' finances must be far worse than she thought.

Agnes returned with the coffee service, Rosette behind her carrying a small plate of petits fours and pralines. When Gabriel walked in with a coverlet and placed it over her, Lottie wondered who else in this room owed explanations. Then Rosette, Gabriel, Agnes, and Abram joined her grandparents, and she knew something truly dire must have happened. The fear that had subsided seeped back into her bones, especially because the faces surrounding her were solemn, not smiling.

"What happened?" Lottie waved away the cup of coffee Rosette passed her and sat up straight on the couch. "PaPa?"

He looked at her grandmother. She nodded. "Lottie, your grandmother and I did not expect tonight to end as it did. Whatever you were doing that caused you to leave the opera, I trust you had a reason. We can discuss that later, assuming you want to do so. What we need to talk to you about must be said tonight, before too much more time passes."

"I don't understand. Why is everyone else here?"

"Your grandmother and I have spoken little of your father and mother. One reason, the one we have always given you, is that to speak of them is painful. And that is no less true because of the other reason, which will help explain why Rosette and Gabriel and Agnes and Abram are here." He leaned forward, his elbows on the chair arms and his hands clasped.

"You need to hear your parents' story," he said. "Not

long after your father met your mother, he came to talk to me. You are very much like him in that regard. You know quite soon what you are passionate about, and you are not easily swayed."

Agnes nodded. "That sure true." Abram leaned close and whispered in her ear. "I'm sorry. You go on."

Lottie resisted the urge to glance in Gabriel's direction, though she suspected what her grandfather just said had much to do with his presence there.

"Charles loved your mother. She was a beautiful young woman, and though you might have inherited your father's eyes, everything else about you is to your mother's credit. But what he loved about her went beyond what most people saw. She was intelligent, an educated woman still eager to learn, charming, compassionate. When I hear 'joie de la vie,' I picture Mignon and her obvious joy for life. And Charles was an important part of that joy. I, we"—he paused to look at Grand-mère, who had not taken her eyes from his face since he began—"both knew how they felt about each another."

He sipped his coffee. It pleased Lottie to hear how much her parents loved one another and answered the question she had about the success of their arranged marriage. But surely everyone had not gathered to hear that.

"Yet, still knowing all that, we didn't want your father to marry Mignon. We—"

"Do you mean he wasn't the man her family selected? Or he was and you did not want him to be?" Lottie wondered if Mignon's parents might have felt the same.

She, not her grandfather, suddenly became the center of attention. "I'm confused," she said. She glanced around the room and felt even more so, seeing their expressions.

"You won't be in a moment," he said.

Lottie heard that hitch in his voice. The kind that went along with the difficult things that had to be said. She could not imagine what he was about to share, and the fact that it caused that reaction in him made her less anxious to hear it.

"The reason we didn't want him to marry her was because…because she was first his placée."

His words must have sucked all the air out of the room, Lottie thought as she struggled to breathe. She latched onto the front of the sofa, the words "his placée" expanding until they filled the room. Everyone was quiet long enough for rage to replace the shock of her grandfather's revelation.

She eyed her grandparents and hoped they saw the depth of her anger, the pool of revulsion that filled her stomach. No one in the room reacted as she did. Not even Gabriel. *They know. They all know.* The enormity of their betrayal ripped apart everything that she thought held them together—trust, loyalty, caring, affection, love.

"Lottie." Gabriel reached for her, and she leaned away from him.

"For eighteen years, I have trusted you, lived with you, loved you. And for eighteen years, you have been traitors. You withheld information from me that changes who I am. Changes the course of my life. You forbade me to pursue what I loved, and you demanded that I love what you pursued. You were marrying me to that man knowing I wasn't white." Lottie spoke as if each fragile word had to be carefully placed on the table dividing them. She wanted to fling them at everyone who hurt her, but then they'd just crash and get lost in the broken confusion.

Her grandfather removed his cravat and paced behind where he and Grand-mère sat. "Paul didn't know at first. I am ashamed to admit that we thought your children would pass. If they didn't, then we would have the money to bring you all home. Then, after I heard about his gambling debt and confronted him, he threatened to tell you the truth before we had a chance to."

"Paul knew? How did he find out?"

"From Serafina," Gabriel said, his voice low.

Lottie stood, no longer caring that she screamed. "What kind of people are you? Who gave you the right?"

"Your mother." The answer and that it came from her grandmother stunned her. She held onto the arm of the couch as she sat. "At first, we were relieved by her wishes for you. It made everything easier for us." She looked at Grand-père. "Most of all for me. I blamed your mother for what happened. I didn't want you to be like her. As time went on, it became increasingly more difficult as you grew and so much resembled her. Finally, I realized that Charles would have rather been happy for a short time with your mother than miserable for the rest of his life without her. But I know that doesn't make up for the way I treated you. For how I distanced myself from you."

Grand-père sat next to Grand-mère and held her hand as she continued. "I loved your father so much, and I lost him. If I allowed myself to love you with the same passion I loved him, I didn't know if I would survive if something happened to you. I don't expect you to forgive me now for what I have done. But I hope we can find a way to love one another."

"My mother? You're blaming this on my mother?"

"No, Lottie, not blaming. They were respecting your mother's wishes and mine," said Rosette. "They wanted to tell you, but it wasn't time."

Lottie turned to Agnes and Abram. "Am I going to hear your names too?"

"No, Miz Lottie," Abram said. "Your grandparents asked us here cuz we raised Charles too." He didn't try to wipe his tears. "We knew Mignon. We loved both them. And we love you."

Lottie directed her attention back to Rosette. "So how can you know this came from my mother?"

"Because your father died in my house, in your mother's arms. And once she knew you were safe, she died the next day. In my arms." She walked over and sat next to Lottie. "I promise to tell you everything, but first this…." She handed Lottie papers that had been folded in three. "She wrote that to you hours before she died. All she told me was I would know when it was time to give it to you, and she made me promise that no one else would read it."

Lottie turned the papers over, and on one of the sections read her name, *Genevieve Charlotte*. In a handwriting she had never seen. Her mother's.

CHAPTER THIRTY-NINE

To my dearest Genevieve Charlotte,

I am certain, my p'tit, that you feel desperately alone at this moment. But, oh, my sweet, please know that even in God's heaven, your father and I are with you as if we sat next to you now. As we have been every day. Watching your life unfold without us. Waiting for this day.

If you are reading this, then everyone who loves you—your grandparents, Rosette, Agnes and Abram—have all respected my wishes. What more could a mother want than to know how deeply her child is loved? For why else would these people, the ones whose arms have held you for all the times your father and I could not, have been so sacrificially committed to honoring the request I made? How many times must they have wanted to tell you what you did not know and yet they did not. Never forget how they loved you, and I pray you live in such a way that makes their sacrifice worthwhile.

Charlotte, for reasons you now understand, I did not know your grandparents. Your father and I lived in Paris because we could be married there and could have a life, for the most part, where our skin color did not determine our options. Of course, we hoped the same for you. Now, about to lose my own, I have to decide the course of your life alone and trust that my decision will not curse the very one I want it to bless. In a few days, Rosette will carry you to the door of two people who are strangers to you. She will have to tell them that their son and his wife died. She will have to tell them that you are their granddaughter. And she will have to tell them that you will live with them. If they could raise you as white, how much less would they need to battle. And if your growing up in their care could be made easier by that, then so be it.

I want you to know that your very birth was a gift to your father and to me. You will see, my precious girl, generations of love in your arms when you hold your child. When you look into her eyes and you realize that, all those years ago, I cradled you in my arms with the same love. That this swell of pride and joy that crashes into your heart and fills it with gratitude and love and hope is what we felt looking into your eyes.

After you were born, there was nothing that would stand in the way of your father's desire to see his parents, for them to see you and me. How would we know that the very desire that brought us to them would bring us fast away?

You won't remember, but before you were taken out of danger of the fever, I told you "we love you" over and over and over again. I covered your face, the face that looked at me with your father's eyes, with kisses. If only I could have made them last a lifetime for you. Loving your father and loving you were the greatest blessings of my life. I will die with treasures many live a lifetime and never find.

God has planted dreams in your heart. Follow them. Find someone to love who loves and respects you, who honors God, and who makes you smile each time you see him. Every day is a miracle.

Know that in everything, God always finds a way.

All our love,
Mama and Papa

1843

Dear Mama and Papa,

We will be boarding soon to leave for Paris, but this visit was so busy, I could not find time to write. The trips are more challenging since Charles Louis decided to start walking before his first birthday. Gabriel told me not to worry, the rocking of the ship would lull him into sleep. Unfortunately, it also lulled me into seasickness.

Nathalie is not returning with us, as she should

deliver any day. Since she and André married, Virgine and Nathalie's parents are outdoing one another with gifts for the child. If they had twins, each child would have more than enough. Nathalie being with child has been a blessing and a curse for Serafina. Ever since her daughter died, she has devoted herself to the orphanages. She tells me she prays Nathalie's child will not struggle at birth, and she does not know if she could ever trust herself to have a child again.

I am surprised our son is not exhausted from being spoiled and coddled by three sets of grandparents. Agnes and Abram strolled him to the French Quarter, where I am certain he was fed all manner of foods no self-respecting one-year-old should eat. They returned him saying they had no idea how powdered sugar found its way to his neck.

Rosette and Joseph allow him to wander the café or the orphanage Joseph is building. Since they purchased Grand-père's land, they have already finished the warehouse. We don't ask Joseph about his comings and goings. Rosette says she trusts her husband, and she keeps him well-stocked in colorful cravats. Alcee begged them to let her join us on our trip back. Rosette promised her that after one more year of learning French, she would allow her. Henri has now adopted Alcee, and we fear she may try to put him in her trunk when the day comes that she sails back with us.

Grand-mère and Grand-père are smitten with their grandson. Everyone in New Orleans has probably "met" him five times because they say to anyone who will stop long enough, "Have you met my grandchild?" They allow him to eat meals in the dining room, saying one can't learn manners too soon. He entertains them so with his few French and English words.

Gabriel has two more years in his college. Switching from engineering to architecture was not nearly as difficult as he expected. He said architecture is engineering applied to buildings. When he finishes, we hope to return to New Orleans so he can work with Joseph, though it depends on the political climate.

I hear the giggles of my son behind me, so I know his father is likely looking over my shoulder as I finish this. Gabriel spends as much times as he can with Charles Louis. When he looks at our son and smiles, I think of your letter to me about seeing the love our parents had for us when we hold our own children.

Gabriel and I have our struggles, but we never forget the journey we endured to have a life together. Gratitude comes quickly then. We know God always finds a way.

Until my next letter.

All my love,
Genevieve Charlotte

AUTHOR'S NOTE

As an author, I'm growing to learn that no sooner does "I don't think I'd ever..." slip from my lips than I'm presented with the opportunity to do that which I never thought I would. Or could.

Writing a historical novel was exactly one of those things I never thought I would or could write. (I say that hoping, after you finish this, that you think I could as well.) I couldn't resist the chance to write about New Orleans, having grown up here and, with the exception of a few years in Texas and a post-Katrina stint three hours away, lived here my entire life.

Rewinding more than 170 years proved quite challenging for someone accustomed to contemporary fiction, where reality is what you write it to be. Historical fiction requires knowing the reality of the time, and knowing requires research. I discovered I loved delving into the past, which meant that for months my family was bombarded with questions beginning with, "Did you know that in the 1840s...?"

But what made this entire experience most fascinating was what happened just days before the manuscript was due. My husband and I had been, for a few weeks, poking and prodding the idea of moving to New Orleans from Abita Springs, a city about thirty minutes away. Trying to find the house we needed seemed to be impossible. Until the day it wasn't.

That it had everything we were looking for isn't the amazing part. That my husband made an offer on it the first evening he walked through it isn't the amazing part. What is amazing is that it was built in the 1840s, the same era in which the novel is set, and the street on which the house is located is the same as the last name of one of my characters.

And so, this novel seemed to birth itself!

This is a photograph of the home we moved to when I wrote the novel. The previous owners had named it Camellia Manor. We recently moved to Texas to be nearer to our children, but I so miss this lovely lady and her stories.

ABOUT THE AUTHOR

A true Southern woman who knows any cook worth her gumbo always starts with a roux, Christa Allan is an award-winning author who writes women's fiction, stories of hope and redemption.

She has been invited to Southern Festival of Books, Louisiana Book Festival, Grand Festival of Art and Books, Pulpwood Queens Weekend and is a speaker at several conferences throughout the year. She is a member of RWA and Women's Fiction Writers Association.

Christa is the mother of five, grandmother of three, and is recently retired after teaching twenty-five years of high school English. She and her husband Ken recently moved to Houston after a lifetime in Louisiana, schlepping along their three neurotic cats and their dog Herman.

You can sign up for her newsletter at
www.christaallan.com

OTHER BOOKS
BY CHRISTA ALLAN

Since You've Been Gone
A Test of Faith
Threads of Hope
The Edge of Grace
Walking on Broken Glass
All They Want for Christmas

WHERE TO FIND CHRISTA

Website:
www.christaallan.com

Facebook:
facebook.com/ChristaAllan.Author

Twitter:
twitter.com/ChristaAllan

Instagram:
instagram.com/christaallan.author

Sign up for Christa's Newsletters:
www.christaallan.com

You can email Christa at:
christa.allan@gmail.com

If you enjoyed *Because You Loved Me*,
and you're ready to be whisked into the 21st century,
here's a preview of *Since You've Been Gone*

PROLOGUE

MY GRANNY RUTH SAYS WE always have choices about falling in love. So maybe you and I should have just fallen in like.

That would have been less painful and less expensive. Because, of course, the wedding and the reception still have to be paid for, even if nobody shows up.

Well, the rest of us showed up. But not you.

That qualifies as grounds for legitimate bridezilla anger.

When the phone shrilled at five o'clock that evening, there was a wisp of hope. Like the scent of perfume after someone's walked through a room and, for as long as the fragrance lingers, you look around to see who's there. But then it's gone, and you know hope's a memory.

An unrecognizable voice from an unrecognizable phone number said you'd been found.

Dead.

Fifty miles away. Headed in the opposite direction of the church.

And on the backseat of your car, a package wrapped in blue.

Baby-blue sailboats.

CHAPTER ONE

S OME PEOPLE LEAD CHARMED LIVES. Lives that unfurl like endless bolts of silk.

I'm not one of them.

My hopsack life had snagged upon disaster. And, for the past month, the threads frayed faster than I could stitch them together.

The appointment I'd just finished left no doubt about the tangled mess ahead.

I found a bench outside the side entrance of the West Shore Medical Building, wished it wasn't the middle of heatstroke-humidity June in New Orleans, and called Mia. Mia of the upscale bohemian wardrobe, wildly curly hair the color of wet sand, and funky rectangular violet eyeglasses. My best friend, who moved six hours away to Houston, has abandoned me in yet another crisis.

Please answer. Please answer. Please... don't go to voicemail. By the fifth unanswered ring, I'd mashed the cell phone against my ear, jamming my earring post into my neck. My silent pleadings were on the verge of running out of my mouth when I heard her voice.

"Hey, Livvy. I'm with a client. When can I call you back?"

The more her design business increased, the more our ability to have conversations decreased. I couldn't bake outside much longer. I was sweating in places I didn't know existed. My mother would be mortified to know I was even thinking about such unladylike bodily functions.

"Sweetie, ladies don't sweat," she'd tell me, the word *sah-wet* dripping off her tongue like sour grape juice. "We glisten." I learned to expect *Gone with the Wind* flashbacks from the woman whose mother named her Scarlett Ellen.

But *sah-wetting* would soon be the least of our lady issues, considering the news I was about to drop on Mia.

"I'm pregnant." I held my breath, willed my somersaulting heart to steady itself, and waited for a sign of life on the other end of the phone.

"Hold on," said Mia, her voice less chirpy. "Wait, no." Her tone now impatient, her fingers probably drumming her desk. "I'll call you back in a few minutes."

My anxiety on pause, I stood and peeled my damp cotton skirt away from my legs where the bench's wrought iron slats had embedded themselves in my thighs. The nearby glass door groaned open, and a gaggle of scrub-dressed people spilled out, yammering about lunch options. The receptionist in Dr. Schneider's office who'd scheduled my next appointment waved to me. I nodded and produced a suggestion of a smile. The least I could do for a woman I'd never met until an hour ago, who now knew more about me than my best friend and my parents.

Mia's name flashed on my phone. I perched on the edge of the bench, and before she could speak, I said, "I'm pregnant." Only this time the weight of the words settled in my throat like broken glass. "What am I supposed to do? I can't believe this is happening to me. My life's already a mess. Isn't it somebody else's turn?" I sounded like a person in the complaint department of humanity attempting to return a defective life.

If God were as compassionate as my mother believed Him to be, then He'd dole out tragedy on a rotating basis. You'd stand in line, then He'd reach into His bushel of adversity, hand one over, and you'd go to the back of the long stretch of mankind. You'd have time to deal with it, dress it in different clothes, ignore it, shove it someplace in your heart before your number was up again.

But no. God dished the trifecta of trials and tribulations in my life. In the past month, Wyatt died on a highway (without leaving a clue as to where he was going), I traded wedding white for funeral black, and now, instead of being a wife, I was going to be a mother. I stopped wearing mascara twenty-eight days ago because I woke up every morning with a tear-stained pillow, cried during the day any time I thought of Wyatt (which was about every ten minutes), and cried myself to sleep at night. After today's revelation, I didn't expect I'd need eye makeup anytime soon.

"You're still there, right?" I walked back inside the medical building, a closer source of cold air than my car on the far end of the parking lot.

"Olivia… I almost don't know what to say."

I knew Mia well enough to know she'd just said volumes.

"I'm not ready for this. I lost Wyatt, and today I found out part of him is still with me. How am I supposed to handle that?" I sat in a chair in the corner of the lobby and hoped I had something in my purse to wipe my already leaky nose.

If only I could be like Holly Hunter in *Broadcast News* and schedule my cathartic crying. My eyes dripped, my underarms dripped, and my emotional reserves dripped. All in a medical building lobby as I waited for Mia to come up with a plan, and I wiped my face with a crumpled Starbucks napkin. I counted on her to save me from myself. Now wasn't the time for her to forgo the life vest when I was drowning in the sea of my own irresponsibility.

"I can only imagine how your parents will react when they hear this. When are you going to tell them?"

The door opened and ushered in the sultry heat and a woman with twins. Her "Sit there and don't you dare move" resonated in the room, and even I shifted in my chair.

"I'm not sure. I need time to process this. What if I lose the baby? Maybe I should wait a few more weeks."

I must've sounded as if I were asking for her permission because, even without seeing her, I knew I'd awakened her hand-waving, finger-pointing, mouth-spitting wrath. "And what if you don't," she snapped. "Postponing the inevitable is always an option. A dumb one. You have to tell them now."

Reality fell over me like the sticky silkiness of a spider's web. "Today? A few days? What's the difference?" I'd lowered my voice so as not to be the main attraction for the audience of three seated near me. "It's not like I'm a pregnant, unwed teenager who…"

"You're right. You're a pregnant, unwed twenty-eight-year-old."

The bite in her voice pushed me against the chair. I picked at a loose thread on my skirt, nibbled my lower lip, and reminded myself to breathe.

"I'm sorry," Mia said, her voice barely above a whisper. "That was mean of me. But in all the years I've known you, your first reaction is to procrastinate. And it's your worst one because you make yourself and me crazy with all your what-if scenarios."

"I know. I know." She made me face my fears but somehow managed to soften the blow. I hated and admired her for that.

"I'm sorry to do this, but I have to get back to Mrs. Nicholls. I told her that while I was taking your call she should pull fabrics she sensed would increase the positive energy in her home. At the price per yard she's looking, her husband may feng shui me into another universe," she said, her wit as sharp as her style. "Go talk to your parents. Call me after you do, okay?"

I promised her I would because she'd be relentless if I didn't. I dropped the phone into my purse, looked up, and made eye contact with one of the twins. She sucked her thumb, forefinger hooked over her nose like a hanger, lids half-drawn shades over her eyes.

I envied her quiet contentment.

Every day since Wyatt died, a tsunami of grief assaulted me, sent me crashing into memories, and sucked my dreams away in its undertow. I didn't know when or how I'd ever experience the soft swell of happiness and comfort without him.

CHAPTER TWO

M IA, HER FUTURE HUSBAND, BRYCE, and I met during our freshman year at Louisiana State University when we waited tables at the Magic Mushroom. By day, it was an unassuming, though always quirky, eatery that New Agers could've hung out in for personal transformation, social consciousness, and gourmet pizzas with names like Aura Artichoke.

As soon as the sun set, the football crowds, karaoke singers, and book-weary students getting turnt up for the weekend guaranteed generous tips. Most of the time, being there didn't seem like work at all. Bryce said some nights he felt like he was earning money just for hanging out with his friends.

After graduation, I moved home for a summer internship with a public relations firm. Bryce and Mia married in August, then moved to Houston where he worked saving the environment, and she opened a design studio to decorate habitats in the environments her husband saved.

And two years later, I met Wyatt, whose first words to me were "Excuse me, would you care for a mushroom stuffed with walnuts and pesto?" Well, he actually spoke to Bryce, Mia, and me, because we were together at the second annual Hope House charity art auction. The center provided support services for abused children.

Bryce, who knew firsthand what those kids experienced, was a generous contributor. Mia and Bryce had donated the catering, which was being provided by his younger brother, Colin, who'd started the business the year before.

My boyfriend at the time, Evan Gendusa, predictably unpredictable, had begged off hours before to study for his bar exam. I was certain he meant as in *law*. Bryce disagreed. "Stools, Livvy. He meant barstools." Either way, I wasn't invested enough anymore to care. A shame, really, considering he turned more heads than I did when we'd walk into a room. We'd known each other since high school, and his parents and mine were friends. We had been together over a year. I couldn't compete for attention with his ego or his law classes.

Being dateless turned out to be perfect. I could devote all my eye time to Wyatt.

On his next pass, Wyatt served mini crab cakes and nodded in Bryce's direction to ask if my husband would want one. Bryce, engaged in an intense discussion of ping drivers and his improved golf game, wouldn't have known what his own wife wanted much less her friend.

My lips slid into a smile—like the ones I'd seen in the Victoria's Secret catalogue because with those bodies, who wouldn't flirt with the camera—and I told him

Bryce was my friend's husband. When he walked away, I checked my mirror to make sure remnants of spinach phyllo weren't wedged between my teeth.

Later, as Mia brushed spring roll crumbs from the top of her baby bump, landing zone for whatever missed her mouth, she asked, "That waiter over there," tilting her head toward Wyatt. "Is he worried you're too thin? You seem to stay in his flight path."

"He's sweet. And, come on, he's not hard to look at, either. What's not to like about a man with blue eyes?" And thick, wavy black hair that just brushed his collar, a grin that could melt chocolate, and a body made for biceps. Of course, I'd have to take that starched white tuxedo shirt off, one button at a time, to know for sure...

"Hel-lo, Miss What's Not to Like Over There." Mia waved her hands in front of me. "How about... he's a waiter?" She said *waiter* like it was synonymous with *drug dealer*. "For all you know, he has someone like me"—she paused to pat her belly—"waiting at home."

Wyatt himself, the possible philandering druggie, saved me from answering by swooping in with a tray of desserts. "Ladies?" He offered an array of coma-inducing indulgences.

Mia reeled in a towering brownie, a slab of red velvet cheesecake, and a mini éclair. "Olivia, do you want something from... I'm sorry, what did you say your name was?"

"I didn't." Wyatt's eyes met mine for the length of a

heartbeat, then he smiled at Mia. "My name's Wyatt."

"No, thanks." Adorable. I glanced at his left hand. No ring. Not even an untanned suggestion of one. I tipped my wineglass in Mia's direction. "I'll share hers."

Mia glared at me. "Only if the baby's full." She slid a benign fruit tart off the tray and handed it to me. "Just in case."

Sometimes with Mia, resistance is futile. I held the tart on my lap like a bomb that would detonate if I moved. One blueberry toppling onto my dress, and I would explode.

Wyatt lingered for a moment, but no chance was I navigating this tart to my mouth while he stood in front of us. His eyes grazed me. My skin shivered watching him. Then he said, "Enjoy," and turned to the next table.

"Was he referring to the dessert or your staring at him?" Mia examined the éclair as if it might be defective, then sent it down to the baby. "You're actually blushing. Hormonal adolescent jolt?" She looked at me wide-eyed, as if she hoped the answer weren't the one she suspected.

I relocated the tart to the table, stood and smoothed the front of my gown, and scanned the crowd for a broad-shouldered waiter with ink-black hair. "I'm getting a drink. Want anything?" And without waiting for her to answer, I said, "It's been months since I've been able to engage in harmless ogling. Really, where could this go?"

Mia shrugged. "Bryce was a waiter when I met him. That's where it could go."

THE THREE OF US STAYED after the auction officially ended so Bryce could talk to Colin. That's how we learned Wyatt and Colin were friends. They'd met during high school, then later worked together as cooks at a French Quarter hotel. When Colin left to start his catering business, Wyatt offered to help.

The next morning Bryce and Mia had reservations for the Sunday jazz brunch at the Court of Two Sisters. Colin had invited Wyatt, and the night before, I had invited myself when Mia told me their plans.

I met them at their hotel. Bryce opened the door, looked at his shoeless wife, and tapped his watch. "Reservations, remember?"

Mia huffed and puffed, demonstrating an alarming contortionist move to reach her bare foot. "If there wasn't a volleyball in my stomach, I might be able to buckle these sandals." She leaned back in the chair, her arms flopped over the side, her face waved the white flag of surrender.

Bryce looked at her, his expression a caress so tender I felt as if I'd just intruded on a private moment. He kneeled in front of her, propped one leg up, and helped Mia with her shoes.

"And this," Mia said to me, "is the kind of man you want to be the father of your child."

As we were leaving their hotel room, she informed me she'd Googled Wyatt and unearthed as much information as she could, "for your own good since you seem so fascinated with him."

By the time the elevator doors opened to the lobby, she'd ticked off all the details on her list: He was twenty-three, she couldn't find any siblings, there was no mention of college, and he worked as the sous-chef at one of the Brennan restaurants. Oh, and there were no known ex-wives or felonies.

"But Livvy," she said, "he may not be Mr. Right. Maybe he's just Mr. Right Now."

"I can live with that," I said as the door opened, and the humidity swooped by to frizz my hair. "I'm not looking for forever."

I learned to be careful what I asked for. Sometimes it arrived in the most unexpected ways.

CHAPTER THREE

I ALWAYS WANTED A BABY.

But, clearly, I wasn't specific about the *when* part of the want.

And now to break the news to my parents. My churchgoing, Bible-quoting, choir-singing mother answered my call before the first ring ended.

"Sweetie, of course your dad and I will be home if you're coming over. I'll send him to the club to pick up dinner. It'll be so much nicer to eat at home. Just the three of us. Oh. My. I'm sorry. You know I didn't mean to suggest three was better than four. I meant it would be more enjoyable and civilized for us to eat at home instead of having to listen to all the racket in the Grill Room. You know, those young parents let their children have their own heads and run around like little heathens... Well, shame on me. That's not the kind of thing I should be saying..."

She paused for a breath, so I jumped into the void. "Mom, I'm ten minutes away. We'll talk when I get there, okay?" My mother's conversations were bait and capture. Interrupting her wasn't impolite; it was survival.

But despite all her yammering, my mother's heart never failed to listen. She shielded me from guests' endless questions after the almost wedding, from the decisions of what to do when the caterer had prepared food for three hundred and no one was there to eat, and from making decisions about Wyatt's funeral because we were the almost family—the only family he had.

I turned past the long stretch of white picket fence that marked the entrance into Wildwood Country Club. Pulling into my parents' driveway, I felt as if a slab of granite had landed on my chest. And I didn't expect that I would leave feeling any better.

"HEY, I THOUGHT YOU LIKED CARLO'S Eggplant Parmesan," my dad said as he picked up my plate. "Your mother's going to have to sew weights in your clothes to keep you from floating away."

"I'm full, really. I'll take the rest home. I won't have to cook for days. And I'm sure I have enough ballast to stay grounded." I sighed, remembering Lily as a volleyball in Mia's tummy.

"Your grandmother will be home in a few days, so you might not have to cook ever again." My mother laughed, but I knew she was serious.

She had grown up in a house where food equaled love. And if someone didn't eat much, Granny Ruth took it personally. Happy people ate, and, unless you wanted to be the focus of her rapid-fire questioning to exorcise the demon blocking your stomach, you ate.

"Maybe you should have joined her on that cruise. It might have been nice to have a change of scenery," said my mother.

"Watching everyone on the Oldies but Goodies cruise dancing to 'Macarena'? No. But it was sweet of her to invite me along," I said.

Mom leaned across the table and patted my hand—a whisper of her familiar almond and cherry lotion followed. When I was younger, she would come into my room at bedtime, rest her warm hand on my cheek, and kiss me good night. The scent would linger even after she walked out.

"Are you sleeping well? Your face looks so drawn," she said.

"I'm sleeping. Mostly."

She and my father exchanged looks. The emotional telepathy of thirty-five years of marriage. Their eyes conveying the words they left unspoken. Would Wyatt and I have experienced that connection?

I'd never know if we would have shared that moment when our hearts could speak for us, because when Wyatt died, his secrets died with him. I hated that answer. I hated it because it was true. I hated it because it swallowed my life whole.

"Well, okay, honey. But remember, Dr. Welsh gave you those pills—"

"Of course, Mom. I remember." How could I forget? The pills I didn't take because numbing the pain of losing someone I loved didn't make sense to me. The grief reminded me what it meant to be alive. And now I couldn't take the pills because I was responsible for the life Wyatt had left me.

"If you think you need something else, maybe something stronger, we can call him. Not now, because his office is closed—"

"Scarlett, we can discuss our daughter's drugs later." He turned and winked at me. "If you get the coffee started, Olivia and I will clear the kitchen table."

For a second, she looked like someone coming out of a trance. In her mind, she had already scripted her conversation with Dr. Welsh's nurse tomorrow, made the appointment, and driven me to the pharmacy.

"Sure. In fact, I just bought a new flavor…"

Off she went in the direction of the pantry, her glasses pushed up like a headband, her dark brown hair gathered into a stub of a ponytail.

My dad elbowed me as I stood next to him rinsing dishes. "She means well, you know."

I nodded and handed him a bowl. "I know, but thanks for the distraction." He smiled, and I wanted to shout, "Please don't be so nice. I'm about to rock your world, and there's no distraction for what I'm going to tell you." Instead, I returned his smile and added one more brick to my wall of guilt.

My mother brewed her Southern Bread Pudding Coffee, the aroma of cinnamon and raisins trailing behind the steaming mugs she and my dad carried to the porch. Its wall of windows faced the tee box behind their house where they watched the sun set. They relaxed in their matching leather recliners facing the golf course, and I sat cross-legged between them on the oversize ottoman.

"Did you two play golf this afternoon?" Since the sun didn't set until a few hours after they closed the office, my parents often came home and played nine holes.

"I wanted to, but my hip wouldn't cooperate." My mother sounded as if she were scolding a disobedient child.

"Scarlett, you make it sound like it has a mind of its own. You really need to make an appointment with that orthopedic doctor." My dad's tone matched hers, as did the look in his eyes.

I pretended to be invisible, having learned years ago that taking sides in these verbal exchanges between my parents sometimes ended in an emotional tug-of-war. With me as the rope.

Mom reacted as she often did when she didn't want to admit my father spoke the truth. She ignored him and changed the subject.

"I love that sundress on you. It's so flattering. Doesn't that red look great on her, George?" Mom leaned over the chair arm and riffled through the basket of *Good Housekeeping* and *Redbook* magazines on the floor.

Dad glanced at me over the rim of his coffee mug. "Um... yes, very nice."

"It's great to see you dressed up. Not in those yoga pants and…" She paused, tilted her head and scrunched her mouth in that way she did when she was suspiciously curious. "So, did you do something special today?"

I drank some water to wash away the anxiety that lined my mouth. But there wasn't anything I could drink to dilute the sludge in my gut.

"You're looking puny. Are you feeling sick? George, you don't think anything was wrong with that dinner, do you?" My mother's eyebrows edged toward each other, a sure sign an inquisition was pending. "Is it indigestion? I'll check the medicine cabinet—"

"Mom," I said, my hand on her arm stopping her from getting out of the chair, "I'm not sick." One breath. Two. "I had a doctor's appointment. I'm pregnant."

Her gasp after the word *pregnant* created a mini tidal wave of coffee that lapped out of her mug and splashed onto the hem of my dress. "Oh my goodness. Look what happened," she said. In her attempt to lean forward to blot it, the mug leaned with her, spilling more coffee in my lap.

I jumped up, more from the surprise than the warmth.

"Now what have I done?" Her voice vibrated, and the flush in her cheeks spread to her neck. "Don't move. I'll find a towel."

"Mom, it's fine. Just wet, that's all."

"You might still have some clothes here. I'll go look. We'll get it clean. It's going to be okay," she said, but her hand trembled, and the mug she placed on the end table performed a little tap dance of its own.

"Are we still talking about the dress? Mom, you heard me, right?" My words scratched like fingernails against a chalkboard.

"Scarlett, Olivia, both of you, please sit," said my dad, folding his newspaper in half, then in half again, creasing the edges as he did.

The silence swelled between us.

We both sat.

I blotted my wet dress with a napkin, glad to have a reason to avoid eye contact. I didn't want to know what I'd see in my parents' eyes.

My dad placed his hand under my chin and lifted my face. "You've walked through hell for weeks. The worst part of it for us has been watching you suffer this pain and not being able to save you from it. Wyatt's accident and being robbed of one of the happiest days of your life… you had no control over any of that. But you had to live with the consequences."

He looked at my mother whose quiet tears streamed down her face and spotted her blouse. "But this, Olivia. You had control over this. I don't understand," said my mother, her face drawn in disappointment.

"I didn't ask you to understand. Nothing about this makes sense. Wyatt and I loved each other. We were getting married. It's not like we were irresponsible teenagers."

"Exactly, Livvy. You weren't. You were irresponsible

adults," my mother said. "There's a reason sex outside of marriage is discussed in the Bible. This is one of them."

Somewhere between the words *irresponsible* and *Bible,* I dropped the reins of my seething anger, and let it rip. "Not the God talk. Not today. Maybe not ever. You know, if Wyatt hadn't died, we'd both be here telling you about this baby. And, whether we were married or not, you'd be thrilled." God had ruined my life. I didn't care anymore about anything He said after He had let Wyatt die, leaving me alone.

"Olivia, you knew your father and I disapproved of your moving in with Wyatt before the wedding. We certainly didn't think you slept in separate bedrooms. But it's obvious to all of us now that our plans often don't work out the way we expect. It would be foolish to think there wouldn't be consequences for your actions." She folded her arms across her chest, her back erect, shielded by her self-righteousness.

My father stood on the sidelines like a referee at a tennis match that was disintegrating into a vendetta. "Scarlett, Livvy, both of you calm down. We can handle this better if—"

"Dad, it's too late for that." I held my hands out in disbelief. "Mom, that's it? That's your compassionate Christian response? If it is, then why are you shocked I'm not buying into this God of yours who's ruined my life?"

"Olivia, please—"

She reached toward me, but I backed away.

"No. I don't have the energy to fight about this.

Wyatt's death should be punishment enough for whatever wrong I've done. Or he's done. Or we've done. I don't even know." I placed my hands on my stomach, "But this baby... this baby... I refuse to let you make this baby a punishment, too."

"We don't have to do this to one another," my dad said. "Scarlett, can we stop with the accusations? All of this fighting isn't going to change the facts."

"Exactly, which is why it's time for me to leave." Before I walked out, I lowered my voice, laced it with sarcasm, and snarled, "By the way, this new life you're ashamed of? It's your grandchild."

My father flinched. The recognition of what this child meant flashed through his face when I said those words.

"Olivia, don't you think there's something very important you've forgotten in all of this?"

It wasn't a question my mother meant for me to answer. When she spoke with such deliberate softness, whatever she had to say would be anything but.

"Wyatt's car wasn't headed in the direction of the church when he had that accident. And we still don't know why. If he hadn't died, you'd be just another bride who'd been jilted at the altar."